ALSO BY TINA FOLSOM

LUTHER'S RETURN

SCANGUARDS VAMPIRES – BOOK 10

TINA FOLSOM

Luther's Return is a work of fiction. Names, characters, places, and incidents are the products of the author's imagination and are used fictitiously. Any resemblance to actual events, locales, or persons, living or dead, is entirely coincidental.

2015 Tina Folsom

Published in the United States

Cover design: Leah Kaye Suttle
Cover photo: Shutterstock, ©The Art of Photo
Author Photo: © Marti Corn Photography

Printed in the United States of America

1

The eight-by-eight windowless cell had been his home for twenty years.

Luther West didn't look back as he walked—ahead of Dobbs, the Kevlar-clad vampire guard—toward the end of the long corridor lined with similar cells. Cells that held other vampires; criminals just like him. Bright light illuminated the corridors in the massive concrete maze located somewhere in the foothills of the Sierra Nevada.

Luther glanced up at the fluorescent tubes above his head. To a visitor they would look ordinary, but Luther knew better. From a control room, the flick of a switch activated the UV tubes located inside the casings. Any vampire caught in the corridor once the UV lights were switched on would slowly, but surely, incinerate.

A painful death. And an effective deterrent for anyone trying to escape.

Apart from that nifty gadget, a vampire prison wasn't much different from a human prison. The idea was the same: punish the perpetrators and keep them away from decent people so they couldn't harm anybody else.

Well, it had worked.

The UV ray guns the guards carried to keep the prisoners in line fulfilled their purpose. Though painful when applied, they ordinarily left no permanent marks on a vampire. The consumption of human blood and an uninterrupted sleep cycle assured that a vampire's skin healed without scarring. However, some of the guards had been crueler than others. And those prisoners who had a hard time submitting to authority and accepting their fate found out the hard way that even a vampire's body could scar.

Luther had been one of them.

To teach him who was boss they'd lowered his already meager

rations of human blood to a near-starvation level and interrupted his sleep cycle every thirty minutes so his vampire body couldn't heal. One week of such treatment, and scar tissue grew over the burns caused by the UV rays, making the disfigurement permanent.

Luther's back and chest bore witness to his early years of defiance. He'd learned his lesson. He subsequently became a model prisoner and kept his true feelings to himself, biding his time. But he'd made enemies early on, and some people held a grudge longer than others.

"Release day?" The voice came from an open cell. He recognized it as that of Summerland, another guard, one who never missed an occasion to show Luther who was in charge.

Luther turned his head instinctively, though he knew the question wasn't meant for him. Behind him, Dobbs stopped, and Luther did the same, anticipating the order to wait.

"West's time is up." Dobbs jerked his thumb at him then looked back at the guard inside the cell. "What you doin'? Thought that V-CON was released last week."

V-CONs—it was what the guards called the prisoners: *Vampire Convicts.*

Luther glanced past Dobbs at Summerland who motioned his blond head toward the interior walls. "Yeah, he was. But he didn't take all his junk with him."

Summerland continued to rip posters from the walls. Movie posters, pictures of beautiful women, actresses most likely. Movie stars. Or maybe singers. One of the women looked vaguely familiar. He'd probably seen her on the screen. A blonde with a rack like Raquel Welsh and eyes like a wild cat. Green like emeralds. The vampire who'd previously occupied this cell clearly had good taste in women. Not so good taste in movies though, if the posters were anything to go by.

Access to movies and television shows was one of the privileges for good behavior. The ex-prisoner must have exhibited model behavior, since he'd even been allowed pictures from the outside. Or he'd bribed a guard.

After all, the prisoners were vampires, and many of them had already lived a long life and accumulated fortunes with which to buy certain services. Luther knew of prostitutes being smuggled into the prison by the guards in exchange for large sums of money. Being a guard at one of the few vampire penitentiaries was a coveted position. It was rumored that many guards had retired as rich men.

Though Luther could have paid for hookers, he never asked for such favors. A woman was the reason why he'd spent twenty years in this hellhole. Women were trouble with a capital T. He would make damn sure to stay away from them. Another lesson he'd learned: never trust a woman's feelings. No matter how much she tells you she loves you. Not even if she carries your child.

With a grunt, Luther pushed back the rising memories and the anger that welled up with them.

"Done chatting?"

"Watch that mouth of yours, West," Dobbs admonished. "You'll get out of here soon enough. When I'm ready. Even if some people don't like that fact. Right, Summerland?"

Summerland narrowed his eyes and shot a venomous look at Luther. "Oh, he'll be back one day."

Luther pulled one side of his lip up in a show of derision. "Don't count on it." Without waiting for Dobbs's command, he pivoted and continued walking in the direction they'd been heading.

He heard the guard's footsteps behind him, but they were suddenly obscured by a noise up ahead. Angry shouts and grunts echoed down the corridor. The moment Luther turned a corner, he saw the reason for the commotion.

A massive, clearly pissed-off prisoner was fighting tooth and nail against his two guards. The guards, Norris and McKay, were both armed to the teeth, but the convict didn't give them a chance to employ their weapons.

Fangs bared and eyes glaring red, underscoring his aggression, the V-CON struck out with such ferocity and skill that the two well-trained guards had to use all their strength just to stay on their feet.

"Ah, shit!" Dobbs cursed. He pressed down the button on his radio.

"Corridor seven. Hostile V-CON, two guards in distress. Employ UV lights. Repeat…"

"Fuck!" Luther cursed, whirling his head back to Dobbs. "Are you fucking shitting me?"

On his release day he would get a last dose of UV rays? What the fuck was that supposed to be? A goodbye present?

But Dobbs merely shrugged and pulled his protective shield over his face. The rest of his body was already adequately protected by his gear, right down to the specially designed gloves.

"Fucking asshole!" Luther charged toward the melee. If he could diffuse the situation quickly enough, Dobbs would have enough time to cancel his command. No fucking idiot prisoner would get him burned on his release day!

"Over my fucking charred body!"

Livid, Luther barreled into the aggressive convict, taking him by surprise. The idiot hadn't expected to be attacked by a fellow prisoner. Big mistake.

Slamming his fist into the jerk's face, Luther yelled: "You're not going to screw up my release day, you bastard!"

A fist flew straight at him, but the V-CON had no idea who he was dealing with. Luther might have been imprisoned for twenty years, and rightly so, but he'd lost not a bit of his lethal fighting skills. At best he was a little rusty, but his muscle memory returned with every second he pounded into the guy.

With stoic calmness Luther accepted the blows the other vampire managed to land.

Another punch, and his opponent finally landed on his back. Now that the hardest part was done, Norris and McKay jumped back into the fray and restrained the V-CON's arms.

But subduing the prisoner had taken too long.

Luther heard the tell-tale clicks of the light tubes on the ceiling.

"Fuck!" he cursed just as the lights flickered for a moment.

Then he felt the burn.

UV lights blasted him as if he were standing under the midday sun.

"Call it off, Dobbs! Fuck!" Luther screamed, whirling his head toward the guard.

He saw Dobbs fumble for his radio and drop it to the floor.

"Fucking imbecile!"

Pain searing through his body, Luther lunged for the communication device and grabbed it. He pressed down the button. Behind him he heard Norris and McKay dealing with the V-CON who was now screaming with pain.

"Disengage UV lights in corridor seven," Luther yelled into the radio. He'd heard the guards often enough to be familiar with their commands, their way of speaking.

"Who is this?" came the crackling reply.

The stench of burnt hair and skin—his as well as the other prisoner's—rose into his nostrils, making him nauseous.

The radio was suddenly ripped from his hand.

"It's Dobbs. Disengage UV lights in corridor seven immediately. V-CON subdued."

Seconds later, the lights flickered again. Luther collapsed to the floor, this time not from pain, but from relief.

"Everything under control," Norris now confirmed.

Luther slanted him a look, scoffing. Yeah, everything was under control now—no thanks to the guards. This was Luther's doing. But before he could tell the guard what he thought of his comment, a shiny boot kicked him in the side, knocking him against the wall. Automatically, his fangs descended and his lips peeled away from his teeth, showing his attacker his pearly whites.

"Summerland!" Luther hissed under his breath. Figured!

He'd saved the guards from severe injury and possibly death, and this was his thanks for it?

The boot came his way a second time. Luther reached for it, but Summerland was jerked back.

"Let him be!" Norris ordered.

Luther glanced past the stunned guard, witnessing how Norris still held on to Summerland's shoulder.

"Better help get the newbie settled." Norris motioned to the subdued vampire whose face and hands were covered in angry blisters. He'd gotten the full brunt of the UV lights, lying on his back when the lights had come on.

Luther had been able to look away from the rays, but his nape and the back of his head had sustained significant damage—nothing some human blood and a good day's sleep couldn't fix.

"And I'm not gonna be the one writing up the incident report," Norris insisted. "I'm due for my vacation."

McKay who held a UV gun to the head of the V-CON—whose hands were now tied with silver shackles—grunted in displeasure. "You sure know how to pick the right time, leaving the rest of us to deal with this newbie." McKay hit the butt of his gun against the prisoner's temple. "Who doesn't fucking know what's good for him."

"Let's go, West," Dobbs ordered. "Unless you like it here so much you wanna stay longer."

In spite of the pain that radiated through his head and traveled down his spine, Luther jumped up, not wanting to show the ungrateful guards that he was hurting. He gave a nod of acknowledgment to his jailor, and continued his walk out of the hellhole that had been his home for twenty lonely years.

2

"My zipper is stuck!"

Katie Montgomery whirled around in the locker room-turned-dressing room-for-the-night. One side of it was reserved for the female members of the cast. Seven-foot-high partition walls separated the area from the section where the male actors got changed into their costumes.

The drama class at the University of San Francisco, a private school, was putting on *A Midsummer Night's Dream* before the Christmas holidays. And as the drama teacher, Katie was responsible for the entire production, including making sure everybody looked the part and knew their lines. In addition she was also playing one of the parts herself, since unfortunately a female student had dropped out early in the semester and Katie couldn't find anybody else for the demanding role.

The hustle and bustle, the chatter, the excitement among the amateur actors reminded her of the years she'd spent on film and television sets in Hollywood. Her name hadn't been Katie then. Everybody in Hollywood knew her as Kimberly Fairfax, the blonde bombshell. Well, she wasn't blonde anymore either—in fact, she'd never really been blonde. Her natural hair color was a rich dark brown, just like her brothers', Haven and Wesley.

She rushed to Cindy, the twenty-year-old girl who'd wailed about her zipper. "I've got it." She stepped behind her and looked at the back of the pastel-blue-and-green fairy costume. "Back in the sixteenth century they had buttons and bows," Katie mumbled to herself. She pulled on the zipper, but it was tight. "Have you gained weight?"

Cindy looked over her shoulder and shrugged sheepishly. "I swear I only have one pastry in the mornings."

Katie tilted her head to the side, but said nothing.

"Okay, and one in the afternoon. But it's really not my fault. I'm just always hungry. And I'm still growing. Besides, we can't all have the same perfect figure as you. I don't know how you do it. You still look like you're in your twenties, and I know for a fact that your first big movie was released when I was born."

Smiling, Katie shook her head. "Just hold your breath for a moment." She pulled the zipper up and patted the girl on the shoulder. "It's all good."

Before her student could continue commenting on Katie's appearance, Katie turned away and looked around to see if she was needed anywhere else. She always refrained from commenting when people remarked on her looks and age.

She was forty-two, but for a witch, age meant nothing. While she wasn't quite as ageless as her vampire brother, Haven, she and her witch brother Wesley aged so slowly they could easily pass for twenty-somethings. It was one of the reasons Katie had left Hollywood and the movie business behind. Too many people had started asking questions, wondering what plastic surgeon she was using to continue looking so young. She was afraid that one day they would figure out that she wasn't human, but a preternatural creature.

Despite her witch genes, she had no powers to speak of. A ritual her mother had performed shortly after her birth had robbed her and her brothers of their witch powers. When her brother Haven had sacrificed his human life twenty years ago to save the world from an evil witch, and become a vampire, the Power of Three she and her brothers were supposed to possess had been destroyed for good.

But Wesley, her eight-years-older brother, had wanted his powers back. And he'd worked for it. Studied the craft. Made mistakes. Practiced more. Now, twenty years later, he was an accomplished witch. He used his powers for good instead of evil. And for Scanguards, the vampire-run security company they all owed so much to.

At least half of them were here tonight. They'd all come to watch Isabelle, Samson and Delilah's daughter, perform. Instinctively her gaze searched for the young hybrid. As the daughter of a vampire and his blood-bonded human mate, Isabelle was an extraordinary creature. She combined the advantages of both species within herself: she had the strength and speed of a vampire without the drawback of being burned by sunlight. And once she turned twenty-one, she would stop aging, just like her vampire father had stopped aging when he was turned over two centuries earlier.

Isabelle wore a seventeenth-century gown in a rich azure color and looked absolutely stunning. The long dark hair that normally cascaded down her shoulders, framing her lovely figure, was fashioned into a medieval hairdo. Already now, at age twenty, men were standing in line to gain her affections. Isabelle had inherited her mother's beauty and her father's strength. She was a force to be reckoned with. It showed when she and her two brothers, Grayson and Patrick, nineteen and seventeen respectively, were of different opinions. Sparks flew when the three got into an argument. All three of them wanted to lead. Only one would finally rule.

But tonight something was different about Isabelle. She didn't look as confident as usual. She seemed rather nervous and looked uncomfortable. Was she having stage fright?

Katie glanced at the large wall clock. In thirty minutes the curtain would rise. This was not the time for anybody to get cold feet. She was walking toward Isabelle, when she heard somebody call her name.

"Katie? Got a minute?"

She pivoted and saw Blake pop his head in the door.

"You can't come in here!" she chastised and rushed toward him.

He immediately retreated. When she stepped outside into the corridor, he was waiting for her.

"Apologies, but nobody heard me knock," he said, grinning disarmingly.

A decade ago Katie would have rolled her eyes and accused him of using any excuse to ogle the beautiful young girls in the dressing room. Not tonight. Blake had changed in more ways than one.

He'd matured and grown into an utterly handsome man with short dark hair, the same blue eyes as his 4th great-grandmother Rose, and a toned body made of pure muscle. The family resemblance to Quinn and Rose, however, ended there. He looked older than his blond vampire forebears now. His ancestors had been turned into vampires in their twenties, while Blake had become a vampire at age thirty-two, twelve years earlier. Quinn had turned him at Blake's insistence.

"What is it?" Katie asked, looking up at Blake who dwarfed her.

"I just wanted to go over security with you."

"But we've already done that. I really don't have the time. We only have—"

"It won't even take a minute of your time, sweetheart," he insisted, turning on his charm.

"Sweetheart?" She laughed. There was nothing amorous going on between her and the tall vampire—they both knew that. "You must be desperate."

Blake chuckled, displaying his white teeth. "You know me too well." He pulled a piece of paper from the inside of the trendy sports coat he'd paired with black slacks and sturdy boots. "Samson's orders."

Involuntarily she had to smile. Even dressed in elegant eveningwear, Blake was always ready for war.

"I have the feeling you enjoy being the head of Scanguards' personal security detail far too much."

He smirked and looked around the corridor, making sure none of the stagehands who were arranging final details could overhear them. "Providing 'round the clock security for thirteen hybrid teenagers is no walk in the park. And don't even get me started on the parents."

Katie knew what he meant. Some parents could be overprotective of their offspring, and Samson was no exception when it came to his three children. Though he did have reason to be cautious. Scanguards had enemies.

"Driving you nuts, are they?"

Blake ran a hand through his hair. "You have no idea. And trust me, those kids have never been safer in their lives than since I took over their security twelve years ago."

"Was that why you wanted to be turned? So the kids couldn't run roughshod over you?"

Blake briefly glanced down the hall where a worker was carrying two chairs into the next room. "That, and the fact that I didn't want to look older than my grandparents."

His serious expression belied the light tone of his voice.

"Sorry I asked."

Blake blinked and gave a sigh. "Katie, I don't mean to—"

She lifted her hand. "You don't have to explain yourself—"

"I love these people," Blake interrupted, motioning to the wall. Behind it was the stage and beyond that the audience waiting for the performance to start. "I love the Scanguards family. They're my family, and I don't want to leave them. Had I remained human, one day I would have had to. I can't do that."

Katie put her hand on his forearm and squeezed.

He met her eyes. "And if you tell any of them about what I just said, I'm going to suck the life out of you," he warned.

"Don't wanna come across as a big softy, that it?"

"Because I'm not."

"No, you're not. And loving somebody doesn't make you weak, it makes you strong."

"Well, let's go over this." Blake pointed to the piece of paper in his hand, clearly embarrassed. "I marked at which points in the play Isabelle is going to be on stage and when she's supposed to be backstage with the other actors. Does that look right?"

Katie skimmed the list of scenes and nodded. "You know your Shakespeare."

He shrugged. "Rose makes me read all that stuff."

She grinned. "Sure she does." The sound of the door opening behind her made her turn her head to see who was leaving the dressing room.

She saw Isabelle freeze as if caught.

"Oh, hey Blake," Isabelle said quickly and a little too cheerfully. "Are you gonna watch?"

"Like a hawk."

Isabelle rolled her eyes. "I meant the play."

"So did I." He pulled her into a quick hug, placing a kiss on the top of her head, before releasing her. Then his gaze bounced back and forth between Isabelle and Katie. "Oh my, if we stuck you two in the same clothes, I swear you could be confused for twins!"

Katie exchanged a look with Isabelle.

"Twins?" they said in unison.

Blake held up both hands. "Okay, sisters. But, boy, if I didn't know any better, I'd say you two came from the same womb."

"Okay, enough of that," Katie said and made a shooing motion. "Don't you have work to do? Because I sure do."

Blake grinned and nodded to Isabelle. "Break a leg, okay?"

Isabelle smiled. "Thanks."

"You, too, Katie. But then you're an old pro," he added and turned.

"Hey, who are you calling old?" Katie protested. "I'm still younger than you!"

Without turning back, Blake waved his hand at her and continued walking down the corridor, before marching through a door and disappearing from view.

"Men!"

A suffering sigh came from Isabelle. Instantly, Katie ran her eyes over her. "Something wrong, honey?"

"It's nothing, it's just…"

"Stage fright?" Katie prompted. "Don't worry, we all get it."

"It's not that. I'm ready for the play. I know all the lines. Not just mine. I know everybody's."

Katie brushed her hand over Isabelle's hair, pride swelling in her chest. Samson's daughter had talent. "Well, that's why I made you understudy for all the major female roles. I've never seen anybody who could retain so many lines in such a short time."

Isabelle smiled unexpectedly and a little of the gloom lifted off her face. "I'm so glad you did. That's why, you know, I was wondering… I mean… Do you think…"

Katie felt her forehead furrow. Isabelle wasn't normally somebody to be nervous or tongue-tied. "What's bothering you?"

Isabelle twiddled the ribbons below her empire waist. "It's Cameron."

For a moment, Katie didn't know who Isabelle was talking about. Then it dawned on her. "Cameron, who's playing Lysander?"

Isabelle nodded and avoided eye contact when she continued talking. "Yes, who's in love with Hermia."

A soft smile tugged at Katie's lips. "Who's played by me."

Isabelle lifted her head. "And in the end you get to kiss Lysander."

"And Helena, played by you, gets to kiss Demetrius."

Isabelle nodded, but didn't comment further.

"I thought you wanted it that way. Isn't that every girl's dream, to be pursued by two men? Like in the play how Helena is pursued by both Lysander and Demetrius because of Puck's love potion?"

"Yes, but Lysander's love isn't real. It's just an illusion."

"But it's a play. It's all an illusion."

Just like Hollywood had been an illusion. A pretty one. One that had made her wealthy, not wanting for anything. But nothing had been real in Hollywood: in the end she hadn't even been able to trust the people closest to her. Betrayal had nearly cost her her life. It was the real reason why she'd returned to San Francisco five years earlier: to return to her family, where she belonged, and to be safe again.

She'd managed to buy back the old Victorian house on Buena Vista Park that had once belonged to her family. And she'd made it vampire safe, so that whenever Haven and his mate Yvette visited, they wouldn't have to worry about sunlight hurting them.

"I'd much rather be Hermia, because Lysander's love for her is real," Isabelle continued. "And you said yourself I know all the lines. I'm your understudy. You know I can do it."

"You want me to switch roles with you?"

"Please."

"You really like Cameron, don't you?"

Isabelle nodded.

"Does he know?"

"No."

"Why don't you tell him?"

"I don't know whether he likes me."

"So you figured if you kiss him at the end of the play, you might find out?"

Isabelle shrugged. "No harm in that."

Katie reached for Isabelle's hand. "Well, we'd better get changed then. I've got everything in my private dressing room."

It wasn't really a dressing room, more a combination office/prop room she'd managed to borrow from the football coach for the duration of rehearsals.

"You're the best!" Isabelle said.

Smiling, Katie steered her to the second door on the right and entered the windowless room, letting the door snap shut behind them.

3

"Never did mockers waste more idle breath," Katie said, dressed as Helena in the long blue dress that Isabelle had worn before the performance, while looking back and forth between the two students who played Lysander and Demetrius.

The lights illuminated the three of them on the old creaking wooden stage of the university. In the chairs below in the auditorium, vampires and their families mixed with humans, who had no inkling about the preternatural creatures in their midst.

Before the performance, Katie had peeked through the curtain and scanned the audience. Both her brothers were in attendance; Haven had brought Yvette and their son and daughter. In the front row, Samson and Delilah sat proudly, flanked by their sons, Grayson and Patrick. Zane and the entire Eisenberg family were sitting in the back, while Amaury and Nina and their twins, eighteen-year old Damian and Benjamin, sat near the windows, which were covered by thick velvet curtains.

Quinn Ralston and his clan, which included his wife Rose, his protégé Oliver as well as Oliver's mate Ursula and their ten-year old boy, Sebastian, sat in the row behind Samson. Blake, who was also part of the Ralston clan, had taken up a post near the entrance door, scanning the room, while occasionally speaking quietly into his intercom and listening to the mic in his ear. Tasked with guarding thirteen Scanguards minors, ranging from ages ten to twenty, he definitely had his hands full, despite the fact that all of them were accompanied by their parents.

Gabriel and Maya were surrounded by their brood, two teenage boys and a girl. Maya was responsible for vampire females being able to conceive, though they were normally infertile. Her medical and research background had finally paid off when she'd developed a treatment that allowed a vampire female to become pregnant and carry a child to term. It had made waves in the vampire community.

Her mate Gabriel, a vampire with a vicious scar marring the left side of his face, was scanning the crowd. As Scanguards' number two, he never forgot his duty. Mixed among the Scanguards people sat the families of the other student actors, as well as many friends who'd come to support their classmates' thespian passions.

"Lysander, keep thy Hermia; I will none: if e'er I lov'd her, all that love is gone. My heart to her but as guest-wise sojoun'd; and now to Helena is it home return'd, there to remain."

Demetrius's delivery was a little wooden, but Katie had to admit he'd proven to be faithful to his character, and she was pleased with the performance so far. Even though she'd slipped into the part of Helena—and as much as she wanted to immerse herself in the character—she was still aware of her role as the director and teacher.

"Helena, it is not so," Lysander responded.

"Disparage not the faith thou dost not know, lest, to thy peril, though aby it dear," Demetrius replied and looked to stage left, pointing his hand in the same direction. *"Look where thy love comes; yonder is thy dear."*

Silence greeted Demetrius's announcement.

"Yonder is thy dear," he repeated, a little louder this time.

Katie's pulse kicked up, while her eyes searched the darkness to the side of the stage from where Isabelle was supposed to reappear as Hermia, Lysander's lover. But all she saw was one of her students dressed as a fairy waiting in the wings. She exchanged a look with the girl, but only got a helpless shrug as a response.

Isabelle had missed her cue! Embarrassed for her star student, Katie cringed. Had Isabelle forgotten her lines under the stress of the performance, or had she mistimed her next appearance on stage? Had she taken a bathroom break and forgotten the time?

From the auditorium, whispers drifted to Katie. The crowd was getting restless, sensing that something wasn't going according to plan. Her gaze shot to the first row. She didn't have to be able to see in the dark like the vampires watching to see Samson's eyes, because they were glowing red now, pointing at her like beacons.

What's going on? he mouthed, his entire face a mask of concern.

Katie had no problem reading his lips. It was a skill she'd learned during her professional acting career, when assistants off camera or off stage would prompt her.

She gave a quick shake of her head at Samson, then stared back at the side of the stage from which the actors entered. Still nothing.

An uncomfortable prickling sensation traveled up her arms. Something was wrong. Isabelle was a responsible person, despite her young age. She was an adult and didn't flake out on her commitments.

The two students playing Lysander and Demetrius stared at her for guidance.

"What now?" Lysander murmured.

Katie didn't reply. Instead she stalked to where the fairy waited in the wings, leaving the stage. She grabbed the chubby girl by the shoulders. "Where is Isabelle?"

"I don't know." Cindy choked down some food, powdered sugar rimming her lips. "She was here just a few minutes ago."

"Go, run to the bathrooms and see if she's there, quickly!"

Cindy instantly followed the command.

From the auditorium, more voices drifted to Katie. People were talking, wondering what was the problem. Just like she was.

"Where is she, where is Isabelle?"

Katie whirled her head in the direction of the voice and saw Blake rushing toward her, entering the backstage area from the corridor.

"I don't know. She missed her cue. She might be in the bathroom. I've already sent somebody there to look for her. Maybe she got nervous."

Blake pressed his finger to the mic in his ear. "Secure the perimeter. Find Isabelle Woodford. I repeat: secure all exits. Nobody gets in or out of this place without me knowing. Got that?"

Before she could tell Blake that he was probably overreacting, heavy footsteps came through the darkness backstage.

"Isabelle?" Samson pushed past Blake, his hazel eyes pinning Katie with a look that could have outclassed the Spanish Inquisition. "Where is my daughter?"

For a moment, Katie was paralyzed. The over six foot tall vampire made an imposing figure. He was power personified. She'd always known that, though she'd also seen his kind side, had experienced it personally many years earlier. But tonight he was something else: a concerned father.

"Check the dressing rooms and the bathrooms!" Blake barked into his mic.

"I don't know where she is; she was supposed to come back on stage," Katie said, replying to Samson. She wrung her hands in front of her stomach, anxiety building inside her.

The sound of somebody running in sandals came closer and Katie peered past the Scanguards boss.

"She's not in the bathroom," Cindy called to her, an expression of regret on her face. "I can't find her."

Blake barked more orders into his mic, some of them so low that Katie couldn't understand them. Past the curtain that separated the backstage area from the stage and the auditorium she heard people running around. Blake's team was seemingly at work to search every corner of the building.

"Cindy, assemble all the other students in the men's dressing room. Go!" Katie ordered. "And stay there until we know what's going on."

The girl looked frightened, but nodded and disappeared.

Samson looked at his chief of personal security. "Anything?"

"My guys are still searching. But there's no sign of her in the bathrooms or the dressing rooms."

"Maybe my dressing room? We were getting changed in there earlier," Katie offered, desperate to be of help.

Blake charged outside.

"What the fuck's going on?" a voice came out of the dark.

A second later, Grayson appeared from between the curtains. He was the mirror image of his father. His hair was as dark as a raven, though he'd gotten his eyes from his mother Delilah: green, just like Katie's. Grayson's green eyes were now flickering red as if he had a hard time controlling his vampire side. "Where is my sister?"

"We don't know yet," Samson said, his voice tight.

Blake came running. "Nothing in Katie's dressing room. We also checked all the closets on this level. My guys are working their way up to the other floors."

"And the exits?" Samson demanded.

"Nobody's getting in or out of this building without me knowing," Blake confirmed.

Grayson took a step toward Blake. "Then why the fuck can't you find her? You're supposed to know where she is at all times. You're supposed to protect her!"

Grayson was a hothead, just like Blake had been in his youth, but deep down he was like his father: fiercely protective of his family. If Katie had ever had any doubts about Grayson's loyalty to his siblings despite their constant rivalry, his anger at Blake now expunged them entirely.

Blake peeled his lips back from his gums, flashing the nineteen-year-old just enough fang to demand respect. "Isabelle was playing a different part from the one she was supposed to."

Katie expected Blake to point the finger at her, but to her surprise, he didn't. Instead he took the blame on himself. "I didn't adjust her security detail in time." He narrowed his eyes at the hybrid. "But I can assure you, Grayson, I *will* find your sister. She's my responsibility, and I don't—"

"It's my fault," Katie cut in, putting her hand on Blake's forearm. "I'm to blame. She begged me to change roles with her. And I agreed." She turned her head to Samson. "I'm sorry. It was all last minute. I—"

Samson cut her off with an abrupt movement of his hand. Then he looked back at Blake. "Search every inch of this building and the grounds. She has to be here. She *has* to."

"Samson!" Delilah's strained voice came from behind him.

He spun around.

Katie noticed their wordless exchange. As a blood-bonded couple they were able to communicate telepathically. Seconds passed in silence. It made Katie even more aware of the goings-on around her: stagehands rummaged through the area where spare furniture was kept, turning over each item. Scanguards staff rushed through the corridors, opened every door, checked every closet. Different voices calling for Isabelle could be heard throughout the building. Katie knew that others would be outside the building, searching the surrounding parking lot, adjacent buildings, and streets. There was any number of hiding places, though Katie knew that Isabelle wasn't hiding. She sensed it in her gut. Could feel it in her veins. Just like Samson and Delilah sensed it.

With every second that passed, reality encroached on the make-believe world of the stage behind her: Isabelle was gone.

Katie watched as Samson pulled his wife into his arms and pressed her to him, gently caressing her head.

"We'll find her, sweetness," he promised.

More people now crowded into the backstage area. Zane, the bald vampire who could scare the living daylights out of anybody, marched toward Samson, clearly agitated. He had a special connection to Isabelle: he was her godfather, the first person Isabelle had ever bitten. Besides her parents, he was the closest confidant she had.

A sob tore from Delilah, and Grayson exchanged a look with his father. Samson nodded and transferred his wife into his son's arms.

"She has to be here, Mom," Grayson comforted her.

"Nothing in the basement," Zane reported to Samson, then turned to Blake. "How about the surveillance cameras?"

"I've already sent Eddie to check the video footage," Blake replied, just as Amaury joined them.

The linebacker-sized vampire with the shoulder-long hair exchanged a quick glance with Samson. "The upper floors are clear, too."

Blake touched his mic and listened for a moment. Then, "Bring him in! What are you waiting for? Now!"

Instantly, Katie could see all the vampires backstage go on alert. Their eyes started to glow, and she could see their mouths become fuller as their fangs extended.

"Who?" Samson asked Blake.

"My guys found an unknown vampire lurking in the parking lot. They're bringing him in now."

When the assembled vampires' eyes narrowed a few moments later, Katie realized that they could already hear the intruder being dragged in, though it took another few seconds for Katie's ears to perceive the sound of the struggling individual.

Everybody was rushing toward the door, anticipating the suspect's arrival. Their broad backs obstructed Katie's view. Anxious to find out what was going on, Katie stepped onto a footstool and looked over the vampires' heads, just as three of Blake's men brought in a defiant vampire.

Oh my God! He looked ferocious, and the black hair, black lashes, and dark complexion made him look like the devil. His eyes glared red, and his fangs were extended. He was big, broad-shouldered and muscular. He wore casual clothes, but there was nothing casual about his demeanor. Power and strength radiated from every pore of his body. She was inexplicably drawn to that power. Drawn to the vampire beneath the surface.

The sudden silence in the room pulled her out of her observation and made her snap her gaze upward, back to the captive's face. The strange vampire had stopped struggling and was staring at Samson.

"Luther!" Samson hissed.

4

It had been a bad idea to show up in San Francisco wanting to make things right, Luther realized now. Apparently twenty years had done nothing to lessen Samson's hatred for him. Nor Amaury's. Both his former friends glared at him as if they were ready to rip his head off. Maybe they should. Maybe it would all be for the better.

"Oh my God, it's him, it's Luther," the tearful voice of a woman broke the hate-filled silence.

He didn't have to break eye contact with Samson to recognize the voice: Delilah, the woman he'd almost killed so many years earlier.

"It was him, it was him!" she now yelled with a fury he didn't quite understand.

If he'd known that everybody at Scanguards held a grudge for such a long time, he would have never come.

"I paid the fucking price," Luther ground out.

What else did they want from him? The council had sentenced him to twenty years, though they could have given him fifty, but Amaury's mate, Nina, had pleaded for leniency. Maybe she shouldn't have. Maybe he didn't deserve leniency.

"Release him!" Samson commanded the guards who were restraining him. When they hesitated, he added, "That's an order."

When the men took their claws off him, Luther felt a sense of surprise wash over him. Had he misjudged Samson?

A balled fist punched him in the face so fast and so hard that Luther was catapulted back. He lost his balance and crashed against the wall. Before he could jump back up, Samson was already on him.

"Where's my daughter?" he yelled and delivered a second blow to Luther's jaw.

Luther's head snapped to the side, and he tasted blood. His own blood. "How the fuck should I know?"

When the next blow came, Luther blocked it with his forearm and pushed back. But Samson didn't give up so easily. Fury coursed through Luther, giving him wings. He reared up and barreled toward his former friend, delivering an uppercut to Samson's chin, yet still holding back his true strength.

Samson's eyes blazed with unbridled rage, while his friends stood back a few paces, allowing their boss to do as he pleased. Luther gritted his teeth. He hadn't come to duke it out with Samson as if they were two thugs. That hadn't been his plan. Far from it.

But apparently it was what Samson wanted.

Another punch veered toward Luther's temple. In a lightning-fast move he raised his arm, preventing Samson's claws from reaching their target, while kicking his foot against his opponent's knee. But Samson didn't go down as expected. Sure-footed, he barely swayed before drawing back his arm for another blow.

"Stop it!" Luther yelled.

"What did you do to my daughter?" Samson repeated, flashing his fangs.

"I have no idea what you're talking about!"

But his words fell on deaf ears. Samson's claws came toward him. Luther moved, but the wall at his back and another vampire who stood too close made it impossible to get out of the path of the lethal instrument fast enough. Sharp barbs, as deadly as knives, sliced across his shoulder, leaving deep cuts from which blood oozed instantly. The metallic scent permeated the air in the corridor, inciting the need in the assembled vampires to show their vampire side.

Fangs flashed. Fingers turned into claws. Eyes glowed red. Men turned into bloodthirsty vampires. He'd seen it often enough—prison had been a perfect microcosm of what happened on the outside.

Samson slammed his full body weight against Luther, pinning him against the wall. Though Luther could have pushed him off, what would have been the point when at least seven other vampires were surrounding them, ready to interfere should their boss be in danger? Not even Luther could beat those odds. So he didn't even try.

"Go ahead, slice me open!" he challenged his old friend. "But it won't change my answer. I don't fucking know where your daughter is."

At least now he could guess that the slightly hostile treatment he was receiving had nothing to do with what had happened twenty years ago. Rather, he seemed to have stumbled into an incident that was only just unraveling. And he sure had no interest in sticking around to find out what this was about. If Samson couldn't keep tabs on his daughter, it wasn't Luther's goddamn problem.

Through narrowed eyes Samson watched him intently, as if he could find out the truth by staring at him. Luther didn't blink. He had nothing to hide.

From behind Samson, another vampire appeared. Luther had never seen him before, but he knew nevertheless who he was. After all, he was a younger edition of Samson himself—and a hybrid. He had to be his son.

"He's lying. He has to be lying!" the young hybrid spat. "Dad, you can't possibly believe Luther! Not after all he did!" It appeared Samson's offspring knew who he was—and what he'd done in the past. Mistrust spewed from the boy's eyes.

"Grayson!" Samson growled, tossing his son a warning look. "You take care of your mother and Patrick; I'll handle this."

Reluctantly, Grayson retreated a couple of steps. By doing so, he gave Luther a view of the people standing farther back. In the door frame of what appeared to be a backstage area, a woman stood dressed in a long blue period dress with an empire waist, which accentuated her full breasts. Outside he'd seen posters about a play when he'd arrived. Apparently she was one of the student actresses.

For a moment, the sight of such female perfection made him forget that he was in the middle of a confrontation. One thing was immediately evident: she wasn't a vampire. However, she didn't appear fazed by the show of aggression the vampires around her demonstrated.

Luther slowly lifted his eyes from her cleavage to her graceful neck and the beautiful oval face framed by dark brown hair, which was upswept with curls dangling from it. She looked like she didn't belong in this century. As if she was a time traveler, a mirage from a different era. Not quite human, but something more. She was beautiful, and the sight of her filled him with an odd sense of yearning. A longing he didn't understand.

"I'm asking again, where is my daughter?"

Intrigued and at the same time irritated, Luther tore his gaze from the dark-haired beauty and glared back at Samson.

"I don't fucking know. So take your hands off me."

"Luther?"

At the sound of Eddie's voice, Luther spun his head to the side. His protégé, the young man he'd turned into a vampire over twenty years ago, came toward him.

"Hi Eddie, been a long time," he said dryly.

Only once, Eddie had visited him in prison, and back then they'd gotten into a physical fight. He wasn't expecting Eddie to take his side now either.

"What're you doing here?" His protégé seemed genuinely surprised and interested.

"He abducted Isabelle," Samson claimed.

"No, he didn't," Eddie contradicted his boss.

Luther raised an eyebrow, surprised that Eddie would give him the benefit of the doubt.

Eddie moved closer, addressing Samson directly. "Blake asked me to check any surveillance recordings from the cameras inside and outside the building. We have a visual. Isabelle was taken. But not by Luther. If he's behind it, he didn't do the dirty work himself."

Well, so much for Eddie's confidence in him.

"Who? Who took her? Did she get hurt?" Samson asked, easing off Luther and reaching for his wife's hand.

Luther recognized true fear in his old friend's face.

"All I could see on the tape is that some guy grabbed her outside the dressing room. She struggled, but she couldn't shake him. Which suggests that he's a vampire or a hybrid himself—we don't know for sure, since a video can't capture a vampire's aura. But with Isabelle's hybrid strength she would have been able to defeat any human."

"Did you recognize him?"

Eddie shook his head. "I only got a partial of his face. And no voice. There's no audio on the recording."

"Run what you've got through our database at HQ; see whether we can get anything with facial recognition."

Eddie nodded. "I already sent all the footage to the server at HQ."

Samson turned back to Luther, narrowing his eyes. "Who took Isabelle?"

"Didn't you hear Eddie? It wasn't me!"

"One of your men?" Samson continued grilling him.

Luther sucked more air into his lungs. "I don't have any men. I was in prison for twenty years. Remember?"

"Oh, I remember." A dangerous undertone colored Samson's voice. "And now you're out. And back here. On the night my daughter disappears."

"I've got nothing to do with that."

"We'll see." He motioned to Zane and Amaury. "Cuff him and take him to HQ."

"You're making a big mistake," Luther warned.

Samson went toe to toe with him. "No, you're the one who's making a mistake by showing up here." He tossed a sideways glance at his subordinates. "Interrogate him downtown." Then he swung around and looked back at Eddie. "Did the guy on the video touch anything? Doors? Walls? Anything at all?"

"There's a chance we can get some fingerprints off the door, but it means we'll need to get fingerprints from everybody else too in order to rule them out."

"Do it!"

"I'll get a team on that," Blake interrupted him, then nodded to Eddie. "You and Thomas analyze the recording and run it through the system."

Not too gently, Zane and Amaury grabbed Luther's arms.

"Welcome back," Amaury gritted.

"I hear we're related now," Luther replied. His protégé Eddie being

Amaury's brother-in-law made them practically family.

Amaury flashed his fangs at him, apparently not too pleased about that fact. "Trust me, that won't have any bearing on how I treat you."

A shove from Zane catapulted Luther closer to the door of the backstage area. The woman in the blue costume still stood there, her lips moving as she mumbled something to herself.

Tears rimmed her eyes. "It's all my fault."

The words registered but didn't make sense. Luther hesitated for an instant, resisting Zane and Amaury's grip, and inhaled.

The scent filling his nostrils made him jerk back in surprise.

The woman wasn't human.

5

Katie's breath shuddered and her heart skidded to an abrupt halt. Luther was staring at her, eyes widened, lips parted, still showing the tips of his fangs. His nostrils flared. Though she was used to being around vampires and had never been scared of them, this was different. Luther was different. He wasn't civilized like the others. Anything but. *Feral* came to mind. It fit with his admission that he'd been in prison for twenty years.

His eyes were dark, almost black, but around the rim of his irises a golden hue began to shimmer. It was a sight from which she couldn't tear herself away. Almost as if he was using some unseen power to draw her to him. To entice her to approach. To catch her in his net.

She felt paralyzed, unable to move, unable to breathe for fear he would tighten the invisible chains he'd wrapped around her and suffocate her. In her mind's eye she could see it happening. Her instinct told her to step back, to extricate herself from his spell. But something else inside her, something purely female—and purely wanton— overrode her sense of self-preservation.

This man was danger personified. Her entire life, she'd tried to avoid danger, tried to stay safe, but suddenly that very notion seemed cowardly. Danger suddenly called to her. Tempted her. Told her to throw caution to the wind. To live a little. To take a risk.

Luther's eyes narrowed, and his lips moved. *You*, he mouthed.

But before she could figure out what he meant by that, a voice broke the spell she seemed to be under. "Katie!" It was her brother Wesley.

Luther's head whirled in Wes's direction, his look changing to one of battle-readiness.

The moment Wes reached them, he pressed a quick kiss to the top of her head. "Hey, love, you okay?"

Katie could only nod, before Samson interrupted, "We need you to find her, Wes."

With a regretful look, Wes shook his head. "Sorry, Samson, but she's a hybrid. Her vampire side prevents me from *scrying* for her. I have no way of locating her. Not with witchcraft anyway."

When a low growl came from Luther, Katie's gaze instantly shot to him, but already Zane and Amaury were dragging him away.

"Can't you try, Wes?" Delilah insisted, giving Wesley a pleading look. "Please can't you find my baby?"

Wes closed his eyes for a moment. "I wish I could help. But there are limits to my craft."

"Oh no! As a baby she was telepathic, but it went away when she started to speak. I wish she could still communicate with me. Oh, Isabelle, where are you?" A sob tore from Delilah and she buried her head in her son's chest.

Grayson exchanged a look with his father. "What now, Dad?"

Samson turned to Blake. "I want every one of our men out there looking for Isabelle. Call in anybody who's on leave. I want every corner of this city searched. Tap into every surveillance camera, every traffic camera, every video feed. I want my daughter found."

"I'm on it." Blake nodded, a look of confident determination on his face. He looked at Delilah. "We'll find her. We'll get her back. I promise you."

Then he waved at John, a vampire who'd joined the ranks of Scanguards two years earlier after leaving New Orleans and Cain, the king he'd served for almost two decades. He'd needed a new environment after a tragedy had befallen him, and Samson had provided him with a new home and a new purpose at Scanguards.

"What do you want me to do?" John asked, his southern accent still pronounced.

"Take a couple of men and interrogate the audience and the student actors. I also want all the stage hands and any of the University employees who were on site looked at."

"You've got it," John answered and walked away.

While Blake issued more orders, Katie squeezed her brother's hand before releasing it and approaching Samson.

"Samson, I want to help. Please tell me how I can help."

He glanced at her, giving her only the briefest of looks. "There's nothing you can do. Scanguards will take care of it." He turned toward his son and wife. "Where's Patrick?"

"He's with Damian and Benjamin."

Samson nodded. "Join them and make sure everybody gets home safely."

Katie felt somebody tug at her sleeve and pivoted.

"You should go home, too," Wesley suggested.

"I can't, Wes. It's my fault. I changed roles with Isabelle. I didn't tell Blake."

"Go home, Katie," Samson snapped behind her.

She whirled around and stared into his furious eyes.

"I don't want to see you right now. Can't you understand that?" he gritted from between clenched teeth.

Oh God, yes, she understood it. He knew it was her fault, and he was trying hard not to let his anger out on her. She had broken protocol by not telling Blake about the role change so he could adjust his security detail accordingly. It was her fault that there'd been moments where Isabelle hadn't been guarded.

"I'm so sorry."

"You heard my father," Grayson interrupted, a protective arm around his mother's back. "Leave!"

"Let's go." Wesley put his arm around her. "I'll take you home."

Reluctantly Katie allowed her brother to lead her toward her dressing room. Out of earshot of the vampires, she stopped and turned toward him.

"Wes, please, I want to help. I feel responsible. If I hadn't changed roles with Isabelle, she would have been on stage, and maybe this would have never happened."

"You can't know that. Whoever took her probably just waited for the right moment."

"But one of Blake's men would have been there had he known Isabelle was going to be on her own backstage. I should have told him."

She felt tears well up in her eyes. But she couldn't cry. Crying meant admitting defeat.

Wes opened the door for her and motioned to the interior. "Get changed. I'll wait here for you, and then I'll take you home."

When the door closed behind her, silence suddenly greeted her. The voices and sounds from the corridor were muffled in the small room. She reached behind her back, trying to find the zipper, but the fabric tightened across her chest, making it impossible for her to reach far enough back to open the dress.

A sob tore from her chest. "Damn dress!" she cursed.

Frustrated, she ripped the door open. "I can't get this stupid dress off," she wailed at Wes who stood there.

"Oh, Katie," he murmured, reaching his arms out to her.

"I'll take care of it, Wes," Yvette suddenly interrupted.

Katie looked at her sister-in-law as she came toward them, grateful for her concern. Yvette, beautiful with her long black hair and elegant in her figure-hugging red dress, ushered her back into the room and closed the door behind them.

"Hey, honey," Yvette murmured and pulled her into a sisterly embrace. "It'll be all right. We'll find her. Scanguards takes care of their own."

Katie sniffled and lifted her head to look at Haven's mate. "I feel responsible."

"Don't," she demanded. "Now let's get you out of this dress."

With expert hands, Yvette helped her get undressed.

Katie wiped her tears from her eyes. "Are the kids scared?"

Yvette rolled her eyes while she handed Katie a T-shirt. "The younger ones maybe, but the older boys are all suddenly turning into Rambo. Even Cooper."

"But he's only sixteen!" And in Katie's eyes, her nephew was still a child, though he probably wouldn't have liked to hear that.

"Don't I know it? But he hears the twins talking about joining the search and off he goes, begging his father to let him help, too."

"But Amaury's boys are hellions! They aren't like Cooper." Cooper was a lot more sensible. More the thinking kind.

"Yeah, and guess who they got that from. Damian is cut from the same cloth as his father, and Benjamin is just like Nina. And together they're unstoppable once they've gotten something into their heads. No wonder Amaury and Nina stopped having any more after those two."

Katie sighed and pulled her jeans up. "Aren't all hybrids like that? Thinking they're invincible?"

"All hybrids of the Scanguards family sure are. They see their parents and what they do for a living, and they think that every vampire is like that: a fighting machine out to right all wrongs. They're gonna have a rude awakening one day when they realize that not all wrongs can be fought and defeated. I try to instill that in Lydia and Cooper, but whenever they get together with the rest of the bunch, they want to be superheroes!"

"Can you blame them?" Katie put her hand on Yvette's forearm, thankful that her sister-in-law was preventing her from spinning out of control. "They see their parents as superheroes, and they want to be just like them. Your kids want to emulate you."

Yvette raised an eyebrow and tilted her head to the side. "Why do I suddenly feel like you're trying to butter me up, sis?"

"I'd never do that," Katie claimed. "Though there is one thing you could do for me, since you have Level A clearance at HQ."

Yvette shook her head. "The answer is no."

"You don't even know what it is."

"The answer is still no."

6

Zane slammed his fist on the table, clearly enraged. The silver chains with which Luther was tied up rattled from the impact. They didn't do any damage to his ankles, since those were covered by his pants, but the shackles around his wrists were another story. They burned painfully into his flesh. But he didn't flinch. There was nothing Zane could do or say to make him change his answers.

"As I already said, I have nothing to do with the disappearance of Samson's daughter."

He blinked against the glaring lights in the underground interrogation room. The room was two stories high, with only one door and a mirrored window high up, facing the table Luther sat at. He assumed that somebody was watching from up there.

"Very odd coincidence then that you showed up here the same night, don't you think?" Zane flashed his fangs. "Care to explain?"

Not particularly. "Maybe I was in the mood for a cable car ride or a stroll down the Embarcadero."

The back of Zane's hand slashed across Luther's cheek, whipping his head to the side. But Zane would have to be a lot more forceful to do any damage. The time in prison had increased Luther's tolerance of pain to a level that, to most other vampires, would appear impossible.

"That's enough, Zane!" a voice came from the door.

Luther shot the newcomer a glance.

Eddie marched into the room. "Take a walk, Zane, I'm gonna have a word with him."

Zane growled, but stepped back. "I'll be back with my instruments later." He turned and walked out, slamming the door behind him.

What he meant by instruments was pretty clear: the bald vampire with the short temper intended to inflict pain by torturing him. What a waste of everybody's time.

"Didn't get a chance to say hi earlier," Luther said to Eddie instead, turning his attention to his protégé. "You look good."

"You don't."

Luther shrugged, motioning to his shoulder and face, both of which sported fresh wounds, which had already stopped bleeding. In a few hours he'd be as good as new. "Hazard of the trade."

Eddie remained standing and leaned over the table, placing his hands flat on its surface. "Why are you here, Luther?"

"Can't I look in on my protégé?"

"You didn't come to see me. Not after what happened the last time we saw each other. We both know that. So cut the crap."

Luther dropped his gaze to Eddie's hands. The gold ring on Eddie's ring finger was hard to overlook.

"So you're married now. Who to?"

"He's married to me!" Thomas's voice came through the loudspeaker and echoed in the empty room. "Now answer his questions."

Only mildly surprised, Luther looked up at Eddie. "Congratulations. So I was right then." And though he didn't want to admit it, he was pleased for Eddie. At least he'd found himself and the happiness he deserved.

"Why are you here, Luther? You still hate them so much that you want to make them suffer? Is that it?"

"I'm all fresh out of hate." It was the truth, but it didn't make him feel any better. Because the disappointment still sat deep within his bones, still gripped him day and night and didn't let him go. No matter what he tried, he couldn't shake it, couldn't get over the betrayal. And the guilt that surfaced with it. Because in part, he was to blame, too.

"Fine, you don't wanna talk. Then let's watch a little movie together." Eddie's voice sounded calmer now. He motioned up to the window, giving his lover behind the impenetrable glass a sign. "Thomas, run the surveillance footage."

A moment later, a panel in the wall retreated and in its place, an oversized monitor appeared. The image on it was black and white and grainy, but Luther had no trouble recognizing the place where the video had been taken: in the corridor of the university.

Samson's daughter, dressed in a long burgundy gown, her hair in an upswept hairdo, looked not unlike Katie. In fact, with their hair made up the same way, and wearing similar dresses, they could easily be mistaken for sisters. Though, of course, in reality Luther would never mistake Isabelle for Katie. Something had stuck out about her. Something he didn't see in Isabelle, something about the eyes.

But before he could think on it more, a man appeared on the video. He seemed to say something to Samson's daughter, though there was no audible sound. Luther had expected that. Eddie had mentioned earlier that the video didn't have any audio.

The struggle was short. Despite her hybrid powers, Isabelle couldn't shake her attacker. But her lips moved, and Luther leaned forward.

"Who is he?" Eddie asked.

Luther shook his head, watching Isabelle's lips move again and again. *I'm not in Berlin?* It didn't make any sense. Was he reading her lips correctly? Why Berlin? No, he had to be wrong. *I'm not Amberly?* That didn't sound right either. For a moment he tore his gaze from the monitor.

"I don't know him. The angle of the camera. It makes it impossible to see his face."

He watched as the man dragged his victim away, his hand over her mouth now to prevent her from screaming.

"I can't help you."

"That's not good enough." Eddie turned toward the observation window. "Lie detector?"

"I'll set it up," came Thomas's voice through the speakers.

"Lie detector?" Luther scoffed. "Haven't you forgotten one tiny detail? I'm a vampire. Polygraphs only work on humans."

A proud expression crossed Eddie's face. "Thomas invented one especially for vampires." He leaned closer. "Just a word of warning: the UV blasts sting."

"Well, that's just perfect, isn't it?" As if he needed any more burns on his body.

7

Katie ducked into a niche and watched as Thomas left the observation room. The moment he turned a corner, she rushed toward the closing door and jammed her foot between door and frame before it could close again. She peered through the gap and saw her brother Haven sitting at the controls.

Relieved she slid into the small room and closed the door behind her.

Haven whirled his head to her, growling. "What are you doing here, Katie? Didn't you hear Samson?"

She walked to him and pulled the chair next to him out from underneath the console.

"How did you even get in here? HQ is practically on lockdown."

Katie shrugged, giving him a sheepish smile. "Sorry, but I had to come. I know in my gut that I can help. I have to do this." She leaned toward him, giving him a brief hug.

Haven was a big softie who loved her and couldn't deny her anything. As if he wanted to make up for the time when he hadn't been there for her. A long time ago, he'd risked life and limb to find her after she'd been abducted as a baby. He'd since made peace with the man who'd taken her, because it had been vital to keep the balance of power in the vampire and witch world.

"Please," she murmured, employing all her sisterly charm. "Just let me watch. Maybe I'll see something that will help us find Isabelle."

Haven sighed. "If Samson catches you here, you're on your own."

She kissed him on the cheek. "You're the best."

He rolled his eyes. "Apparently somebody else is even better, otherwise you wouldn't even have made it inside headquarters."

She opened her mouth to respond, but Haven lifted his hand. "I don't want to know whether it was Wes or Yvette. Then at least I won't have to get mad at either one of them."

Katie smirked. "That's why we all love you."

"Yeah, right." He turned back toward the window and looked down at the goings-on in the room below.

"What are they doing to him?"

"Lie detector test."

"What?"

Katie peered down into the room. Luther's shirt was gone. His hands were chained to the table, his feet to the floor. A big machine on wheels stood next to the table. Thomas, with Eddie's assistance, was placing electrodes onto Luther's chest. She leaned closer to the window, focusing her eyes on Luther's skin.

"Oh my God," she murmured to herself. Luther's chest was marred by scars. She strained, trying to get a better look. Burn marks? By the looks of it, there were many of them, large and small. She could only imagine the pain they must have caused when he'd obtained them.

"I thought vampires didn't scar." Katie exchanged a look with her brother.

"Maybe those are from when he was human."

She nodded and changed the subject. "Does a lie detector test even work on a vampire?"

"This one does," Haven claimed. "Thomas designed it."

"He's kind of a genius, isn't he?"

"Yep, pretty brilliant. Though Eddie isn't far behind."

"How does it work?"

Haven shrugged. "Can't really explain it the way Thomas can, but basically, when a vampire who's strapped to the machine has the urge to answer a question with a lie, the electrodes administer a blast of UV light to his skin, burning him."

"So a lie detector and torture device in one? But how does the machine know if a vampire is lying?"

"In principal it's similar to how a human lie detector works. Something to do with subtle changes in the vampire's aura that the naked eye can't detect, but the machine can. And as soon as it does it sends a signal in the form of a UV blast. Pretty effective, if I may add.

I've seen it in action."

"How?"

"Eddie and Thomas tested it out on each other. Made sense. Because of their bond, they could immediately sense when the other one would lie and then program the machine accordingly."

Curious, Katie peered down into the room. Luther appeared calm, as if he'd resigned himself to his fate. As if he didn't care what happened to him. An odd calmness emanated from him. It was Zen-like. It fascinated her, made her want to know more about him, and find out what went on behind the unreadable façade of his handsome face.

"He said to Samson that he was in prison for twenty years. What for?" she asked, turning to her brother.

"A murder plot."

At Haven's short answer, she gasped. "Murder?"

Her brother nodded. "It was before my time, and nobody talks about it much. But apparently he was trying to kill Delilah and Nina. Delilah was pregnant with Isabelle at the time. The attempt was thwarted by Scanguards, and Luther was put away."

Open-mouthed, she stared down at Luther. "No wonder Samson was so enraged. Do you think Luther came back to finish the job? Maybe kill Isabelle instead?"

Ice shot through her veins at the thought.

"He denies having anything to do with it, and from what I've seen so far, I'm inclined to believe him."

Haven pointed to the monitor to his left, and Katie followed his gaze. An image of a corridor was frozen on the screen. She recognized it. It was the area near the dressing rooms.

"He denies knowing the guy who took Isabelle. And from the partial face we have, so far we haven't found a match in the databases. We'll know more after the lie detector test. But no matter what the result is, Luther is dangerous. He's not like us. He's a criminal."

Katie involuntarily shivered at her brother's assessment. She could blame the air conditioning in the room, but she knew it was her body's reaction to the man who was being interrogated.

Thomas and Eddie stepped back from Luther, giving her a good view of his scarred torso once more. Her fingers itched with the need to caress the marred skin, to feel for herself the damage that had been done to his body. As if she needed proof that he was somebody she had to stay away from. Somebody she should not find as fascinating as she did.

The phone rang, and Haven answered it. "Yeah?"

In the interrogation room below, Thomas gave Eddie a sign to switch on the machine. Next to Katie, Haven jumped up.

"I'll be right there."

She spun her head to him. "What's wrong?"

"We have a lead. Somebody spotted a woman being dragged into a car not far from the University." He was already at the door, when he looked over his shoulder. "Stay out of sight and out of trouble." Then he sighed. "And Katie, I know this whole thing has to be particularly hard on you. But don't let it drag you back to that dark place. It's behind you. It's over."

She nodded automatically, shuddering at the memories, and watched the door fall shut behind him. Then she turned her eyes back to the window. Though Thomas spoke to Luther, there was no sound. Haven had probably switched off the speakers before leaving the observation room. Not wanting to alert anybody below that she was up here watching them, Katie didn't dare try any of the buttons on the console to find the right one to listen in on the room below.

Instead, she turned to the computer screen and shifted into Haven's empty chair. With a click of the mouse, she hit the play button on the screen and watched Isabelle's abduction unfold.

She strained to get a better look at the kidnapper, but the grainy black-and-white picture and the camera angle didn't help. Besides, the man kept his head down as if he knew that there was a camera. Isabelle struggled, and it was evident that she was using her vampire strength against the attacker, but the man seemed stronger than she. A vampire or a hybrid himself.

"Oh God, Isabelle," she murmured to herself. "I'm so sorry."

She reached for her student's face on the monitor, wanting to comfort her, to tell her that she would do anything to find her, when she accidentally touched the mouse again, restarting the video from the beginning.

It was almost too much, having to look at it again. Helplessly, she stared at Isabelle, when she noticed her lips move, repeating the same thing over and over again. *Kimberly.* There it was, Katie's stage name. Was she calling for help?

Katie used the mouse to go back in the video and played it again. This time she only looked at Isabelle's lips. During her time on the stage, she'd learned to read lips—mostly because at the beginning of her career she'd had a hard time remembering her lines and had often needed the help of a prompter.

I'm not Kimberly.

Katie drew back in her chair. Isabelle hadn't called for her to help her. She'd told her kidnapper that she wasn't Kimberly. That she wasn't the one he was after.

The vampire taking Isabelle had mistaken her for Katie.

"Oh God, no. It *is* my fault."

"What are you doing in here?"

At the male voice, Katie whirled around and stared at the tall vampire entering the room.

"I'm Haven's sister…"

"We're on lockdown. Only Scanguards personnel are allowed." Not too gently, he grabbed her by the arm.

She tried to pull free, but he was too strong. Furious, she glanced at the badge dangling from his breast pocket and read his name.

"My brother authorized me to be in here, Jake, and I'm sure he won't be pleased that you're throwing me out."

Jake grinned with an air of superiority. "Nice try, lady, but Haven knows better. Let's go!"

"Goddamn it!" she cursed under her breath. Just as she'd discovered something, some idiot was throwing her out.

Haven was out following the lead they'd gotten; Yvette was probably back at home with her son and daughter, and Wes was nowhere to be seen. Most likely he was still at the university, helping with the interrogation of the students and audience members.

Katie straightened her T-shirt after Jake had unceremoniously deposited her on the sidewalk outside of Mission HQ. For now, there was no way back into Scanguards' shiny headquarters. But she knew how she could help nevertheless, because the realization that the kidnapper had been after her and not after Isabelle, had reminded her of something she'd tried to forget.

Katie dug for her keys and headed for her car. She would be home in less than ten minutes, traffic permitting, and back here shortly after that. And then Samson and the rest of Scanguards would have to listen to her and accept her help. Because she could find Isabelle.

She knew who'd taken her.

8

Bare-chested, Luther remained chained to the table and floor in the interrogation room. The electrodes had been removed and the polygraph carted out of the room. It had been several minutes since Thomas and Eddie had left him, both with unreadable expressions on their faces.

When the door opened anew, it was none other than Samson who entered. Gabriel followed him. The scar that reached from his ear to his chin gleamed under the harsh neon lights, making it look even more pronounced.

The gazes of his visitors immediately shot to Luther's disfigured chest and reminded him of the ugliness of his upper body. A strange look crossed Gabriel's face, and for an instant, Luther thought he noticed his old friend's scar twitching in brotherly compassion. But it had to be a trick of the light.

Samson stopped in front of the table, looking down at him. The stress of the last hours showed on his face.

"You passed the lie detector test."

Samson's words were clipped, his jaw clenched, and it was evident that he hated to make such an admission.

Luther lifted his hands, rattling his chains. "Well, then I guess we won't need these anymore."

Samson snarled. "But I don't trust you. For all I know you managed to beat the machine."

"Why does that not surprise me?" Luther replied dryly. He paused for effectiveness. "Oh yeah, it's because you can't let bygones be bygones!"

The back of Samson's hand hit him across the cheek. He swallowed the insult and faced him stoically, then slowly and deliberately turned his face to the other side.

"Would you like the other cheek, too?" he mocked.

Before Samson could take him up on the offer, Gabriel jerked his friend back by the shoulders.

"Don't! He's just provoking you." Gabriel tossed him an acid look. "Pushing all the buttons again, are we, Luther?"

Luther lifted one shoulder in a half-shrug. "As long as there are buttons to push." And by the looks of it, Samson could be more easily provoked than ever before. Was that what having a family did to a man? Turned him into a powder keg?

Samson's nostrils flared as he visibly tried to get himself under control. "What are you doing in San Francisco, Luther?"

"Like I told Zane already, maybe I was in the mood for a cable car ride. None of your fucking business. Last time I checked this was a free country."

"We'll see about that." Luther watched Samson exchange a look with Gabriel, before his number two nodded.

Samson placed his hands on the table and leaned in. "Here's what we'll do now. Gabriel will use his gift on you. And you won't resist. And if he sees that you had anything to do with the abduction of my daughter, I'm going to rip you to shreds."

Luther clamped his jaw together. "That's an invasion of privacy."

"You have no right to privacy. You forfeited that right when you attempted to kill Delilah and Nina!"

"I paid for that mistake." Dearly. He even regretted it, but there was no way in hell he'd ever admit that fact to the asshole hovering over him, acting all superior.

"Not nearly long enough," Samson claimed. "If it had been up to me and Amaury, we would have locked you up and thrown away the key."

"But it wasn't up to you."

"This time it will be. This time I won't hand you over to the council, but deal with you myself."

Luther pushed the air out through his nostrils. "Not even you can touch an innocent vampire."

"We'll see about how innocent you are." Samson motioned to Gabriel and stepped back.

Gabriel nodded and approached. "You know the drill. I can dig into your memories, but I'll only see what you've seen and heard. I can't read your thoughts or—"

"Yeah, yeah," Luther interrupted him. "Why don't you just get on with it and don't pretend you care about my rights? Like I give a shit."

He watched Gabriel close his eyes and stand in front of him, motionless. Luther felt nothing of the invasion into his memories. It was what made this gift so dangerous: Gabriel could use it without anybody knowing he was doing it.

At the thought of what Gabriel might see, Luther shuddered. He didn't want him to see the cruelties he'd had to endure in prison, and he hoped that Gabriel wouldn't go far enough back in time to see how he'd received his scars. He didn't want anybody's pity. He'd deserved the punishment.

Instead, Luther concentrated his thoughts on something else. Somebody else: the actress. Wesley, the witch who'd suddenly shown up, had called her Katie and kissed her. There was something about her. Her scent wasn't entirely human, but just as he'd thought he recognized what it was, the stench of that male witch had polluted the air around them.

She looked familiar. Had he met her somewhere before he'd gone to prison? It was impossible. She wasn't a vampire. Twenty years ago she would have been a child, not the beautiful woman she was now. It was impossible that he knew her. Maybe she simply reminded him of someone from his past.

"There's nothing, Samson, he was telling the truth."

Gabriel's voice brought him back to reality. Luther lifted his lids to look at the two Scanguards bosses.

"Are you sure?" Samson ran a hand through his hair.

"He's got nothing to do with Isabelle's abduction. He met with nobody after he was released from prison last night."

"What about earlier? He could have planned this long ago."

Gabriel shook his head. "I went far enough back. There's nothing."

Luther caught Gabriel's sideways glance and wanted to curse. Gabriel had seen more than he wanted him to see.

"You've gotta let him go."

Luther lifted his hands, looking pointedly at the shackles.

Samson sucked in a breath. "You're free. But that changes nothing. Leave this city! If you ever come back, I will find a reason to kill you. Do you understand that?"

"You're making yourself perfectly clear."

Luther recognized a serious threat when he saw one. Samson was volatile. As long as the whereabouts of his daughter were unknown, he would lash out at anybody he had a grudge against. And Luther wasn't willing to stick around to play scapegoat.

"Unchain him!" Samson turned and marched out of the room, leaving his second-in-command to execute his order.

As Gabriel untied him, he said, "You'd better heed his warning and head out tonight."

The chains rattled as they dropped to the floor.

Rubbing his wrists, Luther rose from the uncomfortable plastic chair. "I have no reason to stay." He reached for his shirt and pulled it on, not bothering to button up. He grabbed his jacket.

"Don't you?"

Luther stabbed his index finger into Gabriel's chest. "You might have seen my past, but don't presume to know anything about me. I'm not the man you once knew."

Gabriel pointed to the door. "You're free to go. The guard outside the door will escort you out."

Without a word, Luther walked to the door and opened it. Outside, a vampire with a semi-automatic pistol strapped to his side, motioned him to the left. In silence, Luther walked ahead of him, the maze of corridors reminding him once again of prison. This wasn't much different, though there was more activity and more noise at Scanguards HQ.

When they reached the lobby, a fancy entry hall with large glass panels on the side that faced the street, the guard stopped at the reception desk for a moment. Luther took the opportunity to let his eyes wander. It was odd that the entrance to Scanguards was made of glass. What did they do during the day when the rays of the sun flooded this area?

Maybe the glass was made of a special, UV-impenetrable material. After all, twenty years had passed since he'd been on the outside, and even inside the vampire prison he'd noticed technological changes over the years. Perhaps somebody had invented glass that didn't let UV light through.

Involuntarily, he took a few steps toward the glass-paneled exit, wanting to look at the glass from up close. But before his eyes could zoom in on the shiny surface, they were drawn to a poster that had been affixed next to the double doors.

It was an announcement of the play that had taken place tonight. *A Midsummer Night's Dream*, it read. A photo of what appeared to be a dress rehearsal was on the top half of the flyer, while a list of the major players graced the bottom. In the middle though, it was written in large letters: *Directed by former Hollywood star Kimberly Fairfax.*

Words bounced around in his head.

Hollywood.

Actress.

Kimberly.

His eyes snapped to the picture. And then he saw it. Saw her. The woman with the green eyes like a cat. The actress on the posters in the cell. Though her hair color was different, her eyes were unmistakable.

Kimberly.

It wasn't *I'm not in Berlin* or *I'm not Amberly.*

I'm not Kimberly was what Isabelle had tried to tell her kidnapper. Kimberly had been the target, not Isabelle.

"Let's go, buddy," his vampire escort said from behind him and gave him a shove toward the door.

Luther obeyed automatically and stepped outside, where another vampire stood guard. Behind him the door closed. The cool night air whirled around him, and he slipped on his jacket. He turned left and walked to the next corner. Hesitating, he stopped there.

No wonder he'd thought he knew Katie when he'd encountered her in the corridor at the university. She was Kimberly Fairfax, the actress whose posters had been plastered over the other V-CON's cell. The posters Summerland had torn down.

Katie was the intended victim. She'd been the target, and most likely still was.

Goddamn it! This wasn't his fight. He was leaving tonight. Samson had made it clear that their next encounter would be a bloody one. Next time he would strike first and ask questions later.

Luther pulled the lapels of his jacket up, firm in his resolve to leave, when a woman's voice drifted to him from the entrance to Scanguards' headquarters.

"But I have to speak to Samson. It's important."

Luther glanced over his shoulder. Katie. Or Kimberly. Whatever her name was.

"Sorry, Ma'am, but I have orders to deny access to any non-Scanguards associates tonight." The vampire blocked the entrance with his bulky body.

"Please, I'm Haven's sister. Let me see him."

"No family members on the premises tonight. Besides, Haven isn't in right now."

Katie cursed. "Then Blake. I'll talk to Blake."

The vampire didn't move.

"Damn it, why are you so stubborn? I have vital information about the abduction. I have to get it to Samson or Blake. I have to show them this."

For the first time Luther noticed the letters in her hand, which she now waved at the guard.

"Do you have a cell phone, Ma'am?" the guard asked calmly.

"Yes, why?"

"I suggest you use it and call Blake. But I can't let you in tonight. We're on lockdown."

Katie gritted her teeth. "Fine!" Then she walked a few yards in Luther's direction and stopped at the curb, her face turned away from him.

Luther remained in the shadow of the adjacent building, undetected, and watched her as she pulled her cell from her pocket.

With his vampire hearing, he had no problem picking up every single word she spoke into the phone.

"Blake, damn it, why are you not picking up your phone?" She sighed. "It's Katie. I found something. You have to check the video footage of Isabelle's abduction. Read her lips. She's telling the kidnapper that she's not Kimberly. Blake, the kidnapper wanted me, not Isabelle. He got the wrong person." She lifted her hand, holding the letters as if wanting to show them to Blake through her cell phone. "I think I know who it is. I've been getting letters. Some obsessed fan. They are different from the usual fan mail I still get. I think he was threatening me. Threatening to come for me. Blake, please, you need to check this out. The letters were posted somewhere in the Sierras. He isn't far away. He could have found out about the performance tonight. Please, call me as soon as you get this message. You need to see these letters."

She disconnected the call.

Posted somewhere in the Sierras.

The words echoed in Luther's head. The Sierras, where the vampire prison was located.

Shit!

9

Katie shivered. She'd thrown only a cardigan over her T-shirt before leaving her house and jumping back into her car, too excited about what she'd found to look for a thicker jacket in one of her many closets. Besides, she'd not expected to be denied entry into Scanguards, and to have to stand in the cold, arguing with a security guard.

Wrapping her arms around herself to ward off the cold, she ran back one block to where she'd parked her car in a quiet alley. Having spent half her life in Southern California, she had yet to get used to the cool winters in San Francisco, so unlike the balmy weather down south.

Her hand trembled slightly as she dug into her handbag, where she'd shoved the letters back, and pulled out her car key. She turned to the driver's door of her Audi, when a movement in her peripheral vision made her snap her head to the side.

There was... nothing.

She tried to shake off the odd feeling, but a shiver raced down her spine and settled at her tailbone. The sound of somebody breathing made her swivel on her heel.

All her breath rushed out of her lungs when she saw the man who stood less than a foot from her.

No, not a man. A vampire. And an ex-con.

"Luther." She breathed more than spoke the name.

"I see I don't have to introduce myself. Saves me time."

Instinctively, she stepped back. Her back hit the car, effectively trapping her between it and the big vampire.

God, close up he seemed even bigger than before. Broad-shouldered and tall. Her gaze drifted away from his penetrating eyes and full lips to his neck and farther down still. Down to his marred skin. Then she realized it: though he was wearing a shirt and jacket, both were unbuttoned, giving her an unobstructed view of his scarred torso. Oddly enough, the sight didn't disgust her. Didn't repel her. Instead, it fascinated her, made her want to touch him.

"Freak show's over," he grunted.

Embarrassment coursed through her, and she felt her cheeks heat despite the cool night air. The urge to defend herself was automatic. "I wasn't…" His narrowing eyes made her change her tactic. "I thought they'd locked you up."

"Couldn't pin it on me. 'Cause I've got nothing to do with it."

The deep timbre of his voice echoed in the alley and sent tiny vibrations through her body. Like little shockwaves pulsing through her.

"Then maybe you shouldn't sneak up on people associated with Scanguards, or they might change their mind."

"So what's your association with them?"

She lifted her chin. "None of your business."

"You're not a hybrid. Frankly, I'm not quite sure what you are, 'cause as sure as shit you're not human." He sniffed, trying to make his point.

"What do you want?"

Luther motioned to her handbag.

"You're a common thief? Here to rob me? Oh my God! How despicable!"

"I want the letters! Give 'em to me! I want to see them."

"The letters?" How did he know about the letters?

"I know you have them." He made a grab for her handbag.

She tried to hold onto it, but he was too strong. Within seconds, he'd pulled out the letters and was leafing through them.

"What do you want with them?"

He ignored her question and pulled one of the letters from its envelope. His eyes flew over the scribbled handwriting.

"Ah shit!" he cursed under his breath, then looked at the envelope again. He thumbed through the stack. "All postmarked in Grass Valley."

"So what?"

Luther glared at her. "You can't show these to Scanguards."

"You have no say in what I show to Scanguards or not! The

kidnapper wanted me, not Isabelle."

"I know."

"You know?"

"The surveillance recording. I read her lips. She told him she wasn't Kimberly."

"Then you'll understand how important it is that I get these letters to Samson." She reached for them to take them back, but he held onto them. "These letters will lead us to the kidnapper. It has to be him. The things he says in his letters. He says he's coming after me. I didn't take it seriously. I thought he was just some crazy fan."

"Yeah, hazard of the trade, I guess." The sneer on his face negated the notion that he had empathy.

"Give them back to me."

"Can't do that."

"Why the hell not?"

"Because these letters will lead right back to me."

Katie gasped in shock. "You wrote them?"

"I didn't say that," Luther growled, leaning even closer. "But the postmark on these envelopes will suggest that I did. Samson isn't acting rational right now. Once he sees the letters he'll accuse me and draw resources off the search for the real kidnapper. Is that what you want?"

"You're lying."

His face came closer. "Do you know what's near Grass Valley?"

Pressing herself firmly against the car, she shook her head.

"The prison I was released from last night."

Realization hit her. "If it wasn't you who wrote these letters, then you know who it was."

"No, I don't."

She shook her head, not believing him. The intense exchange of looks they'd had earlier in the night came back to her. "When you saw me at the university, you recognized me. You knew who I was, didn't you? You knew because the vampire who took Isabelle showed you my picture, didn't he?"

"No."

"Who are you protecting?"

"Nobody!"

She felt his warm breath on her face and shivered again. "Give me back my letters, or I'm gonna make a hell of a lot of trouble for you."

"You don't know when to quit, do you?"

He lifted his hand and reached for a strand of her hair that had escaped the old-fashioned hairdo she was still sporting. "No, you're not the quitting type, are you?" He looked at her with an unreadable expression on his face. "I should warn you. I'm dangerous. And if you think you can fight me, you're wrong. You're not strong enough compared to me. So give up. Go home."

Katie narrowed her eyes at him. "I'm a witch. I'm stronger than you. So you'd better be careful."

She noticed the surprise on his face. He didn't believe her. And rightly so: even though she'd been born a witch, she had no powers to speak of. While Wes had regained his powers through hard work and practice, and now smelled like a witch again, she knew from other vampires around her that the smell of witch on her was so faint that most vampires dismissed it. She could only hope that Luther believed her. It would protect her, because no vampire took on a witch. And Katie knew she needed that protection.

"A witch. Interesting. Just like that other witch. The one who kissed you."

His comment seemed strange to her. Why emphasize the fact that Wesley had kissed her?

"Well, at least you don't smell as intensely of witch as he does. Who is he? Your lover?"

"None of your fucking business."

"Well, let's find out, shall we?"

Before she could comprehend the meaning of his words, his lips were on hers, robbing her of her next breath and the ability to speak.

Instinctively, she raised her hands, slamming her fists against his chest. But an ant barreling into an elephant would have been more successful at making the massive beast budge. The vampire who was currently keeping her captive with his mouth didn't move an inch—at

least not away from her. He pressed her against the car, leaving no space
between them.

The heat from his chest scorched her, making her even more aware
of the fact that his shirt was open. Her fingers were drawn to that heat,
to the comfort it provided to ward off the chill of the night. Her fists
unfurled, not wanting to beat against the hard flesh any longer. Instead,
her palms searched for the contact of skin-on-skin.

Maybe it was his drugging scent that made her touch him. Or maybe
the imploring press of his lips against hers and the unrelenting strokes of
his tongue. When had she parted her lips to allow him to explore her?
When had she slanted her head to give him better access to her mouth?

He tasted of real man, of power and domination. And of danger. She
could taste that, too. Yet it didn't stop her from responding to him.
Arousal spread through her body. Lust and need collided. Desire flared.
Passion surged. Not even in the make-believe world of the movies had
any of the characters she'd ever played been allowed to feel like this.

Luther's kiss was a demand as well as a challenge. If she backed
down from it, she would lose. He would think her weak. How she knew
that, she had no idea. But kneeing him in the nuts, like she would any
other man in this situation, wasn't an option. Besides, he was no
ordinary man. He was a vampire. The most dangerous one she'd ever
encountered. And if she knew one thing about vampires, it was never to
run, or they would hunt you as their prey.

She tried to remind herself of the many things her brother had taught
her about vampires, but only one thing came to mind at present: a
vampire's lust for sex and blood were intimately connected. If he
couldn't satisfy one, he needed to satisfy the other. And once engaged in
one activity, the other would follow suit. Simple as that. Whatever she
did, she was doomed.

Though at present, that doom seemed rather exciting. Luther's hands
were roaming her body, touching, exploring where nobody had in years.
She hadn't yearned for the touch of a man in a long time. But Luther's
kiss ignited that long-buried need to feel a man's hands on her, to taste
his lips and tongue, to feel his sex grind against her.

Just like Luther did now. The hard outline of his erection pressed firmly against her center, making her knees weak and her mind foggy. His hungry mouth prevented her from forming any protest, even if her brain had been capable of doing so—which it was not. All it seemed to do was send messages to her hands to continue exploring his chest. To caress the marred skin, stroke the angry scars and find the beauty beneath them. To feel his heart beating into her hand.

A vibration charged through her. Was it his heartbeat that sent these waves through her body? A groan came over his lips and bounced against hers, making her tremble in his arms. Involuntarily, Katie rocked her pelvis against his groin and felt another vibration.

She realized then that she was powerless in the arms of a vampire. Powerless, because she wanted what he was offering. A chance to forget.

10

Blake disconnected the call to his voicemail and cursed as he rushed along the corridor of the executive floor at Scanguards' headquarters in the Mission district. At the door at the end of the long hallway, he stopped briefly.

Thomas Brown-Martens, Chief of IT and *Eddie Brown-Martens, Deputy Chief of IT*, it said in bold black lettering. The two had combined their last names after their wedding and blood-bond. Not only did they now share an office and in effect the management of Scanguards' IT department, they spent practically twenty-four hours a day in each other's company. How they could stand that much togetherness was beyond him.

Blake shook his head and knocked quickly, not waiting for an answer before he opened the door and entered.

Two heads spun in his direction. Eddie, pointing at something on the monitor, stood behind Thomas, who was sitting at his desk.

"Hey," Thomas greeted him.

"We were about to call you. I think we found something," Eddie said, staring back at the screen. "Run it again," he told Thomas.

Whatever Eddie and Thomas had found could wait a moment. "I had a call from Katie. I need to look at the video of Isabelle and the kidnapper again," Blake requested.

Thomas motioned him to step closer. "We're looking at it right now."

Blake walked around the desk so he could look at the monitor, and watched the kidnapping unfold once more. This was his worst nightmare come true: one of his charges had been abducted under his watch. Something like this was never supposed to happen. He and his team had been protecting all of Scanguards' children for almost two decades now, and nothing had ever happened. They'd been safe. Heck, nobody had as much as fallen off a bike under his watch. And now this. A kidnapping.

"See, there." Eddie pointed to Isabelle's mouth. "I'm not an expert in lip reading, but I think she's saying *I'm not Kimberly*."

"Fuck! Katie was right." Blake raked a hand through his short hair. Why hadn't he seen this immediately when he'd watched the video for the first time? Maybe because he'd been too focused on trying to get a better visual on the kidnapper's face.

Thomas looked over his shoulder. "That's Katie's stage name. This guy wasn't after Samson's daughter. He wanted Katie. What did she say?"

"She mentioned letters from an obsessed fan. But it doesn't make sense! If it was an obsessed fan, he would recognize that he wasn't abducting Katie."

Eddie nodded. "True. Particularly since the kidnapper had to be a vampire or a hybrid. He would have recognized that Isabelle is a hybrid."

Thomas swiveled his chair around. "Yeah, but did he know that Katie isn't a hybrid? If he's an obsessed fan and never met her face-to-face, how would he know that she *isn't* a hybrid? If he's seen her on TV or in the movies, he wouldn't be able to tell. The cameras can't catch a vampire's aura, nor a vampire's scent."

"Well, it doesn't matter now, why or how. He got the wrong woman. We've gotta find him and get Isabelle back, before he realizes she isn't Katie and hurts her." Blake pulled out his cell. "We'll start with the letters." He dialed Katie's number. "Let's pull prints off them, run them through the databases, and see whether we can narrow our search area with the help of the postmarks. I doubt he'll have written his address on the envelopes." The phone continued to ring in his ear. "Come on, Katie, pick up!"

Thomas nodded in encouragement. "We'll analyze the letters. Maybe he left some clues in his writing. Stalkers like to show their superiority. They think they'll never be caught, so they play with their prey. If there's something in there, we'll find it."

"You've reached Katie, please leave a message." Beep.

"Crap!" Blake cursed. "Katie, I got your message. Call me immediately. We need those letters." He disconnected the call and looked back at his two colleagues. "Do you know where Wesley is? Wasn't he supposed to take Katie home?"

"He's probably still at the university with John, interrogating the audience and the student actors. The forensics team sent the first batch of fingerprints back and we're running them through the system. We're still waiting for the students and stagehands and anybody else who's been backstage to be fingerprinted so we can eliminate their prints and isolate the perpetrator's. Isabelle's we have on file."

Blake nodded, drawing in a few breaths. Just like they had DNA samples of every member of Scanguards and their families in a vault in the basement. "Good. I know you guys are on top of it, but I need everybody to give more than their best in this case. Isabelle is in danger. And I know she's scared. We have to bring her home. That's our first priority. I don't care what we have to do, on whose toes we need to step, or what laws we need to break to make that happen."

"We all feel the same," Eddie said, exchanging a look with Thomas. "Isabelle is just as much our family as the rest of Scanguards."

"Katie needs protection," Thomas added, rising from his chair. "You want me to assign a security detail to her? Once the kidnapper realizes he's got the wrong girl, he'll be making another attempt."

Blake could only agree with Thomas's thought process. "Yes, find out from Wesley where she is. Let's get those letters from her. And then Jake will guard Katie at her house."

"Consider it done," Thomas said.

A knock at the door made them all turn.

"Come in," Thomas answered.

The door opened and Haven entered. His gaze immediately fell on Blake. "Thought I'd find you here."

"You're back already? What about the lead?"

Haven shook his head, regret in his eyes. "Sorry, false alarm. It was a case of domestic violence. It wasn't Isabelle. We sorted the jerk out for kicking his girlfriend around, but the two had nothing to do with

Isabelle's abduction." He motioned to Thomas and Eddie. "Anything new here?"

Thomas and Eddie remained silent, their gazes shifting to Blake.

Blake sighed. "I'm afraid so. We just figured out that Isabelle wasn't the target."

Haven's forehead furrowed. "But if she wasn't, then who was?"

"Katie."

"Fuck!" Haven cursed and turned back to the door.

"What are you doing?"

Haven ripped the door open and looked over his shoulder. "She was in the observation room earlier. I've gotta get her and protect her."

Haven raced into the corridor and to the elevator bank, jamming his thumb on the button to call the elevator.

Blake ran after him. "What the fuck was she doing at HQ?"

"She wanted to help."

"You smuggled her in? That's against—"

"I don't know who she sweet-talked to get in, but you know my sister. She's resourceful."

"Yeah, and one day that trait will get her into trouble."

Haven nodded. "I just hope today is not that day."

11

Luther was losing all sense of time and place. All that mattered right now was the woman in his arms: the softness of her lips, the intoxicating taste of her mouth, the spellbinding touch of her fingers as she gently traced his scars. As if their ugliness didn't bother her.

Just like the faint smell of witch on her didn't bother Luther. He'd always abhorred witches of all kinds—most vampires did—but Katie's scent appealed to him, in fact lured him to her like a beacon guiding a ship to shore. A ship adrift in a vast ocean. A ship that had lost its compass.

Katie responded with passion, despite his demanding kiss and his insistent touch.

Despite the fact that he was a dangerous vampire, a stranger in fact, she pressed herself to his body, and encouraged him to grind his hard cock against her with an ever increasing tempo. The soft cries of passion and lust coming from her throat urged him to roam her body, explore her lush curves, while the scent of her arousal drove the vampire inside him insane with need.

His body heated with every lap of his tongue against hers. Deeper and deeper he foraged into the cavern of her delicious mouth, running his tongue along her teeth, nibbling on her lips, tasting her. He was starving for this kiss, couldn't get enough of it. For over twenty years, he hadn't kissed a soul, hadn't felt this kind of intense connection with another living being. For over two decades he'd only known the touch of his own hand, as he satisfied his base needs during the lonely daylight hours in prison, when it was quiet and most vampires slept.

But none of the orgasms he'd experienced at his own hand compared to the pleasure he felt now kissing this woman, this witch— the actress with eyes like a cat. Green eyes. The eyes that had stared at him from those posters in the prison cell.

Shit!

Abruptly, he released Katie. This was all wrong. Breathing hard, he stared at her. Her lips looked bruised from his kisses. Her hair now fell over her shoulders. Had he been the one to undo the medieval hairdo?

When he met her eyes, he could see it clearly: the lust and passion he'd awakened in her.

What the hell had come over him? He couldn't even remember why he'd kissed her in the first place. But he knew why he had to stop: he had to stay away from women. A woman had been his doom once, and he wasn't going to make the same mistake twice.

"Go!" he demanded roughly, breaking eye contact. "Go home."

"No fucking way!"

Her resolute answer made him snap his head back to her. He narrowed his eyes. "What did you say?"

"You heard me."

She crossed her arms over her chest, drawing his attention away from her face and to her luscious breasts, which only moments ago had been crushed to his chest. Such softness, such comfort they'd provided him.

"I'm not leaving until you tell me what you know about the guy who wrote those letters."

Luther's nostrils flared. "You're not in a position to make demands. Besides, I have no idea who wrote the letters."

He turned on his heel, ready to leave, because the longer he stayed in her company, the harder it would be to extricate himself from it. He knew himself too well; twenty years alone in a cell had made sure of that. Katie was the kind of woman who could get to him, and he wasn't going to allow that.

"But you have a suspicion."

He hesitated for a split-second, but it was enough for Katie to add, "I knew it!"

Luther pivoted and glared at her. "Listen to me. I think it's better you go home and stay out of my business. And for what it's worth, I apologize that I kissed you. Chalk it up to the fact that I was in prison for twenty years." He paused for a moment, before adding a lie to his statement. "Frankly, I would have kissed anything with tits at this point. Nothing personal. Wrong place, wrong time."

Katie pressed her lips together in obvious displeasure. Good, she'd finally gotten the message. Already relaxing, he made a motion to turn.

"Not so fast, buddy!" she said rather calmly. Much too calmly for a woman who'd just been told that the passionate kiss they'd shared meant nothing. "Samson is going to find out about this. I'll show him the letters, and then he's going to hunt you down like a dog."

Luther tilted his head to the side, looking at her for a long moment, before opening his mouth. "May I point out one thing?"

Katie raised her eyebrows in curiosity.

He lifted his hand. "I'm the one who's got the letters. So it appears you have nothing to back up your allegations."

For an instant he thought he saw something flash in her eyes, but then it was gone again, and she even smiled. "Oh, I have copies at home. So do with those whatever you want."

He growled in displeasure.

"Help us find Isabelle. You have the key. You know things we don't," she continued.

"Even if I had any information that could help you find her, Samson has made it clear that the next time he sees me, he'll kill me. This time he won't stop to ask questions. He'll strike first. And despite everything, I rather value my life. So the answer is no."

"If you don't want to help us, I'm going to tell Samson that you lied to him. That you're hiding the fact that you know who's behind this."

"I passed their fucking lie detector test!"

"I know for a fact that the machine isn't all that accurate," she claimed.

Luther narrowed his eyes, but couldn't tell if she was bluffing or not. "Gabriel looked into my memories. He cleared me. So you've got nothing."

Katie brought one hand up and pretended to inspect her fingernails. "You forget that I'm a witch."

"What's that got to do with my innocence?"

"What if I put a spell on you that makes you confess to the crime?"

He sucked air through his nostrils. Had he heard correctly? She was threatening him with witchcraft? No vampire had any defenses against it, and he feared it as much as the next guy. "You devious, little—"

"—bitch?" she offered politely. "Oh please, I've been called worse."

"I was gonna say tramp," Luther corrected her.

Katie pushed herself away from the car and came toward him. "Now here's how this works: you'll lead me to the man who wrote the letters, I'll play bait, and you'll catch the guy. If you don't do it, I'll set all of Scanguards on your tail."

Luther shook his head in disbelief. "Oh my God, you're actually crazy. I mean, bat-shit crazy! Do you have any idea what you're doing? This kind of stuff can get you killed. Hell, it'll get us both killed."

"It won't. Because *you* will keep us safe. You survived twenty years in a vampire prison. Can't have been a cake walk."

No, it hadn't been easy. But right now he almost wished he were back inside and wouldn't have to deal with crap like this.

"I'm sure you know how to protect yourself. Do it, or Samson will be hunting you."

He scoffed. "Do you know what I was in prison for?"

"Attempted murder."

"So you know. And still you won't back down. What makes you think I'm not going to kill you before you can set Scanguards on my ass?"

"If you'd wanted to kill me, you would have done so already." Then her eyes drifted lower and settled on his crotch. "And because you still have a hard on. My guess is you'd rather get into my pants than kill me. So I figure I'm safe as long as I don't let you fuck me."

Luther balled his hands into fists, fuming at her successful attempt at manipulating him. He let out a growl.

"Get in the fucking car! I'll drive."

"Of course you will," Katie answered sweetly. "I guess you won't be needing directions?"

He narrowed his eyes at her. "And not another word out of your mouth until we're out of the city, or I'll be tempted to toss you over the Bay Bridge."

12

Almost three hours later, Katie watched as Luther closed the entry door to a single family home and turned back to her.

"You can't be serious. This is breaking and entering," she whispered.

"The place is empty." He jerked his thumb over his left shoulder, indicating the foyer. "Mail's piling up. These people are probably on a cruise or beach vacation over the holidays."

"You can't know that. They could be back any moment."

Luther marched into the living area. "No Christmas tree in sight. In this neighborhood, everybody has a Christmas tree—unless they're not around over the holidays. All the shutters are closed, and the cars are in the garage. We're safe here for today."

Katie shook her head. "Why did we have to stop anyway? We're nearly there."

Luther rolled his eyes, tossing her an impatient glare. "Let me put it in words you'll understand: 'cause I don't want the sun to fry my ass. We need to wait for nightfall to get into the prison."

"We can't waste time. You could stay in the car. It's got blackout windows, just like all of Scanguards' cars. You just tell me who to talk to. There must be guards there to let us in during the day."

Suddenly he chuckled. "Let us in?"

"What's so funny?"

Luther shook his head. "You really think we're just gonna ring the doorbell and ask them to let us in? I spent twenty years in there. I have enemies. If the guards find out that I disclosed the location of the prison to an outsider, they'll lock me up for another twenty." He scoffed. "And once they figure out what your scent is, they'll shoot you on sight. They don't exactly like witches."

"You said I don't smell much like a witch."

"It's faint, yeah, but given enough time, they'd figure it out. You can't just walk in there and expect to come out unscathed."

Katie's heart started to pound in her chest, constricting at the realization that finding out who'd written those letters wasn't quite as simple as she'd hoped. "But then how are we gonna get the information we need? How will we find the guy?"

"Don't worry your pretty little brain with that. I'll go in. You'll be staying here, waiting for me."

Katie braced her hands on her hips, glaring at him. This big bully was going to leave her behind? "That wasn't the deal. I'm coming with you. Do you really think you can just drop me here and expect me to wait like some submissive little woman who doesn't have two brain cells to rub together?"

He walked toward her until the tip of his boots almost touched her shoes. "Yes, that's exactly what I'm expecting. Though the word submissive doesn't exactly come to mind when I think of you."

Katie pulled in a breath of air. "Oh yeah, then what comes to mind? Go ahead, just say it. You've been holding it in during the entire car ride." And she was sick of his brooding and the silence that had made the drive feel longer than the almost three hours it had taken them to reach the foothills.

That silence had contributed to the fact that she couldn't think of anything else other than the kiss they'd shared. Damn it, she should have pushed him away and slapped him, rather than allowed him to kiss her like that. It had awakened things in her that she didn't know how to handle.

"If you think you can manipulate me, you're wrong. Maybe that works with the humans you normally date, but not with me."

Annoyed by his accusation, she changed the subject. "We're not talking about my love life. I'm coming with you, whether you like it or not."

He tilted his head to the side. "Yeah, that would be *not*. As in—" He moved in closer, bringing his face within inches of hers. "—you're staying put while I break into the prison and get what I need."

"Not without me, you're not." She pressed her lips tightly together, ignoring his masculine scent that tempted her to do something stupid. "Or have you already forgotten that I'm a witch, and that I can make you do anything I want?" It was a bluff, but she hoped he was buying it just like he had before.

When his lips parted, she saw to her shock that Luther's fangs had lengthened and the sharp tips were now protruding from their sockets. Her breath hitched at the sight, and her pulse began to drum excitedly, flooding her body with female awareness.

"Is that what you did earlier? Used your witchcraft to make me kiss you?" Luther narrowed his eyes, but she could see the orange glow around his irises nevertheless. His vampire side was emerging. "Don't you get enough action as is? With those tits and those eyes you should have men lining up around the block. Guess that's not enough. You've gotta force yourself on one who doesn't want you."

Without even realizing what she did, she slapped him so hard across his cheek that her palm stung from the impact. Rage careened through her. Forced herself on somebody? No, no. She was the last person to ever do that, because she of all people knew what it felt like. What it felt like to be forced to do something against her will.

~ ~ ~

Though Luther was used to pain—and a slap from a woman who weighed barely a hundred and thirty pounds wasn't considered pain in his books—the ache from it spread through his entire body. Not physically, but in a different way. As if she'd slapped his heart.

He'd gone too far in his attempt to push her away. Why the hell did she have to push all his buttons?

"Guess I deserved that," he said with a calm he didn't possess and turned his face back to her. He was tempted to offer her the other cheek like he had Samson, but feared she wouldn't get his dry sense of humor.

When she didn't say anything, he searched for words. He was damned if he was going to apologize. Apologies were for wimps, and it would be a cold day in hell, before he apologized for something that she'd provoked.

"Why can't you just accept that it's too dangerous for you to come with me? If I get caught, at least then it's just my ass on the line. But you. Do you have any idea what they'll do to you?"

Shooting her would be the least of her problems. The guards would have a field day with her, playing with her before they killed her. And he sure didn't need another death on his conscience.

"I can look after myself. My brother taught me."

"He a witch too?"

She shook her head hesitantly, as if she wasn't sure it was wise to tell him. "Haven is a vampire."

Instinctively he took a step back. She had a vampire brother? If that wasn't unusual, then he didn't know what was. "So that's why Samson tolerates your presence." He nodded to himself. "And that other witch? Wesley? Are you related to him too, 'cause as sure as shit he isn't your lover."

"How the hell..." She stopped, letting out a breath, before shaking her head. "Oh, why do I bother? Like I give a crap about what you think."

He shrugged. "Likewise." And he'd rather bite his tongue off than ask about that witch once more. However, judging by the way Katie had kissed him, he was certain she had no lover. No woman in an intimate relationship would kiss a stranger like that. Hell, no woman at all would kiss a stranger like that, particularly not one she knew to be an ex-con.

"Fine, now that we've cleared that up, let's get back to our plan of getting into the prison. I'm assuming you have a plan?"

He scoffed. "Has anybody ever told you that you're a pain in the butt?"

"It's come up once or twice."

"I have the feeling you've been around people who are way too polite to tell you the truth. Just to give you a heads-up: politeness isn't my forte."

She stepped closer, seemingly unafraid of him. God, how he admired a woman who didn't back down at the first sign of trouble. Who stood her ground, even if that ground was shaky at best.

"No shit, Sherlock," Katie said in a voice as soft as an angel's, though he knew there was nothing angelic about her.

Well, nothing apart from her lush curves. Or her plump lips. Her sweet tongue.

Fuck!

She was doing it again: ensnaring him with her witchy wiles. Casting out her net. But this time he was on alert. He would be careful not to get drawn in by the seductive gaze of her green eyes that promised unimaginable pleasures. He'd survived twenty years without the touch of a woman, he could survive the next twelve hours until they could get to the prison, get the information they needed, and get out.

After that, she was on her own. Whatever she did with the information they found wasn't his problem. He'd wash his hands of her. Be done with it.

He'd leave California, go north, maybe to Canada, start a new life. Far away from the vampires he'd once called brothers.

"Fine, we'll leave at sunset. Get some rest. You'll need it. We'll have to hike in."

"I'm not tired yet," she claimed.

"Suit yourself."

"I'd like to ask you something." Her voice was even now, almost friendly. That alone made the hairs on his nape stand up in alert.

"I'm all out of answers today."

She walked—no, sashayed—over to the large sofa and sat down in one corner, kicking off her shoes in the process, before folding her legs underneath her.

"You said you had a hunch who wrote the letters. Why?"

"I never said I had a hunch. You assumed it."

"But you *do* have a suspicion. Was it something the guy said?"

"I never met him. Most times we were kept in solitary. So we couldn't form alliances against the guards. There were strict protocols."

"What kind of protocols?"

"How many V-CONs were allowed outside their cells at any one time."

"V-CONs?"

"Vampire Convicts."

She nodded, a serious look on her face. "It must have been lonely."

"I prefer my own company to that of others." It wasn't even a lie. Though it didn't mean that he hadn't been lonely.

"I understand that," she murmured and looked into the distance.

Surprised by her words, he eyed her. What did Katie know about loneliness? By all accounts she'd been a successful actress, adored by her fans, envied by her peers.

She suddenly turned her gaze back to him. "But if you say you never met him, why do you think he wrote those letters?"

"His cell. It was plastered with pictures of you, posters." He pointed at her hair. "Your hair was different. Blonde. That's why I didn't immediately recognize you."

She caught a strand of her hair between her thumb and index finger and twirled it. "I dyed it blonde for a long time. But this is my natural hair color."

"It suits you better." The words were out before he could take them back. To cover the compliment, he added quickly, "One of the guards was cleaning out his cell the day I was released."

"And the V-CON? Didn't you see him?"

"Apparently he was released a week earlier."

Katie nodded to herself. "Enough time to plan this." A haunted look crossed her face. "Stalkers. They love planning. They love the anticipation. It turns them on."

With every word, Luther realized that Katie wasn't talking to him anymore. She was reminding herself of something. Something she'd experienced before.

13

Blake entered a ten-digit code into the dashboard of his black-out SUV and waited for the garage door to Samson's Nob Hill mansion to lift. As the head of Scanguards' personal security, he had access to all the houses where his charges resided, including Samson's.

The early morning sunlight did not penetrate through the specially tinted windows of his SUV, keeping him safe.

When the gate lifted, Blake drove inside the spacious underground garage. Samson's house had changed significantly in the past twenty years. After Grayson's birth, Samson had bought the neighboring house and combined the two houses into one in order to have enough space for his growing family. Now the old Victorian could truly be called a mansion. At over six thousand square feet, it not only housed the Woodford family, but also boasted a garage, which could accommodate up to eight cars, and a command center connected to Scanguards' headquarters, as well as large entertainment and meeting areas on the first floor.

Blake parked in the spot permanently reserved for him, and glanced at the other cars. He wasn't surprised to see Amaury's sports car and Gabriel's SUV parked next to the Woodford family's three cars. But he was surprised to see the BMW Z4 of Amaury's twins. While Amaury could certainly afford to give each of his sons his own car, there'd been no point: Damian and Benjamin went everywhere together.

The moment the garage door closed behind him, shutting out the mid-morning sun, Blake jumped out of the car and marched toward the stairs leading to the first floor. He heard the voices before he even opened the door to the hallway. When he entered, he walked straight into the open-plan living area where most of the visitors were assembled.

Samson, Amaury, and Gabriel stood near the fireplace, talking, while the hybrids were centered around the dining room table, gobbling down mountains of food. Unlike their vampire parents, who only consumed blood, they could sustain themselves on both.

The twins were stuffing their faces, while Grayson paced back and forth. His younger brother, Patrick sat at the table, head in his hands, while next to him, Vanessa, Gabriel and Maya's fifteen-year-old daughter patted his arm in sympathy. Her brothers, seventeen-year-old Ethan and eighteen-year-old Ryder, watched Grayson as if they expected him to explode at any moment.

Neither Delilah, nor Nina, nor Maya were anywhere to be seen. Blake listened intently and perceived the faint sound of footsteps from the upper floor. Well, it was best anyway that Delilah was upstairs with her girlfriends. She was too agitated. And right now, cool heads were paramount. Decisions had to be made.

The door to the garage fell shut behind Blake. Several pairs of eyes immediately landed on him as he walked into the center of the living room. The hybrids jumped up and approached, and the three adult vampires stopped talking and looked at him expectantly. Blake felt the weight of responsibility on his shoulders and the tension that came with it, but he was determined not to let anybody down. This was his greatest trial, the one he'd trained for countless times.

"Any news?" Samson's tight voice cut through the silence.

"We have a positive sighting. A security camera at a gas station. It picked up her red dress. That kind of gown is hard to overlook."

Samson came closer, hands clenched, shoulders lifted. "Is she hurt?"

"We don't know. We couldn't get a visual of her face, and because of the dress's color... Sorry, we couldn't tell if she was injured or not, but we know who her kidnapper is."

Several relieved sighs echoed in the room.

"Who?" Samson ground out, his fangs descending, most likely without him even noticing.

"We ran his picture through facial recognition software and got a match. A small time crook by the name of Antonio Mendoza. Thomas is hacking into the DMV right now to get us an address for him."

Samson nodded. "We need to get him. Now."

"I agree. Let's not wait till tonight. We know he's got Isabelle, but we don't know what he plans to do with her." Blake turned toward the hybrids. "It's going to be a daytime mission, which excludes us." He motioned to himself, Samson, Amaury, and Gabriel. "Hybrids only."

Damian and Benjamin already jockeyed into position. Damian put his arm around his brother's shoulder. "We're in."

"Me, too," Grayson gritted through his teeth. "I'm going to gut that bastard."

Patrick stepped next to his brother. "Not if I gut him first."

"Out of the question!" Delilah's voice came from the sweeping staircase that led down from the second floor.

Blake turned on his heel, watching how she descended, followed by Maya and Nina.

"Mom!" Patrick protested. "I'm going with them to save Isa."

"No, you won't! You're too young. And you're not trained yet."

Patrick spun around, hands at his hips, and faced Samson. "Dad!"

"Your mother is right," Samson replied. "As much as we all want to go in there and bring Isabelle back, we can't." He motioned to the older boys. "Damian, Benjamin, and Grayson can handle it."

"Dad?" Ryder suddenly said, looking at Gabriel. "With your permission, I'd like to join them."

Blake watched as Gabriel exchanged a quick glance with his mate, Maya, before nodding. "Of course."

"It's not fair," Patrick protested.

Grayson turned to him and squeezed his shoulder. "I'll get her back for us, promise. But you need to stay with Mom and Dad. They need you now."

Patrick looked at his brother. "Okay. But if something goes wrong, I'm going to whoop your ass."

Grayson brushed his hand through his younger brother's hair, messing it up. "It won't come to that."

"Well, good," Blake said, steering the conversation back to the task at hand. "The boys need to head back to HQ to get ready. Get yourselves suited up with the reinforced Kevlar gear and semi-automatics. I want you protected against any silver bullets or stakes. We don't know yet whether Mendoza has any accomplices. And you'll be wearing cameras, so I can guide you from HQ."

Gabriel tossed a set of keys to Ryder. "Take the SUV to get to HQ. I want you all riding together." He gave Damian and Benjamin a pointed look. "The sports car stays here."

"Spoilsport," Benjamin grunted under his breath.

"Let's go," Grayson ordered, assuming command just as naturally as his father.

"I'll give you further instructions when I get back to HQ," Blake added.

The four hybrids walked to the stairs leading into the garage and disappeared. When the door shut behind them, Blake turned back to the three male vampires and their mates. The younger hybrids watched them with interest.

"There's something else."

Delilah reached for her husband's hand, her eyes widening in fear. "What is it?"

Blake exchanged a look with Samson, who nodded. He'd filled Samson in earlier. "Isabelle wasn't the kidnapper's target. It was Katie. He mistook Isabelle for Katie. I don't know why or how, perhaps because they looked so similar in their costumes and hairdos. It doesn't matter now." He sighed. "Katie called me earlier. She has some letters that might point to the kidnapper. Some crazy fan. We're trying to figure out whether Mendoza is that man."

"I don't understand," Delilah interrupted. "You just said that Mendoza has Isabelle. So it must be him."

Blake shook his head. "It's possible that he wasn't acting alone. He could have been hired. Do you think a crazy, stalker-type fan would really mistake Isabelle for Katie? I doubt it. He would have immediately recognized that he had the wrong woman. That's why I suspect that Mendoza is working for someone."

"Have you gotten anything from the letters yet? Fingerprints? Anything at all?" Samson asked, pulling his wife closer to him.

Blake rubbed the back of his neck. "We don't have the letters."

"But Katie—"

"Katie isn't answering her phone. Haven is on his way to her house to check on her and get the letters so we can analyze them. If Mendoza isn't working alone, we need to know that, or we're sending the boys into undue danger."

Blake searched Samson's eyes.

A second later, Samson nodded in agreement. "I want all our bases covered. We have to be prepared for when Mendoza realizes that he's got the wrong woman."

Blake set his jaw into a grim line. Yes, once Mendoza realized he had the wrong woman, he'd come after Katie too, and Isabelle would then become a burden to him. They had to get to him before that happened.

His cell phone pinged. Blake pulled it from his pocket and looked at it. "Oh good, that's Haven." He accepted the call. "Hey, what have you got for me?"

"Katie never got home."

Blake felt the blood in his veins turn to ice.

14

The call still echoed in his ears.

"You have to come, Luther!" Samson's voice implored him. *"She's in a bad way."*

Before the last word was even spoken, Luther raced outside into the dark and jumped onto his motorcycle.

Buildings flew past him, lights flashed by him, the wind in his ears drowned out all sounds, but it couldn't drown out his thoughts.

"Vivian, I'm coming! I'll be there."

Minutes became hours. His fingers around the handlebars turned to ice, holding on for dear life. His back was as stiff as a brick wall, his neck frozen in its position, his eyes focused only on the road ahead.

Only one thought filled his mind, repeating on an infinite loop. *It's not time yet.*

The baby was coming too early. Two months too soon.

That's why he wasn't with her, why he'd taken another assignment, thinking she would be safe for a few days without him.

She'd assured him she was fine just before he'd left. "Go, Luther. I don't need you hovering around the house like a caged tiger."

He'd met her eyes and known she was right. They'd fought frequently in the previous months. It was his fault, of course, he knew that.

He'd been too demanding, had wanted to continue the same way with her as before the pregnancy. Wasn't that what blood-bonded couples did?

He needed her, wanted to make love to her every day. But the further Vivian's pregnancy had progressed, the less affection and attention she'd shown him. The less she'd wanted him.

"I'm afraid for the baby," she'd explained. "I don't want us to hurt it."

The baby growing in her belly had become her first priority.

Luther knew it was only temporary. He held onto that belief. So he'd accepted it, been the supportive husband and had put his own needs aside. Only his need for Vivian's blood did he allow himself to satisfy—because as a vampire blood-bonded to a human he could only consume her blood. Everything else would make him sick.

He felt his hunger now as he accelerated his motorcycle into a curve. For two nights he hadn't fed, but that wasn't the reason his hunger surfaced now with unmistakable urgency. As he entered the city and stopped at a red light, he felt it in the pit of his stomach. He knew something was wrong.

When he rested one foot on the asphalt and turned his head to the left, the scent of human blood drifted to him. It came from a couple walking arm in arm to their car. And it tempted him when it shouldn't. Because no blood-bonded vampire lusted after blood other than that of his mate.

"Vivian!" he screamed from the top of his lungs and shot over the intersection, ignoring the cars trying to avoid a collision. "Vivian! Hold on!"

He reached out to her with his mind.

Vivian! Please! Stay with me. I'm here. I love you. Please don't leave me.

But even as he communicated those thoughts via the telepathic bond, he knew that he wouldn't get an answer.

Vivian was no more.

Only rage guided his body now, leading him to his house ablaze with lights on every level.

Luther flung the door open. Upstairs, in the bed where he'd made love to her so many times, Vivian lay, lifeless.

Samson and Amaury stood by the bed, silently staring at him as he entered.

Maybe if she'd died alone, he would have been able to accept it. But his friends had stood by. And done nothing.

"You let her die!" His heart turned to stone. "You could have saved her!"

Had they turned her into a vampire, Vivian would have lived.

"I hate you!"

They offered no excuses.

He didn't hear their condolences, their false words of comfort. False, because they couldn't imagine what he was going through. None of them had a mate and knew what true love meant.

He'd lost Vivian, his mate, the love of his life. The woman he was going to spend eternity with.

"The child?" he asked, not even looking over his shoulder as Samson and Amaury walked to the door.

Samson's hesitation and almost inaudible intake of air told him everything he needed to know.

Luther growled, feeling his fangs lengthen. "Leave my house!"

"Luther, when you're better, we'll talk," Amaury said.

Luther pivoted, glaring at the two vampires who'd once been his best friends. "Leave, or I will kill you both!"

They finally heeded the warning.

Silence descended upon the house. He shed no tears, not for a long time, only stared at the pale face of the woman he loved more than his own life. When he ran his fingers over her face, the coldness of her skin shocked him to the core. Never again would he sense her warmth, taste her sweet blood, feel her body shudder around him in ecstasy.

"We'll be together again one day. I promise you. Just as soon as I've avenged your death!"

But Samson and Amaury weren't the only ones responsible: he, Luther, was the culpable one. *His* child had killed her. It was *his* fault. Therefore *he* had to be punished, too.

15

Blake stared at the bank of computer screens in front of him. Samson was sitting to his left, while Thomas had taken a seat to his right. But this was Blake's operation. He was orchestrating it. And the four young hybrids, Grayson, Damian, Benjamin, and Ryder were his puppets. He wished he could be there with them, but a mission like this was too unpredictable, and he couldn't risk being exposed to sunlight should anything go wrong. The hybrids, on the other hand, didn't have such shortcomings. The sun couldn't harm them, though silver bullets or a stake would kill them as surely as they killed a full-blooded vampire.

That's why he'd had them dress in reinforced Kevlar suits protecting their vital organs. To give them sufficient mobility, their arms and legs were unprotected—though they wore gloves—, as were their heads. Unfortunately, not all risks could be eliminated. That's why Blake had insisted on the hybrids wearing specially designed headbands with a built in camera that weighed no more than an ounce. The cameras were feeding live pictures to the four monitors in the center of the wall in front of him. Each monitor Blake had labeled with a name. This way, it was immediately obvious which hybrid saw what, and Blake and his colleagues could interfere and redirect them should it become necessary.

In addition, a software program Thomas had been working on had been installed in the console. Together with the video feeds from the hybrids' cameras and their exact GPS locations, which were constantly being transmitted back to HQ, a live 3-D video was being created and projected on a larger screen above. It blended the individual camera feeds and created a more comprehensive image, giving Blake a full view of what was happening with and around his charges.

Blake zoomed in on Damian, who was driving the Minivan, which was equipped with a small cell and silver chains to transport a prisoner.

"Remember, take him alive if you can," Blake reminded the four young men via the intercom that fed directly into their earpieces.

A few grunts came as a reply.

Samson leaned in to use the mic. "I mean it," he emphasized.

"Yes, sir," came Ryder's reply.

"Grayson?" Samson prompted.

"Yes, Dad. I heard you loud and clear."

Blake exchanged a look with Samson and muted the mic. "He'll come through when it counts. You've gotta trust him. He's just like you."

Samson scoffed, though an expression of pride crossed his face for a fleeting instant. "That's what I'm afraid of."

Blake turned back to the screens. The Minivan had stopped.

"We're here," Benjamin announced.

"As we discussed, stick to the plan. It's a go," Blake said.

The four young hybrids exited the van.

There was little cover during daylight hours. The house was a ranch style dwelling in a somewhat dilapidated state. The neighborhood wasn't much better: some parts of the Excelsior district were decent, but there were pockets with crack houses and gang-occupied properties the owners had long given up on. At least none of the neighbors would call the police when they saw Grayson and his friends approach the house, looking like ninjas.

The yard in front of the house was brown and overgrown with weeds. A few bushes lined the paved driveway, and a path led past the house to the back of it.

"Two at the back, two at the front," Blake said into the mic.

The twins headed for the front door, while Grayson and Ryder quietly and swiftly took the narrow path to the back of the house. Old household appliances, parts of a bicycle and other trash covered the back yard.

"Doesn't look like Mendoza can spot a good real estate investment," Blake commented.

"When this is over, he won't need any investments anymore." The dry remark came from Zane, who was standing behind them.

Blake didn't take his eyes off the monitors, when he replied,

"You've got that right." Then he pressed the button on the mic. "Enter on Grayson's command."

There was absolute silence in the command room. Nobody spoke, nobody as much as breathed. The air was thick with tension. Everybody's eyes were glued to the monitors.

Blake focused in on the 3-D feed. With a joystick he moved the image on the screen, turning it so he could inspect the house from all sides.

"Going in," Grayson confirmed and gave Ryder a sign.

Ryder kicked the back door in with his foot, lifting it out of its hinges. Simultaneously, the twins did the same in the front. Weapons drawn, all four rushed into the house.

Like a military team, they covered each other as they charged from room to room. They'd trained for scenarios like this, but Blake was surprised at how calm the four hybrids seemed, even though they knew what hinged on this mission. Pride swelled in his chest. One day soon they would make some fine bodyguards.

The kitchen was in disarray, the two bedrooms appeared unused. Blake followed the various camera angles as the hybrids moved through the property.

"Empty!" Damian announced.

"Yeah, the house is empty," Ryder confirmed.

"Shit!" Samson cursed and turned to Blake. "We missed him. He must have taken her someplace else."

"He might have never been there," Blake conceded and pressed the button for the mic. "Boys, look for any signs that Mendoza or Isabelle were there."

"Ok," Benjamin replied.

Samson bent over the mic. "Can you smell her scent? Grayson?"

Grayson marched into the living room, when he suddenly stopped dead. The camera on his forehead picked up what he saw.

"Oh God, no," Grayson murmured. "Please don't let it be her."

Blake felt a lump in his throat that prevented him from speaking. The dust that covered the old worn carpet was unmistakable. In the absence of a fireplace in the house it could only have come from one source: a dead vampire—or hybrid, for hybrids disintegrated into ash when they died just as a vampire did.

Next to Blake, Samson had jumped up. "No! No!"

The sound of pain and despair in Samson's voice nearly tore Blake's heart into a million pieces. He had to be strong now and think clearly, because his boss was in no condition to do so.

"Comb the place! Now!" Blake commanded. "Turn over every piece of furniture. Check his computer. Go through everything!"

Grayson nodded numbly, while Ryder squeezed his shoulder. "Maybe she managed to kill him."

Grayson whirled his head to him. "Then where is she?" He pointed to the sofa. "I can still smell her. She was here." He lifted his head toward the ceiling. "Dad, Isabelle was here. We're too late. Too late!"

A string of vile curses rolled over Grayson's lips.

"He left his cell phone. Wonder why," Damian suddenly said and pulled a phone from beneath a stack of papers. "Must have forgotten it. It was hidden underneath all this crap. Didn't even see it at first."

His brother joined him, reaching for it. "Let me see."

Damian handed it to Benjamin who pressed the iPhone's home button. "Hey, it's not locked."

Blake zoomed in on it. "Is that the voice memo that's open?"

"Yep," Benjamin confirmed. "He must have been recording something."

Damian looked over his shoulder. "Hey, it's still running. Look!"

"Let me see," Grayson demanded and snatched the phone from his friends.

"How long is the recording?" Blake asked.

"Over six hours," came Grayson's reply. "Weird…"

"Go back to the beginning and—"

But Grayson had already had the same idea and pressed the button to replay the voice recording from the beginning.

There were sounds of doors opening and closing, footsteps, some shuffling, voices in the distance, coming closer.

Then, finally, the voice of a man proclaimed, *"Here she is."*

In the middle of it, Thomas's cell phone rang and he turned away, answering it quietly. Blake tuned out his words and concentrated on the monitor.

An angry grunt. *"Who the fuck is that? That's not Kimberly Fairfax!"* It was the voice of a second man. *"What am I paying you good money for?"*

The first man, who had to be Mendoza, replied, *"But that's her. She was right where you said she would be."*

"That bitch isn't Kimberly. Who the fuck knows who she is! Fucking idiot! Should've done it myself!"

"Please, let me go."

"Isabelle," Samson murmured.

"I told him I wasn't Kimberly, but he wouldn't listen!"

"Shut up, you bitch!" That was Mendoza again, but he was cut off by the second man.

"Don't!"

It sounded like a slap. Had the stranger snatched Mendoza, preventing him from hitting Isabelle?

"You're still gonna have to pay for her," Mendoza demanded. *"I did my job. Not my fault that she switched places with that other bitch."*

"Of course." The words of the unidentified man sounded just a little too smooth and accommodating. *"You'll get what's due to you."*

A second later, Isabelle's high-pitched scream tore through the speakers. *"Oh God, no!"*

A chuckle. Then silence. Footsteps.

"Now you and I are alone." It was the voice of the stranger.

"Please let me go," Isabelle pleaded. *"I won't say anything about this. To anybody. I promise. My father will pay you a lot of money if you release me unharmed."*

The man laughed, a cold laugh devoid of any emotion.

"I'm sure he would. But it's not money I'm after."

"Please don't kill me!"

"Oh, I have no intention of killing you. At least not yet. You can be of use to me. You can help me get what I really want."

There was the sound of feet or hands hitting against furniture.

"Don't bother. I'm stronger than you. Now let's go, and don't give me any trouble, or I'll change my mind."

Moments later, the sound of a door being slammed could be heard, then silence.

Blake exchanged a look with Samson. "She's alive."

Pain shone from Samson's eyes. "And as long as he doesn't have Katie, Isabelle is safe. He'll use my daughter to make an exchange."

"That's my thought, too," Blake agreed. "Anything from Haven or Wes?" He looked over his shoulder, to where Thomas was standing now, shoving his cell phone back into his pocket.

"Shit!" Thomas cursed.

Instantly alarmed, Blake rose. "What is it?"

"After Haven couldn't find Katie at home, we had a few men comb the area for her, retrace her last steps…"

The door was ripped open. Haven charged in, a grim expression on his face, clutching something in his hand.

"Where is your sister?" Blake asked.

He stretched out his hand, and Blake focused on the item in Haven's open palm. "We found her cell in an alley around the corner. No sign of a struggle."

"Her car?"

Haven shook his head. "Nowhere to be found. She's gone."

Samson cursed and slammed his fist against the wall. "Fuck! We need to find her. She might be our only connection to the madman who has my daughter."

Nobody in the room said what they were all thinking: what if the kidnapper had already snatched Katie?

"She might be out there doing her own investigation. She was adamant about wanting to help," Haven admitted, though he didn't sound like his usual confident self.

From the corridor, the sound of footsteps came rapidly closer.

Blake squeezed Samson's shoulder. "We'll find her. As Haven said, she might just be out there thinking she can help. Doesn't have to mean that guy got to her. It was three hours before sunrise when she left me the voice message around half past four." He pointed to the monitor, indicating where the boys had just discovered Isabelle's previous location. Then he glanced at the wall clock, making quick calculations in his head. "Sunrise was at 7:20. According to the recording, the kidnapper figured out only shortly before sunrise that his accomplice snatched the wrong girl. He wouldn't have had a chance to get to Katie, not during daytime." Then he addressed Thomas, "Put an APB out on her car."

Wes rushed in. "I have a better idea."

All heads turned to the witch.

"I can scry for her. It'll take me an hour or two. I need something personal to get a lock on her. It'll get us to the general area of where she is. Once we're closer, I'll scry again to get a more accurate location. It's not quite like GPS, but it's better than nothing. I can find her."

"Do it!" Samson ordered.

"I'll get a crew ready," Blake interrupted. "And then we'll pick her up wherever she is and won't let her out of our sight anymore. She must have the letters with her. Once we get our hands on them, we'll have a better idea whether they can offer us any clues that can lead us to the kidnapper."

"I'm going with Wes," Haven offered.

Wes shook his head immediately. "You may be needed here. But I might need some fighting power, just in case. You never know what our dear sister has gotten herself into." He motioned to the monitors. "I'll take one of the boys with me."

"Not on your own, you won't," Blake objected and jerked his shoulder toward the screen. "Any of them will run roughshod over you. I'm coming with you. You'll need more than just one hybrid to back you up." He turned back to the monitors.

"I heard that," Grayson commented.

"You were supposed to." Blake refrained from rolling his eyes. "Guys, mission is over. Come back to HQ. Bring the cell and Mendoza's computer and drop the stuff off with Thomas. He'll run the recording through voice recognition and see if we can get a match." He exchanged a look with the head of IT, who nodded.

"On our way," Ryder responded.

"And I'm coming with you to find Katie," Grayson added.

Blake lifted an eyebrow and gave a wry laugh. "Of course you are." He switched off the mic and turned to Samson. "He's a lot like you, you know."

"Yeah, I'm afraid so."

16

Katie gave Luther a sideways glance as he brought the car to a stop at the end of a dirt road. It was pitch black outside. The moon was obstructed by clouds and the only artificial light around them were the headlights of her car.

Luther had gotten rid of the ripped and bloodstained shirt he'd worn the previous night and helped himself to a fresh one from the closet of the house they'd slept in.

"We're here," he announced and switched off the engine.

Katie was already reaching for the door handle, when she felt a hand on her forearm. She spun her head to Luther. Even in the darkness his eyes seemed to sparkle with gold flecks.

"You can still change your mind and wait here for me."

"Not a chance."

He grunted as if he'd expected her response. "Suit yourself." He opened the driver's side door and got out. Katie followed on the passenger side.

The chill of the December night air was more severe here. They were at a slightly higher elevation than San Francisco, and though it didn't snow at this altitude, she could feel the difference in temperature. Instinctively she shivered despite her cardigan. She always kept a change of clothes in the trunk of her car, but unfortunately a thick jacket had not been part of her emergency overnight bag.

"Should have taken that jacket from the closet."

At Luther's words she glanced at him. "I don't steal."

He scoffed, a derisive look in his dark orbs. "No you don't, do you? You've never even taken as much as a piece of candy as a child? Never committed the tiniest of crimes?"

Her pulse began to race as memories tried to push to the surface. She clenched her jaw. "I don't steal," she repeated.

Luther nodded as if he'd caught her in a lie. "Of course not. You're as pure as the driven snow. Is that why you want to become an accessory now? Because you want to know what it feels like to commit a crime?" A low grunt echoed through the night. He stepped away from the car and walked toward the thicket.

Katie marched after him. "I'm not committing a crime."

He looked over his shoulder. "Oh yeah? What do you call what we're about to do?"

"Investigating." She caught up to him and did her best to keep pace with his long strides.

Luther shook his head. "So you don't steal, but breaking and entering is okay. What other crimes do you manage to justify to yourself? Just so that I'm prepared."

"I don't know what you mean."

"Do you consider killing a vampire a crime?"

"What are you trying to say?"

"Just want to know if your sense of justice extends to vampires. Or whether I'll need to watch my back to avoid a stake in my heart."

"I didn't stake you when you were sleeping."

"I didn't sleep," he claimed, but Katie knew it was a lie. "I was aware of you at all times. If you'd tried anything, I would have had you pinned to the ground in a millisecond."

"That's funny," she responded, "considering you had a nightmare I couldn't wake you from."

Luther whirled his head to her, glaring at her. "That's a lie!"

It wasn't. In fact, she'd awoken from an uneasy few hours of sleep when she'd heard Luther's voice. He'd been resting on the couch. When she'd entered the living room, she'd found him tossing. His hands had turned into claws, his fangs fully extended. But his eyes had been closed.

"I shook you by your shoulders, but you didn't wake."

"I'm warning you. I don't have nightmares."

He looked ahead and increased his tempo, anger rolling off him in waves so violent that she could almost see his aura. It looked like flames were licking around him, trying to consume him.

Equal parts frightened and fascinated, Katie ran her eyes over the powerful vampire, while trying hard not to be left behind. She wasn't used to this kind of tempo, had never been a runner, and felt woefully out of shape for this kind of nightly exercise. If Luther didn't slow down, he'd leave her in the dust. He continued to charge ahead as if he didn't care whether she followed or not.

"Slow down!" she called out to him, but he didn't seem to hear her.

It irked her that he showed no regard for her limitations. After all, she was human, or witch, not a vampire, who could run without breaking a sweat.

Desperate to make him slow down, she searched for something to make him listen. She grasped at something she'd heard Luther cry out during his nightmare. "Who's Vivian?"

Luther came to a dead halt. His shoulders pulled back, his hands curled into fists. But he didn't turn his head, didn't look over his shoulder. Which was almost worse than if he'd whirled around and glared at her.

Only the breaking of twigs beneath her shoes was audible as she caught up with him. When she reached him, she heard the deliberate breaths that came from Luther. She recognized them. Those were the breaths of a person trying desperately not to succumb to a fit of rage or panic. She knew, because she'd been there before. Been at the point where the sheer mention of a name, of an event, catapulted her back to that moment, making her relive her ordeal again.

And at this very moment, she regretted having asked the question. "I'm sorry," she murmured, choking back a tear. "That was uncalled for. It's none of my business. I apologize."

"No, it's none of your business. So stay out of my life, or you'll regret it."

She already did. But it was too late to take anything back. Too late to turn around and start fresh. They were both in this now, and they had to see it through. Soon, she would have the name of the man who'd kidnapped Isabelle, and with Scanguards' help, they would catch the guy and rescue Samson's daughter.

"Now move," Luther ordered gruffly. "If you can't keep up with me, you'd better turn back now."

Katie focused all her energy on her legs. She had to see this through. She owed Isabelle, and more so, she owed Samson. He'd been instrumental in saving her life twenty years earlier, and now was the time to pay back her debt.

Even if that meant duking it out with a vampire who clearly couldn't stand her.

"I'm coming," she murmured to herself.

17

Luther bit back a curse. He knew Katie would be trouble. He just hadn't expected the trouble to start this early. Or his reaction to it to be so uncontrolled.

The nightmares had gotten less frequent than twenty years ago, but they'd never stopped. At least this time he hadn't dreamt the version where his bloody hands clawed into Vivian's pregnant belly. The symbolism of that particular dream didn't escape him. It signified his own guilt, because it had been *his* unborn child that had killed her. He had as much blood on his hands as if he'd killed Vivian with his own claws.

He'd come to the conclusion that there was only one way for history not to repeat itself: he would never commit to another woman.

"You okay?" Luther grunted, glancing at Katie, who walked next to him.

He'd slowed his tempo, knowing his anger had made him unreasonable. It wasn't her fault that he'd had a nightmare, and that she'd heard him call Vivian's name. In fact, he was surprised that she hadn't bolted, and had instead tried to wake him from it.

Luckily, Katie hadn't succeeded, or he might have unwittingly unleashed his rage on her. A fellow V-CON had once found himself at the mercy of Luther's claws, when Luther had awoken during a nightmare. Because of some temporary overcrowding in the prison, several V-CONs had had to double up in cells for a few weeks, until a number of prisoners were moved to facilities in other parts of the country.

Katie didn't reply. Well, maybe he deserved the silent treatment.

"We're almost there." He didn't expect an answer.

"I didn't mean to listen to what you said in your sleep."

He grunted, not knowing how to respond to the apology. *Thank you?*

Yeah, that didn't sound right. He was glad that in the distance ahead of them, a concrete wall appeared. Luther could already see it with his vampire vision, but he knew Katie's eyes couldn't penetrate the darkness like his. He reached his hand out and grabbed her elbow to stop her.

Her breath hitched. "What?" Her green eyes sparkled like precious emeralds in a bed of black velvet. Lush and tempting. More beautiful than any jewel.

"Once we're inside, you have to follow my commands to the letter. Do you understand?"

Katie nodded.

"There's an emergency access tunnel leading into the center of the prison. We'll use it to get in."

"How do you know about it?"

"I designed it."

Her chin dropped. "What?"

"You heard me."

"But I don't understand. Did you dig it so you could escape?"

Luther shook his head. "I was the original engineer when the council decided to build vampire-proof prison facilities. My blueprints became the basis for all current prisons the council operates, even though I left the project to join Scanguards before the first stone was laid."

She still stared at him in surprise. "How can you be so sure they didn't change the design after you left?"

"Because the council didn't want to spend any more money on plans." He paused. "And because my design was genius."

"But if you knew of a way out, why would you stay for twenty years?"

He blew out a breath of air. "I didn't say I knew of a way out."

"But you said you can get us in." A panicked tone snuck into her voice.

Luther nodded. "I can. But it's only accessible from the outside. A fail-safe in case of a prison riot. Nobody can get out in case of a lockdown, but reinforcements will have a way in to help the guards on the inside."

"And you're only mentioning this now?" Katie braced her hands on her hips, an action which involuntarily made his gaze drop to her heaving chest. This wasn't the first time he noticed her perfect proportions, her well-formed breasts, her slim waist, and her shapely hips. A perfect hourglass figure.

He shrugged, finally tearing his eyes away from her. "You didn't ask."

"Well, that's just great," she grumbled. "What else have you not told me?"

Her demanding tone riled him up. "A bunch of stuff that's none of your fucking business." When her lips tightened to a thin line and her eyes narrowed, he couldn't help himself, and continued, "Or did you wanna know about the hookers the guards ferried in from time to time and pimped out to those V-CONs who could afford to pay for them? Would you like to know the sordid details about that?"

Christ, he didn't know why she was riling him up, or why he was fighting back by provoking her. But he just couldn't stop himself.

Katie thrust her chin up. "I don't give a damn who you fucked in prison, or who the guards or the other prisoners fucked. All I care about is getting into that damn building and finding out who kidnapped Isabelle. Can you get that into your thick skull?"

"As long as you can get it into your thick skull that I'm the one giving the orders here." He turned and walked toward the wall. "You coming, or what?"

With satisfaction he heard her stomp after him.

For now he had the upper hand. And it was absolutely necessary for it to remain that way. She needed to listen to him to survive inside the prison walls. Katie knew that. But once they had what they'd come for, he couldn't wait until they went their separate ways. Because a woman like Katie could get under a man's skin, in more ways than one. And that was another thing she knew only too well. Or why else would she swing her hips in that enticing way, and dangle her boobs in front of him as if she were offering them?

Luther suppressed another curse. Maybe Katie had *already* gotten under his skin, because as much as he wanted to regret the kiss he'd stolen from her, he couldn't. For the first time in over twenty years he'd felt alive. And the thought of never again feeling like that drove him half insane. It took all his self control to restrain himself and not pull her back into his arms and bring that kiss to a much more satisfying conclusion. One that he could guarantee would be satisfying for both of them.

18

The hidden entry was exactly how he'd designed it. The mechanism was opened by a sequence that was easily deciphered if one understood the system behind it. It was a combination that changed daily and depended on a number of factors including the longitude and latitude of the prison location, and the time and date. Simple but effective.

Luther wasn't surprised that they'd never changed the system to a random code controlled by the guards inside; he understood the reasoning behind it. In case of a prison riot, reinforcements had to assume that all the guards were dead or unable to communicate, which would delay access to the building if they had to be given the code from somebody on the inside.

When the heavy steel-and-concrete door fell shut behind them, Luther didn't look back. He knew there were no indentations, no ridges, no grooves on this side that would even indicate that it was a door. There was no way out. Even trying to blast a hole with C4 would be an exercise in futility. A deadly one: the force of the blast had nowhere to go but down the long tunnel leading away from the door. Anybody standing in its deadly path would be incinerated.

The tunnel was equipped with low level lighting strips running along the floor, the same type of strips that guided passengers on a plane to the emergency exits.

Luther looked over his shoulder. Katie's emerald eyes sparkled in the dark like a beacon. It wasn't hard to guess why she'd gotten movie roles. Even he could tell that the camera loved eyes like hers, expressive and full of mystery. With those eyes she could capture her audience and make them forget everything around them.

"What is it?" she suddenly asked and stared past him.

Luther forced himself to look toward the end of the tunnel, motioning to it. "Once we're out of the tunnel, you need to do exactly as

I say. Your life will depend on it."

She nodded, her jaw tight.

"Can you see well enough?"

"I'll manage."

He reached for her elbow and noticed her jolt at the contact. "I'll guide you until we're out of the tunnel."

"I don't need—"

He started walking, not giving her a chance to complete her protest. "Just accept my damn help when I offer it. Next time I might not be offering."

He'd never heard a woman grunt, but by God, his ears were not fooling him.

"You're welcome," he ground out and continued marching toward the end of the tunnel.

Her arm felt rigid under his grip. As if she was disgusted by his touch. Less than twenty-four hours earlier she'd sung an entirely different tune. She'd yielded to his touch. None of that submissiveness was evident now. Well, it appeared kissing Katie against her will had been a stupid move. One he wasn't going to repeat.

"Where does this corridor lead to?" she suddenly said into the silence.

"We'll emerge in cold storage."

She gave him a sideways glance. "What's that?"

"You'll see."

He slowed as they came to the end of the tunnel.

"There's no door!" Katie's voice was laced with panic.

Luther squeezed her arm. "There is. It's just not evident. Trust me." He let go of her and ran his hands along the left side of the wall. He felt the indentations almost instantly. His fingers slid into the grooves. With only the lightest of pressure he pushed against the indentations.

A small number pad appeared, and he typed in the same combination as before. A series of clicks confirmed that the code was correct.

"Step back."

The wall moved toward them, swinging to the side. Blue light flooded into the corridor, making him adjust his focus. Cold air blasted him and the low humming sound of a motor reached his ears.

"Stay close behind me," he ordered and stepped forward. A cloud of fog built in front of his face as he exhaled.

"It's a refrigerator," Katie said in surprise.

"I hope you're not squeamish."

"Why would I—" She stopped and let her eyes wander around the large refrigerated storage room. "Oh."

Luther motioned to the bags of blood that were stacked neatly on stainless steel racks, sorted by blood type and age. "They can't let the prisoners starve." Even though some of the guards had surely tried.

"How many prisoners do they keep here?"

He shrugged without looking at her. "The facility is built to hold 480 prisoners."

"That's not a lot of blood for that many prisoners."

Curious, Luther turned to look at her. "Trust me, it's enough."

Katie pointed at the bags of blood. "Maybe for one day. Haven says—"

"Whatever your brother told you doesn't apply here. There are different rules in prison. The daily rations... they are..." He hesitated, not knowing why he even bothered explaining and decided to say no more.

"They're what?"

The honest curiosity in her gaze made him reconsider. He couldn't brush her off now, not when she showed concern about men she didn't even know, convicts, prisoners, *vampires*.

He reached for a one-pint bag and held it up. "This will feed one prisoner for four days."

Katie's chin dropped slowly and her bottom lips quivered from the cold. "That can't be. I know how much Haven and his mate consume. No adult vampire can survive on so little."

"It's a prison, not a country club." He turned toward the door. "Let's go, you're cold."

Her trembling lips and chattering teeth weren't the only indication of her sensitivity to the cold environment. Underneath her cardigan, her nipples were hard. And as much as the sight enticed him, this wasn't the time or the place to act upon it. Nor did he expect a warm reception from Katie should he be so stupid as to touch her again.

Why he'd let his baser instincts rule him twenty-four hours earlier, he didn't understand. If prison had taught him one thing, it was how to control his emotions and his needs. But then, even the best had the occasional relapse. Didn't mean it had to happen again.

Luther walked up to the door. A small window was cut into it, allowing him to look into the anteroom, which was equipped with carts and trays used to distribute the blood every day. He knew the schedule well. It never changed. In an hour, four guards would enter the cold storage and divvy up the rations, then distribute them to the ravenous prisoners.

At the thought of the blood, he felt an acute pang of hunger roil through his stomach. He'd gorged himself on a street person just before he'd been arrested by Scanguards, and considering the amount of blood he'd taken—more than he'd had at any one time during his twenty years in prison—he should be thoroughly sated, but he wasn't.

Katie stood next to him now. Too damn close. He could smell her blood, hear it even as it was rushing through her veins. He could feel the low drum of her heartbeat, the tap-tap-tap of her pulse. Temptation gripped him. He wrenched himself away from it and turned the doorknob.

Luther stepped into the empty prep room. "Close the door to cold storage," he said over his shoulder as Katie followed him. "If the temperature rises in there, the guards will get an alert and show up."

Katie pulled the door closed. "Where to now?"

"Just follow me. And stay quiet. A vampire's hearing is ten times more sensitive than that of a human. Even if you whisper, they'll hear you."

"I know that." And her facial expression told him she didn't appreciate the lecture.

He decided not to comment and opened the door to the corridor just a sliver. Enough so he could listen for sounds.

Footsteps. Coming closer, not retreating.

Luther put a finger to his lips and focused his ears on the sounds coming closer.

"...could take the time off." The voice he heard belonged to Dobbs.

"What, and go where?" MacKay replied.

"To some cool place."

"You mean like Norris? Did he tell you where he was heading?"

"Nope. He was all cryptic about it. He only said that he would leave everybody in his wake."

"Whatever!" MacKay said.

Both vampires' voices echoed in the empty corridor. They were almost at the door now.

"So what would you do on your vacation?" MacKay asked.

A chuckle broke from Dobbs's mouth. "New York City or Chicago. With all those dark alleys at night, hey, that's the ideal hunting grounds. Lots of chicks and junkies who don't even see you coming. That's what I call a vacation!"

Dobbs and MacKay were right outside the door now.

"Cool." MacKay grunted. "Want a snack?"

Shit! Luther suppressed a curse. That's just what he needed now: two heavily armed vampire guards raiding the fridge. His fingers automatically lengthened, and sharp barbs emerged from his fingertips, readying themselves for a bloody battle.

"You know they count that stuff," Dobbs cautioned.

"We can always blame Summerland," MacKay suggested.

"Don't be stupid. That jerk's gonna be up your ass so quickly, you won't even see him coming."

"Don't tell me you're afraid of Summerland." MacKay laughed.

A growl came from Dobbs. "Do whatever you need to do, but don't expect me to cover for you."

Footsteps moved away.

"Hey, wait up, Dobbs."

A second set of footsteps followed the first.

Luther waited until the sounds grew fainter, before he released a breath. Then he looked back at Katie.

Her eyes were glued to his hands. His gaze shot to them. They had turned fully into claws. Deadly instruments. Luther lifted his eyes, meeting Katie's. There was no fear in them, but something he could only interpret as fascination.

19

Katie held Luther's gaze. The orange-red rim around his irises slowly disappeared, turning his eye color back to a rich brown. She'd watched him closely when he'd listened to the guards passing in the corridor outside and seen the tension harden his entire body, readying himself for a fight.

Maybe she wasn't scared of that side of Luther because he reminded her so much of her brother Haven at that moment, of how he'd used his vampire side to protect her. To save her from a human who'd meant her harm. Perhaps that was the reason why she associated glaring red eyes, piercing fangs and hands that took on the form of claws with safety rather than danger.

Katie reached for his hand, but before she could clasp it, Luther turned his back to her and opened the door.

"Come," he said quietly and walked into the corridor.

She followed him, her eyes darting up and down the corridor. She couldn't hear anything. It was eerily quiet. She'd always assumed that it would be noisy in a prison. But maybe that was only the case for a human prison.

The corridor was lined with doors. As she walked past them, keeping close to Luther, she read the signs on them. It appeared that they weren't cells, but rather supply rooms, mechanical and electrical areas, and most likely administrative offices. This had to be the area of the prison the V-CONs had no access to.

Luther guided her through a maze of corridors, turned left, then right, again and again. Within minutes, she had lost all sense of orientation. But Luther seemed to know exactly where he was heading.

At the next corner, he ducked into one of the many niches that held closets. He ripped open one of the doors and jerked her to him, shoving her behind the open closet door. Her mouth was already opening to voice a protest at the rough treatment, when he pressed a hand over her mouth and shielded her with his body. His eyes told her what he couldn't express with his voice: to keep quiet.

She blinked in acquiescence and he removed his hand from her mouth, yet continued to hold her tightly to his broad frame. A few seconds later she heard it: several people came marching down the corridor. Involuntarily she held her breath. But her heart began to pound so loudly in her ears that she was sure every vampire in the entire prison could hear it.

Beneath her fingers, which she realized were suddenly clawing into Luther's shirt, Luther's chest muscles were flexing. Despite the fear of discovery that gripped her, she couldn't help but marvel at the strength that pulsed beneath her trembling fingers. If she were strong like him, she would never again have to be afraid. A yearning went through her and made her aware of her own shortcomings: she was a witch without powers, and right now she hated her mother for having robbed her of the magic she'd been given at birth. If only…

Luther released her.

The corridor was empty again. The guards had passed without noticing them.

"Why didn't they smell me?" she murmured to Luther.

He motioned to the open closet.

She stared at the shelves and noticed the bottles of bleach, soaps, sponges, and rags used for cleaning.

"You really know your way around here."

He put a finger to her lips, before taking her hand to lead her away wordlessly. The spot where his finger had been for such a brief moment tingled, and she wanted to rub her hand over it, not because she didn't like the feeling, but because she wanted it to spread to the rest of her body.

That's crazy, she cursed herself silently, when Luther suddenly stopped and looked at his watch. She cast him a curious look then assessed her surroundings. There were three doors on one side of the corridor, and one on the opposite side. *REC-1* was stenciled in black letters next to the door, right above a keypad.

Katie exchanged a look with Luther, who now turned away from the door and opened the middle door of the three on the opposite wall. He pulled her with him, stepping into the dark room, then pulled the door toward him, leaving it slightly open. In the dim light of the room, which, from the little she could tell, was some sort of storage area, she noticed him looking at his watch again.

She was about to ask him what he was waiting for, when she heard a door opening. She peered past Luther to try to glance through the tiny sliver between door and frame and saw a man, clad in heavy Kevlar gear, emerge from the room opposite, *REC-1*.

A recreation room? It didn't appear so. The vampire wasn't dressed as if he'd just come from a gym.

As soon as the vampire disappeared Luther sprang into action. He flung the door open, charged toward the door with the keypad and typed in a six-digit number. When a click sounded, he pushed the door open and marched inside, waving Katie to follow him.

The door shut behind her.

"We have about four minutes until he'll be back," Luther said.

"How do you know?"

Luther rounded the large desk and plopped down into the office chair. "I know everybody's routine. When you spend twenty years in this joint, you find all kinds of things to pass the time."

Katie looked around. This wasn't a recreation room. The room was packed with filing cabinets, computers, and servers. A records room, yes, that's what this was.

"And the code to the door?"

Luther was already typing away on the computer and clicking with the mouse. He didn't even look up when he answered, "I have exceptional hearing and a musical brain. Every number on that keypad makes a slightly different sound. I can recognize the numbers by their sounds."

"But the guy who left, he didn't punch in any numbers."

Luther looked up briefly, smirking. "The code is changed only weekly. I was on the detail to clean these corridors for the last three years. I can rattle off the code for each and every week that I was here."

Katie blew out a breath. She had to admit she was impressed. Exceptional hearing, a musical brain, an extraordinary memory. What else did Luther have up his sleeve?

"Got it!"

Katie rounded the desk and stared into the monitor just as Luther clicked on the print icon.

"Cliff Forrester?" she read on the electronic file.

"Do you know the name?"

She shook her head. "No. And the letters weren't signed."

The printer on a cabinet along the wall started humming.

"Let's grab this and get out of here," Luther said and stood up.

Katie turned to the printer and snatched the sheet from its tray the moment the printer spat it out. She folded it and shoved it in the front pocket of her jeans.

"Let's go!"

A blaring signal nearly deafened her. The eardrum-piercing high-pitched sound lasted for several seconds.

"Shit!" Luther cursed.

20

"What is that?" Katie stared at him, panic in her eyes.

"Intruder alert." What that entailed, Luther had neither the inclination, nor the time to explain. The shit was gonna hit the fan any moment. "How about some witchcraft now? Otherwise, I'm afraid we're gonna be in trouble."

"Witchcraft?" she choked out, her head moving from left to right and back. "I don't know any witchcraft."

"What?" He ground out the word, making an involuntary step toward her.

"I'm sorry, but I don't have any powers. I was born a witch, but I don't know any spells."

Luther clenched his fist. "Oh that's just peachy, isn't it? I have to fall for the tricks of a witch, and then she isn't even a real witch! Perfect, that's just perfect!" His ears perked up. "Fuck! He's coming back!"

His eyes darted around the room, looking for a weapon.

"I know what to do," Katie claimed and pointed to the wall next to the door. "Stay there behind the door. I'll distract him."

Luther would have laughed, had the situation not been so hopeless. "What the fuck with?"

"Acting." Katie peeled herself out of her cardigan, then pulled her T-shirt over her head and tossed it on the desk. She was wearing a black lace bra that presented her boobs as if on a silver platter.

"What the—" His sensitive hearing picked up the sound of the code being entered in the keypad outside the door. *Shit.* He jumped next to a tall filing cabinet just as the door was swung open. As long as the guard entering looked only at the desk where Katie was standing, he wouldn't detect Luther.

"What're you doing in here? This is a classified area."

The guard—Luther recognized him immediately as Bauer—stepped into the room, hand on his hip where his UV gun was holstered, while the door fell shut behind him.

"Hi!" Katie batted her eyelashes at him, strutting out her enticing female assets, while running her hands over her torso.

"You can't be in—"

"I'm a gift from your colleagues, honey," she interrupted and brought her hands to her breasts, cupping them. "They said you like to play with bad girls like me. And I'm a real bad girl." She pouted. "So, are you gonna punish me for being in here without your permission?"

Luther swallowed hard. Fuck! Was Katie acting? He sure couldn't tell! She looked like she meant it.

"Do you wanna touch 'em?" she continued seducing the dumbstruck guard. Her fingers slowly, deliberately worked the front of her bra. When she finally dropped her hands, her bra fell open in the front, revealing her ample breasts.

Paralyzed, Luther stared at the unexpected sight. His mouth went dry, and his heart stopped beating.

"Fuck!" the guard grunted and took a few steps toward her. "Are you for real?"

Katie brought her hands to her breasts and squeezed them. "Don't you wanna sink your fangs into these babies?"

"Yeah!" Bauer appeared to salivate. "That's what I'm talking about."

Over his fucking dead body!

Luther leapt from his hiding place and jumped toward the vampire guard before he could reach Katie and dig his dirty fangs into her perfect breasts. Before Bauer had time to turn around, Luther pulled the guard's UV gun from the holster and directed the concentrated UV blast at the other vampire's face. The full load hit him in the eyes. A blood-curdling scream came from Bauer and he jerked his hands up to his face to shield it from the attack, but it was too late. Luther had already blinded him.

He aimed another shot at Bauer's open mouth, singeing his lips, tongue and throat so severely that he wouldn't be able to speak until after his regenerative sleep cycle. His vision would eventually return, too.

Luther lowered the gun, then pushed the disoriented vampire down. He landed on the ground, whimpering now in obvious pain, unable to speak.

"Oh my God!" Katie murmured.

Luther shot her a look, ran his eyes over her. She was uninjured. For a split-second, he drank in the sight of her naked breasts and felt a bolt hit him in the groin. She was beautiful. So goddamn beautiful.

"Get dressed."

Luther averted his eyes and looked back at the vampire on the floor. "Bauer, you know I could kill you, and I will if I have to. It depends on you. Here's how this works: I'll take your protective gear and your access card, and you won't struggle. Resist, and you'll die. If you understand me, raise one hand."

The guard lifted his right hand in a one-finger salute, grunting as he did so.

"Big mistake!"

Luther pointed the UV gun at his groin. "I'll let you guess where I'm pointing your weapon now." He jammed the gun between Bauer's thighs.

The guard instantly jerked away, and a second later he raised his hand again, this time without flipping him the bird.

"I'm glad we understand each other," Luther said and looked back at Katie. Her T-shirt now covered her torso again, and she was putting on her cardigan. "Point the gun at him while I get the Kevlar gear off him. If he tries anything, blast his balls. Just make sure you don't hit me."

Katie took the gun from him. "With pleasure."

It took less then thirty seconds for Luther to liberate Bauer from his protective gear and another thirty to put it on himself. Then he used the silver handcuffs on the vampire's belt to cuff him to a steel filing cabinet, being careful not to touch the silver with his bare hands, but donning gloves first.

When he was done, Luther glanced around the room until he found what he was looking for: the protective head gear that would shield him should anybody deploy the UV lights in the corridors. It would also help him avoid detection. Dressed like a guard in full battle gear, nobody would be able to tell who he really was. In the chaos of an intruder alert nobody would take much notice of him.

Which only left one slight problem: how was he going to get Katie out of here without anybody stopping him?

"What are we waiting for?" Katie asked nervously.

"Do you think you can do a little bit more acting?"

"What do you want me to do?"

"I need you to pretend you're a hooker, just like you did earlier."

It was the only way other guards wouldn't see her as a threat and look the other way instead. It was an unwritten code in the prison: prostitutes were tolerated and considered a side business for many guards. With some luck, any guard Luther encountered wouldn't bother him if he thought Luther was simply trying to get a hooker out of the prison before there was a general lockdown.

"You want me to take off my bra?" Katie asked.

"No!" The word shot out of his mouth almost automatically. He ran a hand along his nape. "Just take off the cardigan and the T-shirt. I'll find you something else to wear."

He ripped open a closet, then another one. Just like he'd suspected, Bauer kept a change of clothes in his office, like most guards did. It happened often enough that clothes got ripped or bloodied during fights.

"Here." He took a white dress shirt from a hanger and handed it to Katie. "Put this on, but don't button it. Just tie a knot at your waist so your black bra will show. It'll make you look slutty enough."

Without protest, Katie changed into the shirt. She turned over the sleeves that were too long for her. When Luther saw her transformation, he knew he'd been right.

She looked like sin personified. Her dark hair cascaded over her shoulders, the top of her breasts peeked out from over the black lace of her bra, and at the right angle, one could even see her belly button. Her jeans were tight, showing off her fabulous ass, and her legs were long and slim. Yes, definitely hooker material, though he hated the thought of other men looking at her like that, thinking they could have her in exchange for cold hard cash.

When he lifted his eyes and met hers, he saw something there, saw that she could read him, read the thoughts that were going through his mind as plainly as if he'd spoken them. But she said nothing, didn't comment on what she saw, didn't even flinch or toss him a look of contempt, though she had to think that he was just like all the other vampires: lecherous, and unable to control his need for sex and blood. At the moment those two needs were battling for supremacy, and even though he was doing his best to appear calm on the outside, the storm raging in him had to show on his face and body. He could sense his muscles twitch, his nostrils flare, and his cock thicken, just as surely as he could feel his fangs lengthen.

"Let's go," he ground out and turned abruptly.

"How do you want me to act?" Katie asked from behind him, while he marched to the door.

"You looked pretty convincing earlier. I don't think you need me to coach you on what to do." Luther ripped the door open. Strobe lights on the walls indicated that the intruder alert was still active.

He felt her hand on his elbow and with it a shock of electricity traveled up his arm. He whirled his head to her, a curse already on his lips, when he saw her eyes.

"I'm scared," she murmured.

The curse never left his lips. Instead he lifted his hand and brushed his gloved knuckles over her cheek, surprising himself with the gentle gesture. "I'll keep you safe."

Her lips parted slightly, before he turned his head back toward the corridor and lowered the visor of his protective head gear.

21

The corridor was empty when Katie followed Luther, but even without vampire hearing she could already hear approaching footsteps and commands being shouted. Despite Luther's assurance that he would keep her safe, she knew their chances of getting out of this place alive were minimal.

This had been a bad idea.

A guard came running down the corridor, talking into his communication device as he rushed past them with barely a second glance. Surprised, Katie gave Luther a sideways look. The reflective visor hid his face, and he appeared just like any other guard. Only the name tag would identify him. *Bauer* it said.

"Just how common is it for a guard to be seen with a woman?"

Luther shrugged. "Common enough."

A door opened a few yards ahead of them and another guard dressed in Kevlar gear ran in the other direction. Katie followed him with her eyes when she realized something.

"Why wasn't he wearing a visor like you?" The guard who'd run past them only moments earlier hadn't worn one either.

"Because the UV lights aren't on." Luther's response was clipped; he seemed pre-occupied with deciding which way to turn next.

He gripped her by the elbow and dragged her down a hallway to the left. She almost tripped over her own feet trying to keep up with him and only saw the door in front of them when Luther opened it.

The room looked like a central foyer from which several doors and walkways, as well as stairs, led in a multitude of directions.

Vampires dressed in their protective Kevlar gear seemed to converge here, some strapping on weapons, others speaking into their communication devices.

Neither glancing right nor left, Luther marched through the space as if he owned it. Katie's heart pounded, while she tried to avoid looking at anybody in particular. None of them was wearing the kind of visor that covered Luther's face. Shit! That had to look suspicious.

The door Luther was heading for was closed. Next to it, there was a card reader. From the corner of her eye, she noticed Luther pull an access card from his pocket.

"Hey, Bauer," a voice from behind them called out.

Katie froze.

Luther grunted and pulled her along. Only a few feet separated them from the door now.

"What's with the head gear, Bauer? You know something we don't?"

Luther swiped the access card at the door. A click sounded. He ripped the door open, shoved her through it.

"That's not Bauer! Get them!" At the words, all hell broke loose.

"Intruders in Section K, heading for—"

Katie pivoted and squinted as she suddenly saw the flash of UV lights coming from the guards' guns. Luther ducked and dove into the corridor, slamming the door shut. He jammed the butt of his UV gun into the card reader on this side of the door, smashing it.

"You okay?"

She nodded automatically, meeting his eyes. "Will that keep them locked in?"

He'd already grabbed her arm and started running. "Central command can override any door. We've gotta get out before they can disable my access card."

They ran down the hallway to the next door. Luther swiped his card so fast, Katie's eyes couldn't even perceive the movement. This time he went through the door first, shielding her with his broad body.

"What's going on?" a male voice asked.

She saw how Luther jerked his thumb over his shoulder. "Bit of an uproar," Luther said and stepped aside, giving Katie a view of the room. "Not every day the boys get an eyeful like that." His voice sounded muffled behind the visor.

The vampire guard who'd spoken—she read the name on his uniform, Patterson—looked at her for a brief moment, then glared at Luther. "Can't bring a hooker through here. Rules are rules."

Luther grunted.

"And open your fucking visor when I'm talking to you." The vampire guard narrowed his eyes, his hand shifting toward his weapon, but Luther didn't follow his order and took a step closer.

Pulse racing, Katie took a quick inventory of the room and the guard. There was a computer console that looked like it belonged in a recording studio. Behind it was an arsenal of weapons, and beyond it the only other door. The way out was past this guard.

"Come on, buddy, gimme a break," Luther coaxed. "They're gonna eat her alive back there. And I've already given her more than she can take."

"Lockdown! All stations on lockdown!" a voice came through a loudspeaker. *"Watch out for a male intruder posing as a guard, accompanied by a female."*

Patterson's eyes widened as he reached for his weapon, but Luther was already pouncing. With his full body weight, he slammed into the prison guard. As Luther and the other vampire traded blows and kicks, Katie ran toward the other door, but to her surprise there was no knob and no card reader. She spun around.

"The console!" Luther called out to her, before the guard's left fist flew toward him. He avoided it narrowly and tumbled backward.

Katie rushed to the computer console. Her eyes traveled over the buttons and switches. But there were too many, and they were only labeled with initials. "Fuck! Which one?"

Luther and his opponent crashed against the console, making it rattle. Both men growled and continued fighting each other. Luther had lost his head gear, and Katie knew what this meant: they would recognize him and hunt him should they ever make it out of here.

Frantically, Katie flipped switches and pressed buttons. An alarm began to sound.

"Oh shit!" Luther cursed, freezing for a moment. Time enough for the prison guard to land a blow to his temple, jerking his head to the side.

Luther careened back, trying to regain his balance. Horrified, Katie watched as the guard pulled a smaller gun from his boot and jerked it toward Luther. The metal barrel gleamed under the harsh lights. This wasn't a UV gun. This was a small-caliber handgun. She'd seen Scanguards' people use them—they were usually loaded with silver bullets, and once they hit a vampire, the silver would eat him alive from the inside.

"Fuck!" Katie gripped the first thing her hands reached and charged toward Patterson.

Holding the iPad with its rigid cover in both hands, she threw herself between the guard and Luther, thrusting the tablet in front of the muzzle just as the shot fired.

She felt the impact as the bullet hit the iPad and—luckily!—got stuck in it. The force of it though, pushed her back, making her lose the ground beneath her feet. Arms flailing, she fell with her back against the console. The wind was knocked out of her lungs, and when she pulled in another breath, a scream ripped from her throat.

Pain seared through her flank. She dropped her gaze toward the floor and tried to focus her eyes amidst the blinding pain that wracked her body.

A knife. Covered in her blood.

It came toward her once more, ready to plunge into the same wound it had already caused, but the second hit didn't come. Instead, the guard was jerked back.

Her legs buckled. "Luther," she murmured and closed her eyes, trying to block out the pain.

22

Luther tightened the silver chain he'd snatched from a hook on the wall around the guard's neck and jerked him away from Katie just in time. With his knee, he kicked his opponent in the back, making him not only lose his balance but also the bloody knife in his hand.

Instantly, Luther trained his eyes on Katie: a red bloodstain spread on the white dress shirt, soaking it just above her waist.

"Shit!"

He noticed her sway.

"Hold on, Katie!" he urged her, as he pulled his captive back toward the wall lined with steel conduits. He looped the ends of the silver chain around the thick metal rod and secured it, tying up his prisoner, while Patterson clawed at the chain to loosen it from his neck—to no avail. The silver bit into his skin, burning him, slowly eating away the upper layers.

Angry eyes stared at Luther.

"Don't worry, you'll survive."

"Bastard!" the guard choked out. "I'm gonna get you for this!"

But Luther had already rushed to Katie, who was barely keeping herself upright. "Got you!" He grabbed her with one arm, lifted her off the floor and rounded the console.

"Gotta get out of here," she murmured, sounding breathy.

"I'll get you out," he promised, while he scanned the computer console with his eyes, looking for the right button to operate the door to the outside.

Shit! They'd made some modifications to the original design. Well, it didn't matter. He'd just have to improvise.

From the other side of the door, Luther heard sounds. Something breaking. Fuck! They'd managed to break down the door whose card reader Luther had trashed.

"In here!" Patterson screamed, alerting his colleagues. "He's in here!"

Luther flipped two switches on the console, then hit a button. A buzzing sound came from the door to the outside.

With Katie in his arms, he ran toward it, snatched a semi-automatic gun from the rack on the wall and rushed through the opening door.

Before the door could close behind him, he spun around and emptied the entire clip into the center of the console, where the motherboard was located. Sparks flew and the computer hissed just as the other door to the control room burst open and guards rushed into the room.

The door snapped shut, and the sounds of the guards were immediately muffled.

Luther prayed that the backup lockdown mechanism still worked the same way he'd originally designed it, and that by disabling the computer, the backup would immediately kick in, assess the threat, and lock down the facility.

Luther rushed to the last door, Katie clutched to his chest. He swiped Bauer's access card, and the door to freedom opened. He barreled outside into the open air. The moment the door closed behind him, he heard the sound of a foghorn: lockdown. Relief flooded him. Not even the guards could get out now. It would take at least half an hour for even the best IT expert to override the system and unlock the doors.

Time enough to get away.

"You're safe, Katie. Just hold on for a little while longer," he demanded.

The pickup truck he found in the parking lot was perfect. He carefully laid Katie on the front bench, shucked the heavy Kevlar vest and gloves and hotwired the car. Once the engine started, he pulled Katie's head onto his lap and drove off.

His eyes searched the rearview mirror, but there was no movement, no cars following them as he put miles between them and the prison. For the first time in minutes, he took a conscious breath.

Keeping his left hand on the steering wheel, he reached for Katie with his right. "I'm gonna check your wound. I won't hurt you."

She moaned when he touched her left flank. The dress shirt was soaked in blood, and the smell, now that they were in a confined space, filled his nostrils and made hunger surge inside him. He forced it back down.

As gently as he could, he peeled back the ripped cloth and exposed the wound.

"Shit!"

Her eyes shot open and met his. "Is it bad?" she choked out.

"Just a flesh wound. You'll be all right," he deflected, choosing not to tell her the truth. "But we've gotta stop the bleeding."

Katie pressed her hand onto the wound. "No hospital, right?" she guessed.

He gave her a faint smile. She was smart. He couldn't bring her to a hospital. Not only would it delay their escape, the council that ran the vampire prison had spies everywhere. They would know quickly where to find him. By now they would have identified him from the camera feeds inside the prison.

"I'm so sorry," she murmured, a gurgle in her voice now. "It's all my fault. They'll lock you up again."

"They'll have to find me first. So let me worry about that later." There was something more important to think of right now, because judging by the gurgling sound in Katie's voice, her lung had been punctured. If he didn't act immediately, her lungs would fill with blood and she'd drown in her own fluids.

He lifted his wrist to his mouth, willing his fangs to extend. Then he caught Katie's gaze.

"What are you doing?" she whispered.

"You need to heal." He bit into his own wrist, puncturing his vein, making blood drip from it. He brought the bleeding wound to Katie's mouth. "Drink."

He sensed her hesitate and felt anger well up in him. No vampire offered his blood lightly. This was a gift, one he didn't easily bestow on anybody. "It won't turn you into a—"

"I know that," she interrupted, her voice even weaker than before.

"Then drink, damn it!"

Slender fingers pulled his wrist down to her lips. A warm mouth made contact with his skin. A gentle breath caressed his flesh.

If he hadn't been driving, he would have leaned his head against the headrest and closed his eyes to enjoy the sensation of Katie suckling from him. It had been so long since a woman had done this, since a woman had taken his blood into her body, and accepted him and all he had to offer.

Luther allowed his fist to unfurl and the tips of his fingers to touch Katie's cheek. Her skin was soft and smooth. Warm. Her heat suffused his hand and penetrated the pads of his fingers. Tempted by the tantalizing sensation, he caressed her face with slow, tiny strokes. Katie appeared to suck harder now, pulling more blood from his vein.

Oh God, it felt as if she was sucking his cock, as if her tender lips wrapped around his swollen shaft, taking him deep into her gorgeous mouth.

He took his eyes off the road, looking down at her face. Her eyes were closed again, but she was conscious. She was holding onto his wrist with one hand now. The other lay on her breast, restless, moving.

He knew what was happening to her. While his blood was healing her wound from the inside, the side effects were kicking in. Her body was awakening with sexual desire, with the need to be touched, the need to find release.

The scent of her arousal now mixed with the aroma of her blood and his, creating a combination that became harder and harder to resist with every second that passed. He couldn't let this happen. It was bad enough that he wanted her, that feeling her drink from him aroused him, but he couldn't let her get into the same state he was in.

"It's enough," he ground out and pulled his wrist from her mouth.

She moaned in protest, but he brought his wrist to his lips and licked the incisions. His saliva closed the holes instantly as if they'd never existed.

"Rest now, we'll be there soon." And he hoped that by the time they reached the safe place he was heading for, Katie's wound would be healed and the arousal that came with the consumption of vampire blood subsided.

At least then he'd only have to deal with his own arousal.

23

The gentle rocking of the truck sent her in and out of consciousness, until it finally stopped. No more humming of the engine, no more vibrations beneath her back. No more pretending that the continuous shifting of her hips was a result of the car's movement, when she knew what it really was: a sign of the sexual desire brought on by drinking Luther's blood.

She'd been around vampires long enough to know the signs, but nobody had warned her that the effect of vampire blood would be so intense, or that it would last as long as it did.

Katie felt Luther's thigh muscles flex underneath her nape. Even after he'd fed her from his wrist, he'd kept his right arm across her torso, holding her. Whether to make sure she didn't slip from the bench or for whatever other reason, she didn't know. Nor had she cared. It felt good to feel connected to him, to feel his strength, his protection.

She was aware of him in a way she hadn't known was possible. Every fiber of her body seemed to reach for him, yearning for an even deeper connection, a melding of body and soul. And though she knew it was wrong to give into the desire, she couldn't find the strength to resist.

Luther's blood coupled with the memories of their passionate kiss from the night before conjured up images in her mind's eye that she didn't *want* to suppress. What would it be like if she pulled his hand to her breasts so he could take away the ache that she felt there?

Katie lifted her hand from her stomach, reaching for his, but before she could touch him, he was sliding out from beneath her and placing her head gently onto the bench.

"We're here," he announced and opened the driver's side door.

Katie opened her eyes and looked up, but the light on the truck's ceiling blinded her for an instant. A moment later, the passenger door was opened.

She sat up, slowly, her gaze focused on her midsection where her open shirt was bloodstained. Adrenaline coursed through her and sent her heartbeat into the stratosphere.

She lifted her eyes from the wound and stared at Luther, who stood in the open door. "Oh my God, how badly was I injured?"

"Badly enough." Luther's serious expression said more than his short reply. "Come, I'll take you inside." He reached for her.

Instinctively, she shrank back. If he touched her now, how would she be able to stop herself from throwing herself at him like a sex-crazed groupie? "I'm fine. I can walk."

"Not until I've checked out your wound." The words were said with a finality that didn't allow for any protest.

Luther scooped her out of the truck much more gently than she'd expected a vampire of his size and reputation to be capable of. When she was outside and he kicked the car door shut, she peered into the darkness.

"Where are we?"

He carried her toward a dark building. "At a friend's place." The added *I hope* was mumbled under his breath.

The one-story house seemed to be in the middle of a forest, hidden away from curious eyes.

"No farther!" a male voice came from somewhere in the darkness.

Luther stopped, and Katie instinctively tensed. "I was hoping you'd grant an old friend shelter for a few hours."

"Luther West." Suddenly a man appeared to their right. He lowered the crossbow slightly, but it was still pointed at them, and loaded with a wooden stake.

"Striker Reed." Luther nodded toward the weapon. "Collecting antiques these days?"

Striker grinned, and Katie could now clearly see his fangs peeking from between his lips. "Guns are overrated. I prefer to kill my prey and my enemies silently."

"I'm glad I don't fall into either category," Luther said dryly.

"No, you don't," the vampire agreed. Then he ran his eyes over

Katie, making her shiver involuntarily. She'd never seen anybody with such a cold regard. "Jury's still out on her." He inhaled. "What is she?"

"Human," Luther answered without hesitation. "And she's injured. I need a place to take care of her."

Striker took a few steps closer, his eyes zooming in on her bloodstained shirt. "By the looks of it, you already have." He paused. "But who am I to turn away a friend in need?"

The stranger pointed his hand toward the house. "Mi casa es su casa." Then he walked ahead of them and opened the entrance door. A second later the interior of the house was flooded with light.

Luther carried her over the threshold. "Do you have a room where I can clean her wound?"

Striker motioned to the back of the house. "Spare bedroom has a bathroom with it." He walked ahead and opened the last door on the left.

"Thank you. I appreciate it," Luther said.

Gently he placed her on the bed, removing her shoes in the process.

"Need help?" Striker asked.

Katie's gaze shot to him, and she noticed the lascivious look he ran over her. Instinctively she pulled on her shirt to cover up her bra.

"Actually, yes, there's something you could do for me," Luther said. "I'm looking for somebody."

"Wouldn't have anything to do with the little scuffle at the prison tonight, would it?"

Katie noticed Luther squaring his shoulders as if he expected a confrontation. "How did you—"

"You forget," the stranger cut him off, "that my connections to the council give me unique insight into everything that happens on my turf." He nodded toward Katie. "I suppose you're not really a hooker like my source said."

Katie tilted her head to the side. "Sorry to disappoint you."

Unexpectedly, Striker laughed, then addressed Luther. "Yeah, didn't really think you were into hookers."

Luther grunted something unintelligible, his facial expression dark and stormy.

"Who're you after?"

"An ex-V-CON named Cliff Forrester. He was released about a week ago. I need to know where he is now."

"What's he done?"

"He kidnapped the hybrid daughter of an old friend of mine."

Striker nodded. "Well, in that case, let me make a few inquiries. You guys okay here on your own for a couple of hours?" He chuckled dryly. "Scratch that. Of course you are." He turned and marched out into the hallway.

"Thanks, Striker," Luther called after him.

When the entrance door opened and then closed again a few moments later, the tension in Katie's body finally released. She swung her legs out of bed.

"Whoa!" Luther stopped her, planting himself right in her path. "What do you think you're doing?"

She motioned to her bloodstained shirt. "Getting cleaned up. What else?"

He pressed his palm against her shoulder, forcing her to lie down again. "I'll take care of that. You: stay!" He turned to the door of the en-suite bathroom. "And take off your shirt."

"The bra, too?" she bit out, annoyed by his commanding tone.

He spun his head to her. "Just the fucking shirt, unless you'd rather I help you with that." Then he disappeared in the bathroom.

Katie felt a shiver run down her spine, turning her skin into goose bumps. Her nipples hardened at the same time and she suppressed a curse. Upset with herself for her sophomoric reaction to the order, she peeled out of the shirt and tossed it onto a nearby chair.

She knew exactly why she was reacting like this: because Luther's blood was still coursing through her. It made her irrational, impulsive. It made her want to do things that were wrong—like stripping in front of him and provoking him until he tossed her underneath him and buried his hard cock in her. There, she'd admitted it to herself. But no way would she admit that to the Neanderthal in the bathroom.

All he would do was gloat. His words from the night before still echoed in her ears.

I would have kissed anything with tits at this point.

That had hurt. Did he not find her attractive? Did he not sense the smoldering heat that sparked between them? Was she the only one who felt it? Because it was singeing her, and there were only two things she could do to resolve her current predicament: run as far away from him as possible, or get as close as two people could physically get.

And right now, she didn't want to run. She wanted Luther, even if he didn't want her. And she would use all the feminine wiles at her disposal to get what she wanted.

24

Luther wrung out the washcloth he'd found in the cabinet under the sink and snatched a towel from the rack. He stared into the mirror, but there was no reflection. Not that he needed a mirror to tell him what he already knew: his vampire side was about to break through the surface and make him do things he would regret later. Because another minute in Katie's company, and he'd either choke her to death for flaunting her enticing body and provoking him at every turn, or fuck her until she lost consciousness.

I figure I'm safe as long as I don't let you fuck me.

Her words from the night before ricocheted in his head like a misfired bullet. She knew full well that he wanted her, and she used that knowledge to manipulate him. To play him.

God, he'd even started to care about what happened to her. When the prison guard had stabbed her, his heart had stopped for fear of being too late to save her.

Luther grunted to himself and walked back into the bedroom. Katie lay on the bed, propped up by two pillows. She'd taken off the shirt, but still wore her bra. Keeping his eyes down, he approached and sat on the edge of the bed.

Without a word, he brought the wet washcloth to her wound and wiped over it.

She jerked back.

"Still hurting?" he asked, surprised. The healing process should be almost complete.

"Just cold."

He stopped himself short from apologizing for not having thought of using warm water. He was no fucking nurse. "Hmm."

Carefully, he wiped away the encrusted blood, laying bare the skin beneath. It looked red and angry, still not fully healed. The wound had been deep and the blood he'd given her had gone to her internal organs first, repairing them, but the skin on the outside had still not fully regenerated.

"Will it leave scars?"

"I can make sure it won't." By either giving her more blood, or treating the wound from the exterior.

"How?"

He lifted his head and looked into her eyes for the first time since reentering the room. "Your brother is a vampire. You must know how."

Her eyelashes fluttered briefly, and her lips parted just a fraction. Her breath filled the air between them. "Oh."

"Up to you," he said, shrugging as if he didn't care what she decided, when in fact, he wanted her to say yes. Wanted her to allow him this tiny piece of pleasure.

"I mean, if you don't mind," she said hesitantly. "It would be nice not to have a scar there."

He'd hoped for it, hoped that she was vain enough not to want her perfect body marred by a scar that would be visible if she wore a swimsuit—or made love to a man.

"Fine then."

He laid the washcloth on the bedside table and patted the wound dry with the towel. He noticed his hand trembling with anticipation, his gums itching, his mouth salivating. Seconds passed.

"If you don't want to do it, that's fine. It's not like it really matters. I mean…"

Luther dropped his head to her stomach and brought his lips to hover over her stab wound. "Don't talk."

Closing his eyes, he allowed his tongue to swipe over her skin, coating it with his saliva. The special properties in it would assure that her skin healed perfectly. Slowly and gently, he licked the area, enjoying the warmth of her flesh and the taste of her skin. No more blood was seeping from the wound, but he could taste it anyway. A microscopic layer of residue still coated her skin, allowing him to get a taste of what it would be like to drink from her.

A shudder traveled down his spine and sent a spear of electricity into his balls. He knew exactly what was coming now.

Fuck!

Beneath his tongue he felt her skin mend and regenerate. He knew he should stop now, but he couldn't tear his lips from her. Instead, he continued to run his tongue over her now perfect skin and press his lips to it.

Katie's hand on his nape as she suddenly touched him, almost made him jump from the bed, but her moan held him back. Her tender fingers caressed his nape, then slipped underneath his shirt and stroked the sensitive area between his shoulder blades.

He had to be dreaming. That was the only explanation for this. Maybe he'd passed out. After all, he'd given her a good pint of his blood on the drive here, and he hadn't fed in a while.

"Luther." Katie's breathy murmur drifted to his ears.

He lifted his head and looked at her face. Her eyes were half closed, her lips parted. He'd never seen a more tantalizing sight.

"Please, don't stop," she begged, her hand sliding back to his nape, trying to pull him back.

He resisted and shook his head. "We can't. Please don't make me do this." Because he knew why she was reacting like this.

Her eyes opened wider. "I want you."

He threw his head back, groaning. "No. You don't. It's the blood talking."

"No, it's not." Her fingers dug into his nape, trying to pull him to her.

"Hasn't your brother told you what happens when you drink a vampire's blood? That it causes sexual arousal?" But it wasn't real. It was just an illusion.

"This is different," she insisted, sitting up and bringing her enticing semi-nude body closer to him.

When she put her other arm around him, he gripped both her wrists and forced her back into the pillows. "Once it wears off, you'll regret what you're doing now." And she'd hate him for not having stopped her.

"I won't!"

"You can't know that! My blood in you makes you want me. It'll pass," he ground out, still pressing her into the pillows so she couldn't make an attempt to kiss him. Because once those lips touched his, he'd be lost.

A strange smile spread on her mouth, almost as if she knew something he didn't. "Drinking your blood didn't cause this."

"It did."

"Then why did I let you kiss me last night?"

"You didn't let me kiss you. I forced you."

"And I could have stopped you any time I wanted to."

"May I remind you that according to your own admission, you don't have any witch powers?"

"True, but I do have a really strong knee that I know exactly how to use against any man forcing himself on me, vampire or not." She licked her lips and turned her head to look at where his hands were circling her wrists, keeping her immobile. "I don't mind if you want to hold me down like that. If that's how you like it."

"Goddamn it, Katie. I'm warning you," he hissed, holding onto his self control by a mere thread.

"If you don't want me, you can close your eyes and imagine I'm somebody else. Just imagine I'm one of the hookers you had in prison."

"I've never touched a hooker in my life!" Luther growled. "Damn you, Katie, you'd better not be blaming me later or I might just wring your pretty little neck."

Surprise—or was it satisfaction?—flashed in her eyes, but he didn't give her a chance to respond and sank his lips onto hers. He had to still this inexplicable hunger for a woman he barely knew.

Her mouth welcomed him. Soft lips greeted him and an eager tongue stroked against his, inviting him to a sensual duel. One he could neither win nor lose.

Slowly, he released her wrists. He felt her hands on him immediately. Katie didn't waste time: she unbuttoned his shirt and touched his chest, caressing him as if she didn't even notice the many scars that marred his once-perfect skin. As if she didn't see their ugliness.

He was convinced that Katie wanting him was a side effect of her drinking his blood, but what man—vampire or not—was strong enough to resist a siren's call? He knew he'd pay for it later, but right now, he didn't care what punishment he'd have to endure. All he needed was a few minutes of ecstasy in Katie's arms. And nobody was going to get in the way of it, not even Luther himself.

"Katie," he murmured, releasing her lips for a moment.

"Don't stop," she begged, her voice drugged with lust. The sound made his cock even harder.

"I couldn't, even if I wanted to." He shrugged out of his shirt, then stood and shucked his shoes and pants.

When he lowered his boxer briefs, an audible intake of breath came from Katie. He looked at her. Her mouth had dropped open and she was staring at his cock, which now curved against his belly, hard and heavy.

"Take off your jeans, Katie," he commanded, "because if I have to do it, I'm afraid I'm going to shred them."

She lifted her eyes to meet his gaze. Not breaking eye contact, she opened her pants and shimmied out of them. Beneath the denim, she wore black lace panties matching her bra.

When her hands went to the front clasp of her bra, he stopped her, "Don't. I'd like to do that."

Luther put one knee onto the mattress and joined her on the bed.

25

The old mattress depressed under Luther's weight, but Katie barely noticed it. Her attention was focused on Luther's beautiful body. She'd never seen a man like him, certainly not naked and this close up. He was magnificent, the embodiment of power and strength.

Not even the many scars on his torso could take away from that. On the contrary, they seemed to add to the image of the powerful vampire who now brought his body over hers and pressed her into the sheets.

When she felt his strong thighs spread her legs and slide into the space between them, a contented sigh came over her lips.

"Is this what you want, Katie? A vampire like me in your bed?" He slid his palm over her breast, caressing her through the lace. "Touching you?" He rocked his cock against her center. "Fucking you?"

She arched off the mattress, pressing against him, wanting more of the delicious friction he provided. "Don't be a tease."

He chuckled. "You mean like you? Like you teased me until you got what you wanted?"

"I haven't yet gotten what I wanted."

Luther lowered his face to hers. "Oh yeah, and what is it you really want, Katie? Aside from being fucked by me?"

She held his penetrating gaze, pushing back the thoughts that leapt to the forefront of her mind. To forget and feel safe again. Luther could at least help her attain one of those things, the other she had to find within herself.

"I just want to feel you inside me. That's all I care about."

"That I can give you," he said, before he brushed his lips against hers. "Many times over."

His kiss was passionate and all-consuming, his hands gentle and more tender than she'd expected. He didn't rush it, instead, he explored her thoroughly. Just like his tongue licked and stroked her with unwavering confidence, his hands roamed her body like a man who had all the time in the world.

Katie let her hands travel over his body, caressing his strong muscles, exploring every ridge and groove. When he pulled back, she wanted to protest, but he put a finger to her lips to stop her.

He trailed his hand down one side of her neck and ran it between her breasts until he reached the clasp of her bra. He looked up and locked eyes with her.

"I would never close my eyes while making love to you." He unhooked the clasp with one hand.

Her heart skipped a beat. "Luther, you don't—"

"I mean it." He peeled away the cups of her bra and exposed her bare breasts. "When you showed your boobs to Bauer, you nearly gave me a heart attack." He brushed his knuckles over one breast.

"Vampires can't suffer heart attacks," she said between a sigh and a moan.

"When you invited him to sink his fangs into your breasts, it looked real, like you meant it. I couldn't tell if you were acting."

Luther dipped his head to her breast and licked over her nipple.

A strangled moan tore from her throat, and she thrust her breasts toward him, silently asking for more. But he held back.

"Or weren't you acting? Did you mean it when you invited him to sink his fangs into your tits?" There was an angry undertone in Luther's voice.

Katie sucked in a breath, when Luther's lips suddenly closed around her nipple and sucked on it.

"Oh God!" she cried out, suddenly aching for more, for something deeper.

Luther looked up at her. "Did you want it?"

"No!" she protested. It was the truth. She hadn't wanted the prison guard's fangs in her. In fact, she'd been disgusted by the thought.

Luther's eyes turned darker. He growled softly, then kissed her breasts, nibbling and sucking on them. She loved the way he devoured them, almost as if he were feasting on them, while farther below, he rocked against her in a slow but steady rhythm, igniting her desire for him even more.

"Take me," she begged.

Finally, he listened to her and slid one hand down to the juncture of her thighs. He slipped his fingers underneath the thin lace fabric and combed through the soft curls. When he slid past her center of pleasure, she undulated her hips.

Luther groaned. "Fuck, Katie, go easy."

But even though he cautioned her to take it slow, Luther apparently didn't feel that the same rule applied to him, because a second later, he bathed his fingers in her wetness, caressing her folds, exploring her.

She gasped at the delicious sensations he sent through her body. She spread her legs wider, urging him to give her more. She felt him probe at the entrance to her channel, and sighed. Finally, he drove a thick finger into her.

Katie pressed her head into the pillow, arching off the bed. Then Luther's thumb was on her clit, spreading her juices over the sensitive organ.

"Yes!" she encouraged him.

A second finger joined the first, adding more friction.

"God, you're tight!" Luther groaned. "You're gonna make me come in ten seconds."

"I don't care," she cried out. "Just fuck me already."

He pulled his fingers from her and freed her of her panties so fast she could barely blink. She tried to slip out of the open bra, but he stopped her.

"Leave it on. It's sexy." He positioned himself at her center, his huge cock rubbing against her wet folds. Then he locked eyes with her, and in one long continuous stroke, he seated himself in her.

Her eyelids dropped, her breath rushed from her lungs, and her heart stopped beating. He filled her completely. "Oh God!" Katie wrapped her legs around his thighs, imprisoning him.

"Perfect," Luther grunted, the chords in his neck bulging. "You're fucking perfect!"

Luther began to thrust, deep and hard. Every time his cock drove into her, his pelvic bone slammed against her clit, making her shudder. Her heart beat erratically now, her breaths came in shallow pants, and her head swam with a myriad of sensations. The passion and wildness Luther unleashed on her was something she'd never experienced before. None of her previous lovers had ever taken her this hard and made her body hum so intensely with pleasure that she thought she was floating on a cloud.

She felt weightless, held by strong vampire arms, safe despite the powerful thrusts Luther delivered. In his eyes she saw the same lust and desire that she felt radiate back at her. Like molten lava, his eyes glowed. They looked like flames now, like the flames that raged inside her and threatened to incinerate her. And what she saw peeking from his lips now should have scared her, but instead the sight of his white fangs flashing fascinated her. They had descended fully, ready for a bite. She knew it, had seen her vampire friends and family often enough to interpret the signs. To know when somebody was about to lose control of his human side and unleash the power that was pure vampire.

And while she saw all the signs in Luther's face now, written as clearly as if printed on a piece of paper, she felt no fear. No regret at having taken this risk and put herself at the mercy of a vampire who'd committed unspeakable crimes. Because the payoff was worth it. For once in her life she could forget the bitter memories of her past and live only in the moment. The moment of ecstasy.

She turned her head to the side and swept away her hair, exposing her neck. "Luther."

26

His name rolled over Katie's lips like the call of a siren leading a sailor to his doom. Luther recognized the invitation. Temptation curled through his body, making him thrust faster and deeper. As if sex could wipe away his need for blood. He knew it wasn't so. If anything, his desire to drink from Katie had increased several fold the moment he'd plunged his aching cock into her.

He knew he would succumb to it, particularly now that she was offering him what he so desperately needed.

"Katie," he ground out.

When she stretched out her hand as if to touch his fangs, he snatched it, and pinned it to one side of her head. Without a word, he dipped his head and took possession of her lips, willing his fangs to retract. They did, but only halfway. He didn't have the strength to bend them to his will. His vampire side was ruling him now, and the vampire in him wanted blood.

Luther pumped harder into her, thrusting and withdrawing. Her wet and warm sheath was like paradise. Too good to stop. And too good to continue. He'd been teetering on the edge of his climax for several long minutes now, pushing back his urge to come whenever it tried to overwhelm him. But as Katie's muscles squeezed him harder with every thrust, and her juices enveloped him in her silken depth, he realized he was losing the fight with his self control. A few more seconds, and he would have to give in to his release.

He ripped his lips from her, breathing hard. "God, Katie! I need you to come with me."

With wide eyes she stared up at him.

"Tell me what you need."

"Bite me!" she demanded.

Luther threw back his head, almost howling like a dog. "No!" Damn it, not only was it wrong that he was sleeping with her, knowing she was drugged by his blood, but accepting her blood would be the lowest to which he could sink.

"Luther, please."

He looked back at her, slowly shaking his head.

But she didn't accept his answer. "You asked whether I was acting when I invited Bauer to dig his fangs into my breasts. I wasn't."

Luther froze in mid-stroke, shock coursing through him. "What?" He grabbed both her wrists and pinned them on either side of her head.

"In method acting we portray only the emotions we feel. When I invited him to bite me, I didn't offer it to him. I offered it to *you*."

All the air rushed from his lungs. "No, that can't be." He tried to shake the image from his mind's eye. "You don't know what you're doing, Katie."

Katie wiggled her hands free and slipped them to his ass, gripping him firmly, shoving him deeper into her. The action made his cock jerk inside her, sending him dangerously close to the edge.

His fangs automatically lengthened again, and this time he couldn't force them back into their sockets. From the sparkle in Katie's eyes he could tell that she'd noticed it, too.

Slowly, he began to thrust again, in and out, while his gaze drifted down to her bouncing boobs. They rocked with every thrust from side to side. Hard nipples sat on the top of each breast, pink and ripe for the taking.

"Right there," she murmured.

"Yes, right there," he agreed and increased his tempo, while taking her hands again and pinning them to either side of her head. He lifted his gaze back to her face. "You can't escape now."

Her breath hitched, and he could hear her heart thunder. The sound of her blood rushing through her veins made his glands salivate. He swallowed hard. "You won't be able to stop me."

Katie's chest heaved. "I know."

He searched her face for any sign of fear, but found none. Did she have any idea what she was doing? Or had the lust drugged her to a point where she couldn't be held responsible for her actions? Did she realize that freely offering blood to a vampire other than to save his life meant submission?

"You'll feel my fangs the moment you start to climax."

He drove his cock deeper, enjoying how her muscles clamped around him, holding him like a tight fist.

Her lids lowered halfway, and a moan left her lips. "Luther, yes!"

He shifted his position slightly and drove deeper once more. When he felt her muscles spasm around him, he let go of the last vestiges of his control and gave in to his release, joining her in her climax. As his semen shot from the tip of his cock, he lowered his face to Katie's breast and scraped his fangs against her soft skin.

"Luther!" she cried out and thrust her breast into his mouth.

He opened his mouth wider and set his fangs on either side of her nipple.

"Get the fuck away from her or you're dust!"

Luther reared up, letting Katie's breast slip from his mouth.

Shit!

27

Several things happened all at once. Luther spun around, pulling out of her, and jumping up from the bed. In the blink of an eye he snatched one side of the sheet and pulled it over her naked body, shielding her. Katie shot up to a sitting position, glaring at the three men who'd burst into the room: Blake, Grayson, and an utterly pissed-off looking Wesley.

She didn't get the time to glare back at her brother, who'd been the one issuing the threat directed at Luther. The sound of something smashing against the wall tore her gaze to Luther. He'd trashed the chair and broken off a wooden leg to use as a makeshift stake.

Improvised weapon in hand, he leapt toward the three Scanguards men. The three lifted their weapons—small-caliber handguns—and pointed them at Luther.

"No!" Katie screamed and jumped up from the bed, unconcerned about her nudity. "Don't hurt him!"

She charged toward them, but Luther blocked her way, holding her behind his broad body with one arm.

"Stay back, Katie!" he growled, his other hand holding the stake above his head.

"How dare you order my sister around?" Wesley spat, glowering at Luther.

"Wes, stay out of this!"

She peered past Luther's arm and could see how Wes ran his eyes over Luther's nude body, a look of disgust on his face. Then he met her gaze.

"How could you, Katie? What happened? Did he force you?"

"I didn't fucking force anybody!" Luther snarled.

Grayson flashed his fangs. "I should kill you right here and now."

"Oh look at the little pup! Feeling all strong in the company of his friends," Luther scoffed.

Grayson made a move toward him, but Blake pulled him back. "Stand down, Grayson! Now!" Blake exchanged a look with him. "I'll handle this."

Grayson took a deep breath. His jaw set into a grim line. Grudgingly he said, "You're the boss." It was clear that at this moment he wished he were in Blake's shoes.

Blake looked back at Luther before his gaze landed on her. He slowly shook his head. "You disappoint me, Katie." There was a resigned tone in his voice. "I thought I could trust you, and what do you do? You're sleeping with the enemy. Literally!"

"Blake, please…" she started. "I can explain."

He motioned to Luther, who had lowered his weapon. "It's pretty self-explanatory from where I stand." Disappointment spread in his eyes. "But to let him bite you?" He shook his head.

"He didn't," she said.

"He was about to," Wesley interrupted, "if we hadn't gotten here in time."

Katie looked at Wes. "Damn it, Wes, I'm an adult. Don't treat me like a little child. I can make my own decisions."

"You're still my sister."

"Still doesn't give you the right to interfere in my life."

Hands at her hips, she tried to walk past Luther, but he pushed her back behind him. "You're naked, Katie."

Then Luther exchanged a look with Blake. "If you don't mind, a little privacy so Katie can get dressed without you guys ogling her."

Blake gave a stiff nod. "Two minutes. And don't try to escape out the back. We have another man watching the outside. You wouldn't get far."

Blake shooed the other two out before turning away and closing the door.

Alone with Luther, Katie let out a breath of air. "Shit!"

Luther turned to her. "You could say that." He ran his eyes over her. "Let's get dressed. Those guys saw more of you than they ever should have."

He took the towel from earlier and brought it to the juncture of her thighs, gently wiping away his semen. "This wasn't exactly how I imagined this ending."

"It's not over," she said.

Luther took the towel and cleaned himself off, before turning to collect his clothes from the floor. Katie closed the clasp of her bra and searched for her panties.

"Is there something between you and Blake?"

The sudden question surprised her and made her spin around to look at him. "Why would you think there's something between me and Blake?"

Luther shrugged. "He seemed hurt, as if you'd betrayed him."

Katie rolled her eyes and reached for her panties, pulling them on. "Men! We're friends. Have been for a long time."

"Maybe he wants more," Luther hedged.

Katie pulled on her jeans while Luther stepped into his pants and zipped up.

"Blake is under stress because Isabelle was his responsibility. He's just lashing out."

"You do know that we can hear you, right?" Blake's voice came from the other side of the door.

Katie cursed. "Damn it, Blake, what part of privacy did you not get into your thick skull?"

A grunt was the answer, then footsteps shuffled away.

When she turned, she caught Luther grinning at her.

"What?" She walked to where her bloodstained shirt lay on the floor and picked it up.

"Looks like you know how to handle these guys."

She gave a one-shouldered shrug and fed her arms into the sleeves. "They're just big boys with toys. Underneath it they're—"

"I can still hear you, Katie," Blake warned from the hallway.

"Screw you, Blake!" she cried out. Maybe she was overreacting a bit, but damn it, Blake and the others had interrupted her at the height of sexual ecstasy and prevented her from feeling Luther's bite. She felt cheated out of an experience that she'd been told was out of this world. Who wouldn't be a tad pissy about that?

She charged toward the door, but Luther pulled her back. He leaned down to her and whispered into her ear, "Don't let him rile you up. Though you do look utterly sexy when you're mad!"

She didn't get a chance to reply, because Luther's warm lips captured her mouth for a kiss that robbed her of her breath.

28

"Let's deal with this," Luther said and opened the door to the hallway, leaving the bedroom ahead of Katie.

The three men from Scanguards were pacing in the living room when he entered followed by Katie. He walked up to Blake, but before he could start explaining, Wesley took a few steps toward Katie.

"What the fuck happened to you?" He pointed to the bloodstained shirt. Then he charged at Luther, fists raised. "You hurt her, you fucking asshole?"

Luther blocked Wesley's punch with ease, pushing him back without fighting back. He didn't think it wise beating up Katie's brother. "I didn't hurt her," he ground out.

He felt Katie's hand on his arm as she moved to his side. "I got injured. It wasn't Luther's fault."

Well, that was a blatant lie on Katie's part, because it had been his fault. He hadn't kept her safe like he'd promised.

"How?" Wes hissed, his eyes narrowed in suspicion, approaching slowly.

"I got stabbed by a prison guard."

"A prison guard?" Blake interrupted.

Before either Luther or Katie could answer, Wesley snatched the edge of Katie's shirt and lifted it by a few inches. "You're healed." He turned his head to look at Luther. "You gave her your blood."

Not a question, but a statement. Though it sounded like Wesley wasn't pleased about it.

"I had no choice. Her lung was punctured. She would have died."

Next to him, Katie sucked in a breath and grabbed his elbow. "What?" She shook her head in disbelief. "Why didn't you tell me how bad it was?"

"I didn't wanna worry you. Besides, you're fine now."

"Fuck!" Wesley cursed. "Jesus Christ, Katie, what did you get yourself into?"

"How much did you give her?" The question came from Blake.

Luther exchanged a look with the vampire. "Enough."

"Well, that explains that. So you decided to get quid pro quo for saving her life, didn't you?"

He knew Blake was referring to the fact that Katie would have been aroused by his blood, whether she was attracted to him or not. Considering that her brother already seemed to be annoyed with her, Luther decided to shoulder the responsibility for what had happened in the last hour. After all, it was his fault. He'd given into her demands to have sex when he knew full well that she wasn't in the right frame of mind to make a decision.

"Yes, I did. I took advantage of Katie." Though he didn't regret it. Making love to her had been the best thing he'd done in over twenty years. And if he had to pay for it now, so be it.

"You didn't!" Katie shot back at him, bracing her hands on her hips. "I told you already, it had nothing to do with your blood. Idiot!"

"Let me handle this," Luther said through gritted teeth. "It's better this way."

"But you're distorting the facts!" Katie protested.

"Stop!" Wesley raised his hand in a plea for silence, his face red with rage. "I don't think I wanna know the facts about what happened in there." He motioned to the bedroom in the back. "I have a feeling I know more than I ever wanted to know. But what I do wanna know is what the fuck you're doing with him and why you got stabbed by a prison guard. Maybe we should start with that."

Blake folded his arms over his chest, looking at them expectantly. "I'd like to know that, too. And start from the beginning."

"And you'd better not leave anything out," Grayson added, aggression rolling off him.

Luther caught his look. There was no love lost between them. No surprise. The young hybrid clearly knew all about Luther's past, how he'd tried to kill his mother. Hell, Grayson wouldn't even be here today if Luther had succeeded. Somehow he couldn't blame the guy, though that didn't mean he had to like him.

"You got my message about the letters?" Katie asked, looking at Blake.

He nodded. "I called you back right away, but got no answer. When we couldn't find you, Haven searched your house, but found no sign of the letters."

Luther tossed her a sideways glance. "So there are no copies in existence."

Katie gave him a sheepish smile. "I bluffed." Then she looked back at Blake. "I have the letters. They're in my purse in my car."

"We didn't see your car outside," Wes commented.

"We had to abandon it when we fled the prison," Luther explained. "I can give you the exact location."

Blake nodded, then motioned to Katie. "By prison I'm assuming you mean the vampire penitentiary near Grass Valley." He shifted his gaze to Luther. "From which our friend here was just recently released."

"Yes, the vampire prison. When I couldn't get a hold of you and ran into Luther…"

Luther clasped her forearm. "Maybe I should explain from here." He looked at the three Scanguards men. "When I saw the letters, I realized that somebody connected to the prison had to have sent them. So I decided to help Katie locate the person who wrote them."

That Katie had practically blackmailed him by threatening to set all of Scanguards on his ass and use witchcraft on him—witchcraft she didn't even possess!—was immaterial. He was certainly not going to admit to the men standing in front of him that he'd been tricked by a woman.

"You could have let us do that. No reason to get involved. Samson told you to stay out of our way," Blake said.

Luther scoffed. "Yeah, and the moment you learned about the letters coming from the prison, you would have put two and two together and chased me instead of the real culprit. Samson isn't acting rational right now. He would have just—"

Grayson jumped at him, baring his fangs. "How dare you talk about my father like that?"

Luther didn't budge an inch. "You're just like him, hothead!"

"You fucking—"

"Shut up, Grayson!" Blake ordered and pulled him back. "He's right. Samson would have pulled resources off other leads and chased down Luther. And considering that Katie is still alive and Isabelle isn't here, I'm inclined to give him the benefit of the doubt that he's got nothing to do with Isabelle's kidnapping." He lifted his chin. "Go on."

"I'd seen a cell of one of the V-CONs plastered with posters of Katie. I figured he was obsessed with her. Had to be him. I had to find out his name, and I could only do that from inside the prison. So we broke in."

"How?" Blake asked.

"You don't need to know the details about that. What's important is that we got the information we were looking for and got out."

"Apparently you ran into a few problems." Blake motioned to the bloodstain on Katie's shirt.

"They kind of don't like it when you break in and then try to break out again," Luther said nonchalantly. "Anyway..." He turned to Katie. "The printout."

Katie dug into her jeans pocket and pulled out the folded sheet. Blake reached for it and unfolded it. His eyes flew over the information printed on it.

"Cliff Forrester. You sure?" he asked.

Luther nodded. "Has to be him. He was released a week ago. He had ample time to plan this. And the letters he sent to Katie over the last year seem to suggest he was preparing to come for her."

Blake looked up. "Good work." He handed the piece of paper to Wesley. "Call HQ and give them this information."

"And what do we do about him?" Wesley asked, glancing at Luther.

Blake took a step toward Luther. "Thank you for your help. In light of all this, let's forget what happened here. But I think it would be best for all involved, if you left the area like Samson suggested."

"Well, that's just not gonna happen," Katie snapped.

Luther spun his head to her, as did the others.

"Excuse me?" Blake said.

"You heard me. Luther risked his life to get us this information, and now you're gonna just dismiss him?"

"By the looks of it, he risked *your* life, too!" Blake grunted. "So excuse me, if I'm not too keen on having him around. Nor will Samson or Amaury tolerate him getting involved in this."

"Well, he's *already* involved. Without him, you wouldn't have anything! Maybe his methods are a little unorthodox, but at least they produce results. We now know who's got Isabelle. Now we just have to find him." Katie crossed her arms over her chest. "So you have a choice here: either you let Luther help us find Isabelle, or you turn around now and I'll investigate with Luther on my own."

"Out of the fucking question!" Wesley interrupted, grabbing her bicep. "*You* are coming home with us!" He glared at Luther. "You're not staying with him! It's gonna get you killed!"

Katie tore her arm from her brother's grip. "He saved my life! So make your choice."

Luther tapped Katie on the shoulder. "Katie, just out of curiosity: were you gonna ask me whether I wanted to stay involved in this?"

"No."

"Thought so."

And strangely enough the fact that she didn't give him a choice in this turned him on. Katie was a force to be reckoned with. A woman who knew what she wanted.

Luther grinned and exchanged a look with Blake. "No use fighting her. I tried. And look what it got me into." What exactly he'd landed in, he wasn't quite sure yet. But it was a welcome change from the monotonous life he'd spent in prison.

"Yeah, that's our Katie," Wes confirmed. "Once she's got something in her head, you can't stop her."

And oddly enough, Luther didn't want to stop her. Had they been alone, he would have pulled her into his arms and continued where they'd been interrupted, because a strong woman like Katie was a bigger turn-on than anything else he'd ever encountered.

29

"My father will never allow it!" Grayson protested, glaring at Luther. "He hates you!"

Blake put a hand on the young hybrid's arm, then looked at Luther. "I'm afraid Grayson is right. There are several people at Scanguards who'd rather drive a stake through your heart than let you get anywhere near this investigation," Blake stated calmly. "Unfortunately we're running out of time. We know the kidnapper already knows that he's got the wrong woman."

Katie's breath hitched. They had news from Isabelle? Why hadn't anybody told her? "How? What happened?"

Blake took his eyes off Luther. "We were able to identify the vampire who kidnapped her."

"Cliff Forrester?" Katie asked. "So you already knew." She pointed to the piece of paper, then glanced at Luther. "I got you into all this trouble for nothing?"

Blake shook his head. "It wasn't Forrester who took Isabelle. It was a guy named Antonio Mendoza. He was a hired gun."

"You think Cliff Forrester hired him?"

"It looks like it. Mendoza took Isabelle and was waiting for the man who hired him to take her off his hands, but when the guy showed up, he realized immediately that Mendoza got the wrong woman. He killed Mendoza and took Isabelle with him."

"How do you know that?" Katie asked. Her heart beat as loud as a drum, and she knew the vampires in the room could hear it.

Blake motioned to Grayson. "We sent four of the hybrids to Mendoza's house when we identified him from the surveillance video. The house was empty, but apparently Mendoza didn't trust the man who'd hired him. He turned on a voice recorder before he let Forrester into the house. It recorded everything. The moment he saw Isabelle, he knew she wasn't you. He killed Mendoza for his stupidity. But we know he'll keep Isabelle alive."

Katie swallowed hard. She knew exactly what that meant, even if Blake didn't say it. "He's going to want to do an exchange."

Silence descended on the room. Nobody said anything. Nobody moved.

Luther's voice cut through the quiet. "It won't come to that. There's another way."

Katie lifted her lids to meet his gaze. "It's my fault that he's got Isabelle. I put her in danger. Had I not changed roles with her, this would have never happened. If I—"

"It doesn't matter whose fault it was," Luther interrupted. "I won't allow an exchange. Once he's got you, what's to stop him from killing Isabelle anyway?" He shook his head and looked past her to the other men in the room. "We'll find him. I know how."

"And what do we tell Samson?" Wesley asked calmly.

"Nothing," Blake said. He nodded to Grayson. "Are you with us?"

"Do I have a choice?"

"No."

"Guess you have my answer then." He took a step toward Luther, lifting his chin. "One false move, and you're dust."

Katie caught how Luther acknowledged the threat with a simple nod.

"How will we find Forrester?" Blake asked.

Suddenly Blake, Luther, and Grayson snapped their heads toward the door. A moment later, Katie heard it, too. A sound outside. Their sensitive vampire hearing had picked it up a few seconds earlier. Wesley drew his weapon, just as Blake and Grayson did, while Luther grabbed her and pushed her behind his back, shielding her from whatever was outside the door.

When the door opened, Katie peeked past Luther. Relieved, she went around him, though he tried to hold her back.

"I'm fine." She pointed to the new arrival. "That's John, he's with them."

The tall vampire with the southern accent stepped into the room, his eyes quickly scanning the room. Apparently satisfied with what he saw, he addressed Blake, "Somebody's approaching."

"Vampire?"

"Yeah."

"That must be Striker," Luther said. "He owns this cabin. I sent him out to get info on Forrester."

John furrowed his forehead. "Are you talking about Striker Reed?"

"You know him?"

"I know *of* him." John tossed his colleagues a sideways glance. "I'd suggest you lower your weapons, guys, because that dude is trigger happy, and if he finds you in his house uninvited and armed, he'll shoot first and ask questions later."

"Your friend has a point," a voice came from the hallway behind them.

Katie spun around and stared right into their host's glaring red eyes, a gun leveled at them.

Luther's arms locked around her, pulling her into the protection of his body. "Striker, don't!" Luther yelled. "They're friends."

"Then tell them to put down their weapons."

"Guys, please," Luther said over his shoulder, his arms still around her, pressing her against his warm body.

The gesture made her feel protected, and the knowledge that Luther's first instinct had been to protect her, sent a pleasant tingle through her body.

Slowly she noticed Striker relax. Then he pulled one side of his mouth up. "When I said make yourself at home, Luther, I didn't mean you could invite your friends for a party."

Katie felt Luther's muscles relax, but he didn't let go of her. She was glad that he kept her in his embrace, giving her a chance to enjoy a few more moments of closeness.

"It was kind of last minute," Luther said with a chuckle, "and a little unexpected. Not to say inconvenient."

At his last words, Katie lifted her face and caught Luther's gaze. Did he regret the interruption of their lovemaking as much as she did? The look in his eyes seemed to suggest it.

Striker approached, holstering his weapon at his belt. "Don't you wanna introduce me?"

Luther released her from his embrace, albeit seemingly reluctantly. He motioned to the other men in the room. "These men work for Scanguards: meet Blake, Grayson, Wesley, and John."

All the men nodded.

"This is Striker Reed. He was the council's best tracker."

"Still am," Striker threw in and grinned. "I just don't work for them anymore."

"A tracker?" Katie asked.

"I find people," Striker said cryptically.

"People who don't want to be found," Luther explained, turning to her. "Mostly escaped criminals. It's one of the most dangerous jobs out there. There are few vampires who make the cut to be a tracker, and even fewer who want the job. Though I hear the council doesn't take no for an answer when it sets its sights on a capable candidate."

Striker pulled one side of his mouth up and tilted his head to the side. "Something like that." Then he exchanged a look with Luther. "I have a location for you."

30

Sitting in the back of Scanguards' blackout SUV, Luther casually glanced over his shoulder. John and Grayson were following them in Katie's Audi, which they had retrieved from the place in the woods where they'd left it behind. They'd ditched the stolen truck. Wesley was driving the SUV and Blake sat in the front passenger seat, his cell phone glued to his ear as if it were permanently attached. He'd been talking to headquarters since they'd left Striker's cabin, conveying all the information to his team and receiving an update on what Scanguards had been able to find out on their own.

Next to Luther, Katie was sitting silently, her head leaning against his shoulder.

"You tired?" he murmured, keeping his voice low. With a little luck, Blake was too distracted by his phone call to listen in on their conversation, and Wesley didn't have a vampire's sensitive hearing.

"Just a little," she admitted and snuggled closer to him.

He lifted his arm and put it around her, pulling her against his chest, inhaling the scent of her hair. "Sleep a few minutes. I'll wake you when we get there."

"I'm too agitated to sleep."

She lifted her head from his chest. Even in the darkness her green eyes sparkled. Instinctively, he cupped her face with one hand and tilted her chin up, gazing into her emeralds. The temptation to kiss her was overwhelming, but he knew he couldn't allow himself such intimacy in the presence of Katie's brother and the vampire who seemed to carry a torch for her.

"I know," he said instead. "We'll find her, Katie, I promise you. You can count on Striker's intel. If he says that Forrester was seen in the area just recently, then it's the truth."

"I just hope we're not too late."

He brushed his hand over her hair, caressing the soft strands. "He's not stupid enough to kill her. She's his bargaining chip to get to you. She's safe as long as he doesn't have you."

And by God, he'd move heaven and earth to make sure Forrester didn't get his hands on Katie.

"Luther?"

"Yes?"

"About earlier," she started, hesitating.

He glanced to the front of the SUV, but Blake was still on the phone and Wesley seemed to be concentrating on driving.

He lowered his face to Katie's, bringing his mouth close to her ear. "We'll talk about it later."

She gave a slow shake of her head. "I just want you to know that I regret nothing." She took a breath of air. "And that I wish we hadn't gotten interrupted. I wanted you to—"

He stopped her by putting a finger over her lips. "Don't. Maybe it was better that they stopped me."

Because if he'd bitten her, he would have gotten even deeper into this, whatever this was. And he knew he couldn't get involved. He couldn't make a commitment. Not even to a woman like Katie. No matter how much he was drawn to her. He would only hurt her in the end, just like he'd hurt Vivian, and just like Vivian had hurt him.

Katie's hand curled around his wrist. "You don't mean that."

He sighed. "Katie, you don't know me. I'm not the man you think I am." He motioned toward Blake. "If you're looking for something, you'd be better off with a guy who's decent and... well, nice. I'm none of those things."

"Decent? What does that really mean? We look at people and think they are good and decent, but once we dig under the surface, we see what they're really like."

"Katie, I was in prison for twenty years, for a crime I committed, a crime against innocents. I'm not a choirboy."

"You saved my life today, without even blinking an eye."

He scoffed. "Yeah, after endangering it. What did you expect me to do? Let you die? I was responsible for you in there. I promised to keep you safe, and I didn't keep my promise. That alone should tell you to stay away from me."

"That's honor, Luther. You acted out of honor, and that makes you good inside. And even now you're with us, because you know it's the right thing to do. You're helping us find Isabelle even though you don't have to."

"I needed a ride into the city," he deflected.

Katie chuckled. "I'm sure Striker would have given you a lift to the next town where you could have rented or bought a car."

Luther closed his eyes and shook his head. "Can't I win a single argument with you?"

"You can try," she hedged, "but I'm very competitive."

"You could have warned me about that earlier."

"And spoil the surprise?" She lifted her face and pressed a quick kiss on his lips.

"Don't do that," he murmured, motioning toward the front of the SUV. But the brief contact had given him an appetite for more. "Or I'm gonna have to use mind control on you to make you behave."

"Would you really do that?"

"Don't test me," he warned and slid his hand onto her thigh, squeezing it.

Her breath hitched, and he slid his hand higher. Even through her jeans he felt the heat that radiated from her sex, scorching his palm.

"Trust me, you don't want me to embarrass you in front of your brother."

"Okay," she said breathlessly.

"Good girl."

He withdrew his hand from her sex and took a deep breath. This woman was driving him crazy. He shouldn't be drawn to her like this, shouldn't allow himself to be caught up in her net, but he couldn't help himself. Maybe if he hadn't abstained from women during his time in prison, sex with Katie wouldn't have had such a profound impact on him. But he couldn't forget the few minutes of sheer and utter ecstasy he'd felt in her arms. And he wanted more, though he knew nothing good would come of it. He'd only hurt her, and in turn himself.

"I just got word from Haven," Blake suddenly said, turning to look over his shoulder.

"Haven?" Katie asked, her voice shaking a bit.

"Yeah, he and Eddie are already there. They're waiting for us a quarter mile from Forrester's hideout. We should be there in a few minutes."

"What did you tell Haven?" Katie asked.

"Just what he needed to know. That we have a lead on the kidnapper. And that Luther got us that intel. That's all." Blake's gaze shifted to Luther, then back to Katie. "I'm sure you'll want to fill him in on the rest yourself."

"Thanks, Blake, I appreciate it."

"I'm assuming Haven and Eddie know not to tell Samson I'm involved?" Luther asked.

"I've briefed them. The official story we gave Samson was that a contact within the prison system pointed us to Cliff Forrester after we examined the letters Katie received. We kept it as vague as possible."

Luther nodded, satisfied. Not because he was afraid that Samson would make good on his threat to kill him, but because he didn't want Samson to react irrationally and jeopardize his daughter's rescue. Once this was all over, Luther would disappear back into the shadows as if he'd never been here. Samson would never need to find out that Luther had assisted. He wasn't here to get credit for his help.

Minutes later, Wesley stopped the SUV on a rural road without street lights and turned off the engine. Behind them, John brought Katie's Audi to a stop.

"Let's go," Blake said and exited the car.

Luther reached for the door handle and opened the passenger door, stepping out into the darkness. In front of them, a minivan was parked. Next to it stood Eddie and another vampire. It had to be Haven, Katie's brother. Luther ran his eyes over him. He was slightly taller than his witch brother. Haven glanced past Luther, searching for the person who exited the car behind him.

Luther turned and reached for Katie's hand to help her out.

"Katie!" Haven called out and walked to her. He pulled her into his arms and pressed a kiss on the top of her head. "You scared the shit out of me when you disappeared. Don't you ever do that again."

"I'm sorry."

"What the fuck are you doing with him?" Haven slanted Luther an annoyed look.

Katie peeled herself out of his arms. "Everything's fine."

"If I find out that he—"

"How about we postpone the pleasantries until later?" Blake suggested, drawing everybody's attention to him. John and Grayson had joined them.

Luther nodded. "Fine by me." He noticed Eddie acknowledge him with a quick glance.

"We all know what to do?" Blake asked, looking at the assembled group. "Grayson, you'll stay with Katie. The rest of you, let's go. Haven and John will approach the house from the back. Luther, you'll be with me, Eddie, and Wesley. Questions?"

"Let me come with you," Grayson demanded. "John can watch Katie."

"No!" Blake protested, then looked at his colleagues.

Luther lifted his hands. "If you could spare a weapon, I'd be of more use…"

"You brought extra?" Blake asked Haven.

Haven already turned to the van and pulled a semi-automatic handgun from the interior. Luther followed him and took the weapon.

"Thanks."

"Don't thank me yet." Haven's narrowed eyes made his position clear. He suspected that something was going on between him and Katie, and he didn't like it.

Dropping his voice to a murmur, Luther said to him, "Your sister is an adult. She makes her own decisions."

"And not all of them smart ones," Haven hissed back.

Blake's barked command interrupted them. "Let's go. We're not on a picnic here."

Under cover of darkness, they reached the house moments later. It was an old ranch style home in need of a good paint job and yard work. Nobody had lifted a finger here in years. According to Striker's information, it belonged to Cliff Forrester, and neighbors had seen him a few nights ago, after he'd been released from prison.

There was no light coming from the interior, no sounds either. Blake gave a sign to spread out. Via his mic and his earphone he communicated with John and Haven who approached from the other direction.

"Anything?" Blake whispered into his mic.

Luther didn't hear the response, but Blake pointed to the front door a moment later, indicating that he was going in first. Luther watched from a few feet away as Blake approached the entrance without making a sound, his weapon drawn. He saw Blake's lips move, but no sound emerged.

Blake tested the door. There was a sound of a floorboard creaking, then Blake pushed the door open and charged in. Eddie was on his heels. From behind the house, similar sounds could be heard, and Luther took it as a sign to charge in after them.

It was evident immediately that the place was empty. Disappointment curled through Luther. There was no sign of Forrester or Isabelle. They'd come too late.

"He's gone," Haven confirmed.

"Any outbuildings in the back?" Blake asked.

John shook his head. "Shed's empty, too. There's a motorcycle in it."

Light suddenly flooded the interior and Luther pivoted, aiming his gun at the person who'd entered behind him. He quickly lowered it again, not wanting to shoot Wesley. The witch might not take it too kindly.

"Search the place for any evidence that Isabelle was here," Blake ordered.

The search didn't take long. The place was only sparsely furnished.

"He was definitely here. There's a newspaper from a couple of days ago," John confirmed and motioned to the bedroom he'd just exited.

"And the bed's been used."

Haven nodded in agreement. "Looks like he left in a hurry." He motioned to the hallway, where a set of keys hung on a hook on the wall. "His keys are still here."

Blake turned, giving Luther an assessing look. "Could Striker have tipped him off?"

"Not a chance," Luther said firmly. "I trust him. He wouldn't have alerted Forrester."

"Fine. John, bag everything that's not tied down. Grayson can help you. Bring it back to HQ and have the team sift through it. The rest of us, we're leaving now and heading back to San Francisco."

"No problem," John agreed. "I'll take Katie's Audi back and meet you at HQ."

31

"What are we gonna do now?" Katie asked.

They'd just crossed the Bay Bridge with the blackout SUV and were back in San Francisco. Another half hour and the sun would be up. Eddie and Blake had taken the other van back, while her two brothers were chauffeuring her and Luther back into the city.

"*You* are going to do nothing," Haven said pointedly from the driver's seat, briefly looking over his shoulder. "You've done quite enough for one night."

Judging by the way he said it, he didn't mean it to be a compliment.

"But—"

Haven growled. "Blake is on it. Thomas has already gotten a picture of our suspect and is distributing it to everybody. They'll be analyzing the letters to see if there are any clues in them as to where he'll be. And they're checking into all connections this Cliff Forrester has in California. If he's got another hiding place, a garage, a car, or a storage unit, we'll find it. He won't get far."

"But there must be something else I can do," Katie insisted. "Why don't we set a trap for him? I can be the bait."

Next to her she felt Luther tense. "Hell, no!" he growled.

"Hate to agree with him," Haven ground out, "but that's just not gonna happen. You'll be staying at your house, under constant guard. I've already alerted HQ and they're sending someone over. Until then, I'll be watching you."

Katie opened her mouth to protest, but Luther was faster.

"That won't be necessary. I'll be watching Katie. There's no need to send over a man from Scanguards."

Haven scoffed, glaring over his shoulder. "No fucking way. You're not staying with Katie." He motioned to Wesley and himself. "One of us is gonna keep an eye on you at all times."

Wes nodded in agreement and turned halfway to look at Luther. "Did you really think that after what happened to Katie while she was with you, we'd let you stay with her?"

Luther snarled, but Katie took his hand and stopped him from responding.

Instead, she glared at her brother. "What are you pissed off about? The fact that I got stabbed in prison or that I slept with Luther?"

Haven slammed on the brakes, bringing the car to a full stop on the side of the street. Katie was jerked forward. Had she not been wearing a seatbelt, she would have hit the back of the driver's seat.

"What?" Haven yelled and spun around. His eyes glared red and his fangs descended. "You slept with this scumbag?"

Katie's gaze shifted to Wes, stunned. "You didn't tell him?" She'd been sure that Wesley had filled Haven in before they'd left Forrester's house. Why else would Haven be so adamant about keeping her away from Luther?

Wes lifted his hands and made a grimace. "I can keep a secret, you know." He jerked his thumb toward Haven. "I knew how he'd react."

Haven glared at his brother. "And rightly so! Do you really want your sister to be influenced by somebody like him?" He pointed at Luther. "He's a convict. A murderer."

Katie glanced at Luther, but he took the accusation in stoic silence, his jaw set in a grim line, his eyes watching Haven. She felt the need to defend Luther.

"He isn't the only killer in this car," she said and locked eyes with Haven. "So don't be all righteous now. You were a vampire hunter for over a decade and killed your fair share."

"I killed for you, Katie!" he hissed. "To find you and get you back! And now you throw that in my face?" He jerked the car door open and jumped out.

"Ah, shit!" Katie cursed and undid her seatbelt.

Luther put his hand on hers, but she shook her head and opened the passenger door. She jumped out and ran after Haven, who was marching along the deserted sidewalk.

"Haven!"

He looked over his shoulder, a wounded look on his face, but he stopped. When she reached him, she took a deep breath.

"You did so much for me," she started. "More than any brother should ever have to do for his sister. You sacrificed for me and for Wes. And I know you think I'm ungrateful. I'm not." Tears stung her eyes, but she pushed on. "When we found each other twenty years ago, you gave me the family I always wanted. And what did I give you? Only trouble."

"Oh, sweetheart," he murmured, shaking his head. "The trouble is all worth it as long as I know you're happy."

A tear ran down her cheek. "But I'm not happy, Haven. I've never been able to forgive her for what she did to us. For what she did to you."

Haven reached his hand out and wiped away her tear with his thumb. "You have to move on. Our mother was consumed with the need for power. She paid for it."

"Have you forgiven her?"

"In my own way."

Katie hadn't. "Then you're a better person than I. How can a mother do that to her children? How could she do that to us? To rob us of our powers and claim them for herself, knowing it would endanger us all? I can't forgive her."

As a result of her mother's actions, they had all suffered. Her father had disappeared one night never to return, and a vampire had killed her mother and abducted Katie when she was just a year old. At age twenty-three she'd been reunited with her two brothers.

"I still blame her for taking my powers away. Because if I'd had powers, I would have been able to prevent him from—"

Haven put a finger over her lips. "Don't, Katie. Five years have passed. What happened to you was terrible. But you have to let it go. He's dead. He'll never hurt you again."

"But the fear is still with me."

"I'm so sorry, sweetheart."

She slowly shook her head. "When I'm with Luther, that fear... it disappears. When he's near me, I'm not afraid anymore. I can breathe again, live again." And forget the nightmare that had rocked her world five years earlier and made her turn her back on Hollywood and her former life.

"Oh Katie." Haven sighed. "Why him?"

"I don't know. But with him I feel safe. Please don't take that away from me." Tears now streamed down her face, blurring her vision. "I need him."

Haven's arms came around her, pulling her to his chest. A sob tore from her throat, while Haven caressed her back, comforting her.

"And what if he doesn't want you?"

"I don't know, Hav."

"Okay," he agreed. "He can stay with you. When he leaves, I'll be there to catch you."

"Like you always are," she murmured, but hoped that this time she wouldn't have to rely on her brother's help. "I love you, Haven."

"I love you, too, sweetheart."

32

Luther followed Haven to the door that led down to the garage in Katie's Victorian mansion. Katie was already walking upstairs to the second floor.

"I'm taking a shower," she announced and disappeared.

The moment she was out of earshot, Haven cleared his throat. "If you hurt her, I will kill you."

"I'd do the same if I were in your shoes," Luther admitted.

"Good. Then we understand each other." Haven reached for the doorknob.

"One other thing."

Katie's brother looked over his shoulder.

"I haven't fed. Any chance you could send over some packaged blood, given that I can't leave Katie alone?"

Haven motioned to the end of the corridor. "Katie keeps blood in a fridge in the pantry. You know, for visitors like me and my mate. Help yourself."

"Appreciate it."

With a grunt, Haven disappeared. Moments later, Luther heard the garage door being operated and a car drive out. When the garage closed again and everything went quiet, Luther relaxed. From above he heard the sound of a shower running.

Instinctively he felt the need to run up there, but he pulled himself back. He was here to protect Katie, not devour her like a hungry beast. And he was hungry, starving in fact. Drawing on every last ounce of willpower, he marched toward the kitchen and entered it. In the pantry he found a small refrigerator. Its only ingredients were bottles of blood, neatly stacked in rows, sorted by blood type.

He reached for one, not caring what type it was and popped the twist top open. He gulped the liquid down greedily until the bottle was empty.

But he wasn't satisfied yet. He tossed the empty bottle into the recycle bin next to the door and pulled a second bottle out. Only when he'd emptied that bottle too, did he feel somewhat better. In prison, he would have had to survive on this amount of blood for several days, which had taught him to control his hunger. That's why he was so surprised at the amount he needed now to satisfy his hunger.

However, deep down he wasn't sated. He knew why. Because the reason why stood underneath the shower on the second floor. His feet carried him up the creaking wooden staircase. On the landing, he inhaled and caught her scent. The door to the room at the end of the long corridor was ajar. The sound of the shower was coming from there. Katie's master suite.

He hesitated. It was best to show restraint. Katie had been through enough during the preceding night. She needed to rest. And he needed to cool down. Maybe a cold shower would help bring his priorities back into focus.

Luther walked along the corridor, the rug underneath his feet swallowing his footsteps. He opened several doors, until he found a bathroom. He slipped inside and closed the door behind him. It wasn't long before he'd shed his clothes and was standing underneath the spray of the shower, willing it to wash away the need that was twisting his body into knots.

What had he gotten himself into? He'd taken on the responsibility of protecting Katie from a crazy vampire. And if he failed, not only would he forfeit his own life, worse, he would never be able to forgive himself.

He tilted his face to the ceiling, letting the water rain down on him. "Why?" Why was fate so cruel as to put this woman in his path? Katie, who made his heart beat with excitement, who was offering him a second chance, a chance he didn't deserve. And because he didn't deserve this, he knew how it would end: fate would take it all away again.

He turned off the water and stepped out of the shower stall. With a towel he found in the linen closet, he dried himself off, then wrapped it around his lower half and turned to where he'd set down his clothes.

He froze in mid-turn.

Katie stood in the open door, wearing only a thin red robe, her hair towel-dry.

"I was looking for you," she murmured. Her eyes trailed down his body.

He couldn't help but notice how her lips parted and how she pulled in a breath of air. Her chest lifted, drawing his gaze to her breasts. Hard nipples pressed through the thin fabric.

Involuntarily, Luther groaned.

When her hands went to the belt of her robe to loosen it, he took a step toward her and grabbed her hands, stopping her.

"Don't."

She lifted her lids and locked eyes with him. "Luther, please, I need you."

He shook his head. "I have nothing to give you. I can't promise you anything, Katie."

"Then don't make any promises. I'm not asking for anything. All I want is today. It doesn't have to mean anything beyond the here and now."

He sighed, knowing he'd already lost that argument. "Oh, Katie." He released her hands. "And tomorrow? What's gonna happen then? You know I can't stay." He made an all encompassing gesture. "This is not my life. It won't do either of us any good to pretend we can change that."

"What are you afraid of, Luther?"

She raised her hand and reached for his face. He let it happen, allowed her to trace the contour of his lips.

"Aren't you tired of running?" she asked softly.

"I'm not running."

Katie smiled as if she knew better. "It takes one to know one, Luther. We're both running, and we both need a break. Just for a few moments. Just to catch our breath."

"Damn it, you're making this really hard," he cursed and ran a hand through his wet hair. "I took some blood from your pantry, but I'm still hungry." When he gazed into her green orbs, he knew he didn't have to explain what he meant by that. "We're alone. This time, we won't be interrupted. Nobody is going to stop me once I start. Nobody is going to rescue you from me."

"Oh God, I hope not." She opened her robe and let it slide over her shoulders. It fell to the floor with a soft whoosh.

Luther sucked in a breath, knowing there was no way back now. He pulled on the towel around his waist and let it fall. His cock had already pumped full with blood and rose instantly.

"The first time will be quick and hard," he warned her and pressed her against the wall next to the door. "But one thing I can promise you: you'll come with me."

He already reached for her thighs, spreading them as he lifted her legs off the floor. Holding her suspended against the wall, he moved into her center and brought his cock to her sex.

"Yes." She moaned her agreement.

On his next intake of breath, he sliced into her, seating himself in her wet channel. "Yes!!" he cried out, closing his eyes for a brief second.

Fuck, it felt good. His chest heaved, pumping more air into his lungs, while farther below his hips started to move of their own volition.

He looked at her half-closed eyes. "Yeah, you just stay like that and take my cock deep inside you. You like that, yeah?"

"Yeah, oh yeah." Her words were breathless.

Her hands gripped his shoulders now, her fingernails digging into his skin.

"Yeah, you just hold on tight, baby, 'cause I'm gonna ride you hard."

He thrust into her to the hilt, before pulling almost entirely out again, while his heart was beating at triple its normal rate. He moved his head to hers, opening his mouth wide to show her his fangs. They were fully extended and ready for a bite.

She removed one hand from his shoulder and brought it to his face. With her index finger, she rubbed over one fang. A bolt of adrenaline charged through him, sending a lightning strike into his balls.

"Fuck!"

Nobody had touched his fangs—a vampire's most erogenous zone—in decades.

"Do it," he heard her murmur.

Luther lowered his head to one breast and captured the hard nipple in his mouth. He sucked on it, licked his tongue over the delicious bud. Then he set his fangs to either side of it. The contact of fang on skin nearly robbed him of all his senses. He opened his mouth wider, then slowly, he closed it and drove his fangs deep into Katie's warm and soft flesh.

Hot blood rushed into his mouth and covered his tongue. His taste buds ignited, the flavor exploding in his mouth as the liquid ran down his throat and coated it.

"More!" It was Katie's demand, though it mirrored his own desire. His own need.

He sucked harder, pulling more blood into his mouth. God, she tasted good. He'd almost forgotten what it felt like to feed from a woman while making love to her. It was out of this world amazing. Indescribably erotic. Breathtakingly consuming.

"Yes, yes!" Katie's encouraging cries drove him over the edge.

He slammed his cock into her with more speed and force than he'd ever fucked a woman. He was out of control now, unable to stop or slow down.

He ripped his fangs from her and licked over the incisions. Fangs still dripping with blood, he captured Katie's lips and devoured her mouth with the same passion he'd fed from her, when finally, thank God, he felt her spasm around his cock.

Relieved, he let go of the last thread of his control and pumped his seed into her, filling her tight channel with everything he had. Waves of pleasure rocked his body and extended his orgasm beyond what he'd thought was possible. Again and again, a wave of pleasure washed over him as he continued to thrust into her, while she moaned in obvious ecstasy.

"Yeah, baby, that's it," he encouraged her and teased another few seconds of pleasure from both their bodies.

33

Katie felt weightless when Luther carried her to the bed and laid her onto it as gently as if she were a precious doll. He pulled the duvet back, and she slid underneath it. Luther joined her, pulling her into his embrace.

Katie let out a contented sigh. Her heart was still racing, and perspiration covered her body. But never in her life had she felt better.

Luther brushed his knuckles over her cheek. "Thank you." He touched his lips to hers, giving her a kiss so tender she could barely believe that this was the same man who'd taken her with such ferocity only moments earlier.

She slid her hand to his nape and pulled him back down to her. "Thank *you*."

He chuckled, and the sound reverberated in her heart and made hope spread inside it.

"I wasn't exactly expecting a *thank you* after the way I took you." He held her to his naked body, one hand sliding down to her backside, one thigh wedged between her legs. "I'm assuming that means you didn't mind me being rough."

She gazed into his eyes. His irises were still shimmering golden, a sign that the vampire in him was waiting in the wings, ready for more. She combed her hand through his damp hair. "As long as you take me, I don't care how."

He groaned. "Katie…" He stroked his hand over her torso, caressing her. "Next time I'll be gentler." He dropped his gaze to the spot where he'd bitten her. His lips parted and he looked like he wanted to say something, but hesitated.

"I loved feeling your fangs in my breast," she encouraged him.

"Your blood is sweet." He touched her breast, playing with her nipple and turning it hard again.

She moaned and arched her back, eager for more. Luther had awakened something in her. A hunger she'd never experienced before.

"Give me a few minutes," he murmured, "and I'll give you anything you want."

"I'd like that."

Luther smiled and brushed a strand of hair out of her face. "You're an insatiable woman."

"Do you mind?"

"I'd hate it if it were different." He rolled onto his side and pulled her into the curve of his body, so her back pressed against his chest and her behind slid against his groin.

"Hmm."

He pressed a kiss to her neck. "How did you convince your brother to let me protect you, when he clearly didn't want me around you?"

She sighed. "Haven is a big softy."

"Could have fooled me."

She turned her head to look at him. "I told him that I feel safe with you."

"Then why did you cry?"

"I—"

"I saw it in your eyes when you got back in the car."

She looked away. "It's complicated."

"It's okay, you don't have to tell me. I was just surprised that he would cave so easily. He seemed pretty dead set against me getting anywhere near you."

"He was," Katie admitted. "But he knows how important it is for me to feel safe. And I haven't felt safe in a very long time. He couldn't deny me my wish when I told him I needed you to stay with me. All these years Haven worked so hard to make me feel safe. To help me forget…" She hesitated, waiting for the panic to set in that she always felt when she thought back to the events of five years ago that had almost cost her her life. To her surprise, it didn't. The darkness didn't encroach this time. Didn't swoop down on her and engulf her like it usually did.

Luther took her chin between thumb and forefinger and gently turned her face to him. "To forget what?"

She dropped her lids halfway. "There was a stalker back then. He did terrible things. He…"

Luther's nostrils flared, and she felt his body around her tense. "What happened?"

The concern in his eyes made her continue. "I trusted him. The studio had assigned him to me as an assistant. He was invaluable. Always there when I needed him. Nobody saw it. Nobody realized how disturbed he was. He wasn't right in his head, but he was smart. So smart that he fooled everybody."

She felt Luther's arms tighten around her. "What did he do to you?"

Katie turned her face away, looking into the distance. "He was driving me to a meeting with a producer, or so he'd said. I didn't even get suspicious when he drove up that deserted canyon. He was all cheerful and chatty. Just like always. But when he stopped at an old house, I felt it. I knew something was wrong. I felt a prickling sensation on my nape, and I pulled out my cell phone. The last number I had called was Haven, because he was coming down to LA on business the next day and wanted to visit. I pressed the recall button. I heard it ring once, then a fist hit me in the face, and I was knocked out."

"Fuck!" Luther cursed, shooting up to a sitting position.

She reached for his hand, squeezing it, turning to him. "When I came to I was in a dark room, tied up. I saw it then. He was crazy. Mentally ill. Delusional. He wanted to turn me into a doll he could play with. A doll that did everything he wanted."

"Did he rape you?" Luther ground out through clenched teeth.

"No." She scoffed. "He couldn't get it up. He was impotent." She searched Luther's eyes. "It was the root of his obsession. He thought if he had me, his problem would go away. I had a certain reputation in Hollywood. They called me the modern day Mae West." She shook her head, a smile forming on her lips. "It was all just an image. The studio wanted me to be a sex symbol, to hit the tabloids with lover after lover. It sold movie tickets. Everything in Hollywood was just for show. A big illusion. A person said or did one thing, but when you looked behind the façade, you saw something different altogether. It was one big stage. One big illusion." She sighed. "In reality, most of the men the paparazzi photographed me with were hired by the studio to play my lovers. I had few boyfriends. But just like everybody else, my assistant believed in the image I portrayed. He became convinced that if he had me, he'd be cured."

"What did he do to you?" Luther gritted. The tips of his fangs were showing now, and the rim of his irises shimmered golden.

"He kept me locked up. When he realized that he wasn't able to rape me, he decided to hurt me instead. To take his anger out on me, he used a knife..."

"Oh God, Katie." Luther threw his head back, growling.

"Haven found me. He traced my cell phone. He was able to heal me with his blood. I was lucky, there were no scars. Nobody would ever find out."

Luther drew her against his chest. "Oh Katie, I'm so sorry for what happened to you." He took a deep breath. "You think he's come back to finish what he started. You think it's Forrester?"

"No. It can't be him. The man who'd kidnapped me was human. Haven killed him. Ripped him to shreds in front of me and buried his body in the woods. He'll never come back." She sighed. "And even though I know that, even though I've seen it with my own eyes, the fear never truly left me. I turned my back on Hollywood and my career, thinking if I left that life, I would feel safe again. But I didn't. Not until I met you." She reached for his face, cupping his cheek. "That's why Haven agreed to let you stay. He knows how much I need this. I know it's just for a little while, but when I'm around you, that darkness that's always hovering over me, it retreats. You're chasing away my demons."

Luther took her hand and brought it to his mouth, pressing a kiss into her palm. "I'm so sorry, baby. I wish you would have never had to experience such horror."

She turned fully and slung her arms around him. He'd called her baby. Just like he'd done when he'd taken her in the bathroom. But this time it was different. Not spoken in the heat of passion, but meant as a true sign of endearment.

"Will you stay with me, until all this is over? Until Forrester is taken out and Isabelle is back? Just until then. That's all I'm asking. After that, I think I'll be strong enough to finally put all this behind me."

He nodded slowly, his expression serious. "I'll be here for you."

"Thank you." She pulled his head down to her and offered her lips to him.

34

Luther looked into Katie's eyes and saw hope flicker in them. How could he refuse her anything now? She'd been through so much and yet asked for so little. The vampire in him still seethed with rage and wanted to hurt the man who'd caused her so much pain. But he pushed the beast back. What Katie needed now was tenderness. He still remembered what tenderness felt like, despite the long years without it. He knew he was still capable of it.

It felt strange at first to kiss her softly, to mould his lips to hers and not make any demands. To allow her to take the lead and give her liberty to take from him what she needed. To set his own needs aside and only respond to hers. Her need for tenderness and protection.

He held her in his arms like in a protective cocoon, cradling her to his body, keeping her safe. When her lips parted on a sigh, he took his time to explore her. Slowly and carefully, he licked his tongue against hers, waiting for her to ask for more.

Then he drew his head back by an inch. "Tell me what you want."

"I want to feel you inside me again," she murmured.

"Are you sure? If you just need to be held, I'll hold you. I don't need anything in return."

She brushed her fingers over his cheek, her lips tilting upward into the beginnings of a smile. "Don't tell me this big bad vampire is suddenly going all soft on me."

Luther felt a chuckle build in his chest and didn't stop it from coming over his lips. "Soft, huh?" He ground his pelvis against her. "Does that feel soft to you?"

"Thank God, no."

"Good, 'cause the only thing that's soft around here, is your delicious body. Now, if you want me to go all bad vampire on you, fine, but personally, I'd rather make love to you slowly and gently. I'd like to take my time, draw out the pleasure."

"I was hoping you'd say that."

He pressed her back into the sheets and rolled over her. Braced on elbows and knees, he began to plant soft kisses on her face and neck, dipping lower to her enticing cleavage.

"Has anybody ever told you that your blood tastes of sin and innocence all at once?"

"Nobody ever drank my blood before today."

At that admission, male pride rose in him, and he hummed his approval against her flesh, teasingly biting her without breaking her skin.

"I'm not just talking about your blood, Katie. Your skin, your hair, your lips, all of it tastes of that same sin and innocence. Inviting and forbidden at the same time. I'm surprised no other vampire has ever bitten and tasted you."

He licked over her breasts and captured one nipple in his mouth.

Katie moaned and arched her back, thrusting her tantalizing flesh deeper into his mouth. "Maybe they were all afraid of my witch blood."

For a second, he let the tasty nipple pop from his mouth and chuckled. "Or one of your brothers."

"Neither of them is here now."

"We'd better take advantage of that then," he teased and headed for the other breast. He licked over the hard nipple, before closing his lips around it and pulling on it.

Beneath him, Katie sighed, and he realized how much his body responded to her sounds of pleasure. He filled his hands with her breasts, squeezed and sucked, until Katie was twisting underneath him, her body glistening, her heartbeat pounding against her rip cage. Like a drum, it beat in his ears, communicating with his own heart.

Farther below, his pelvis rocked against her center, his hard cock sliding against her sex without entering. Just teasing her and himself. The scent of her arousal filled the room now.

"You should be made love to twenty-four hours a day," he murmured. And maybe that's what he should do: make love to her until neither one of them could move another limb. Until they were both completely sated.

"Let me feel you," she begged, her hands reaching for him, pulling him closer.

He complied with her wishes and aligned his cock with her drenched sex. The tip of his erection touched her entrance, and a moan came from Katie.

"I've got you, baby," he assured her and drove into her, descending into her warm cave slowly and evenly, inch by inch, without haste. He felt her more intensely now, partially because he'd had her blood, but also because he wasn't rushing it. He perceived every muscle inside her, relishing in the warm wetness of her inner sanctum. She trusted him with her body, and he sensed that trust physically.

Seated to the hilt, he gazed into her face. "Look at me, Katie."

Her eyes opened wide. "Luther." She traced his lips with her finger. "Show them to me."

"My fangs?" he asked, though he knew what she meant.

"Yes. Let me see them."

He couldn't have stopped them from descending even if he'd tried. Peeling his lips back from his teeth, he presented them to her. "Aren't you afraid when you see me in my vampire form?"

"No," she said in a breathy voice and lifted her pelvis to force him deeper into her, while she pulled her lower lip between her teeth.

"My God, it turns you on, doesn't it?"

The green in her eyes suddenly seemed to sparkle. "Yes. I've never seen anything more beautiful or exciting." Her hand trailed down to his marred chest, and she caressed it lovingly, as if she were touching the softest silk. As if she didn't even feel the ugliness under her palm.

"Don't you see my scars?" he asked, wanting her to acknowledge them.

"They're part of you." She met his eyes. "I wouldn't want you any other way." Then she laced her hands behind his nape and pulled him down for a kiss.

Her lips were demanding this time, and he knew playtime was over. It was time to satisfy the woman in his arms, to give her what she so desperately needed: beautiful memories to replace the horrible ones.

"I'm all yours," he assured her and started to move inside her.

Katie's interior muscles held him tightly. They wrapped around him like a vise. On every descent she relaxed, on every withdrawal she clamped around him as if she didn't want him to leave. He felt the pressure inside his balls build and had to use every ounce of his strength to ward off an imminent orgasm. It was difficult not to give into the pleasure that she gave him so freely. Not to let himself go and accept everything she offered him. Because for him, too, this moment meant forgetting the past. He, too, needed to make new memories to deal with the old ones, the ones that haunted him in his sleep.

He whispered sweet nothings to her, telling her that he desired her, that she made him feel good. That she was perfect.

She thanked him with gestures: a tightening of her delicious channel, passionate caresses with her hands, and her ankles crossing below his butt to imprison him. And unlike the prison he'd inhabited for twenty years, this was a prison he didn't want to flee. It was a prison of softness and warmth, of tenderness instead of cruelty, of belonging instead of loneliness. With every plunge into the center of her body, he felt himself drawn deeper.

Had it really been over two decades since he'd felt such joy? How had he survived without the warmth and comfort only a loving woman could provide?

Eager to gobble up what Katie gave him, knowing that soon all this would come to an end, he unleashed his passion on her. Soon he would turn his back on San Francisco again, but until that happened, he had to fill the void in his heart with the illusion that there was somebody in his life who cared enough about him to grant him a few hours of bliss.

What had Katie said earlier? That Hollywood had been one big stage, a pretty illusion. Maybe this here was the illusion he needed to go on with his life. To lay the demons of his past to rest. To forgive Vivian and himself.

He gazed into the passion-drugged face of the beautiful woman beneath him and found her looking back at him. Her gaze was open, and he felt as if he could see into her soul.

"Oh, Katie," he rasped. There was so much he wanted to tell her, to give her, to make her feel.

It was then that he felt her clench around him. Her orgasm caught him unaware, and it was too late to hold back his own release.

With a guttural moan, he thrust into her again and joined her in ecstasy. Before his eyes everything blurred. A sensation akin to floating gripped his body and carried him away to a place where nothing mattered, where the world was in order. Where everybody was happy.

35

Katie pulled the pizza out of the oven and placed the hot baking tray on the stove.

"I'd almost forgotten what it smells like in a kitchen when somebody's cooking," Luther said from behind her.

She looked over her shoulder, smiling. Luther was leaning against the kitchen island, wearing sweats and a T-shirt, both belonging to Haven, for whom she kept a small closet in her house in case of emergencies, while Luther's own clothes were in the dryer. Katie had slipped into yoga pants and a T-shirt after they'd slept for a few hours. But a text message had awoken them.

"That's not surprising," she said. "You haven't been around humans in a long time." She turned to switch off the oven.

"My wife liked to cook."

Katie froze, surprised that Luther was revealing something from his past. She hesitated, but then asked as casually as she could, "Vivian?"

"Yeah, she would spend hours in the kitchen. I think she always found it a pity that I couldn't eat what she concocted."

"Well, I'm not much of a cook," Katie admitted. "I didn't make the pizza. I get it frozen from Pasquale's, and just shove it in the oven." The sound of the garage door interrupted her. "Just don't tell them. They think I actually make it from scratch."

Luther's hands were suddenly on her shoulders, and he turned her to face him. "Another illusion? That of the perfect aunt?"

"Don't we all try to show others what they want to see?"

"Are you doing that with me, too? Showing me what I want to see?"

Slowly she moved her head from side to side. "I can't pretend with you."

"Good."

Luther gripped her chin between thumb and forefinger and dipped his head to hers. His kiss was gentle, but full of heat nevertheless.

The door to the kitchen was flung open, and Luther immediately released her.

"Mmm, pizza!" Cooper said, charging in. "I'm starving!"

The closing door almost hit his sister Lydia in the face. She stopped it with her palm and thrust it open again. "Cooper, you have no manners!" she chastised her younger brother, then tossed a long suffering look at Katie. "Sorry, Aunt Katie, he still hasn't learned to knock. I keep trying, but he's a lost cause once he smells pizza." Her eyes darted to Luther, then quickly back to her. "Sorry to interrupt."

"Hey, Lydia, so good to see you!" Katie greeted her with a smile and pulled her into her arms. She squeezed her niece tightly and ran her hand over her long red hair. "How are you holding up?"

Nineteen-year-old Lydia drew her head back and sniffled. "I miss Isabelle. She's my best friend."

"I know, honey, I know."

"We'll get her back," Luther said from behind them.

Katie released her niece and turned sideways. "This is Luther, he's been helping us. Luther, that's my niece Lydia, and—" She pointed to the sixteen-year-old hybrid already cutting the pizza in slices. "—my nephew Cooper. Haven and Yvette's kids."

Luther offered his hand to Lydia. "Your mother is Yvette? But that's impossible."

Lydia hesitantly shook Luther's hand and quickly released it. "I'm adopted." Then she pointed to Cooper. "But unfortunately Mom had *him* later."

Cooper grinned, chewing on a slice of pizza. "You'd be bored if you didn't have me to boss around, sis." He stretched his free hand out to Luther and shook it. "Nice to meet you."

"Likewise." Luther looked quizzically at Katie. "I guess we're not talking about the Yvette I knew a long time ago, because she's a vampire."

"Oh, Mom's a vampire," Cooper said casually. "That's also why she sucks at cooking." He grinned at Katie and pointed to the pizza. "This is amazing! You're the best cook in the world, Aunt Katie!"

Katie rolled her eyes. "Why don't you at least sit down while you're eating?"

She turned to the hanging cabinets and pulled three plates from it, then placed them on the table, while Cooper put the baking tray with the pizza in the middle of the kitchen table.

Luther pulled the chair back for her and motioned her to sit. She could sense that he was still baffled about Cooper's comment and looked over her shoulder. "Maya, Gabriel's mate, is a doctor. She pioneered a fertility treatment for vampire females. It was successful." She ran her hand through Cooper's dark mane. "And this boy here is one of the results."

"Hey, I'm not a boy. I'm a man!" Cooper protested.

Lydia laughed and scooped a slice of pizza onto her plate. "Yeah, right."

"So vampire females don't have to be infertile anymore," Luther said, clearly digesting the news. "How does it work?"

"I'm not a doctor, but the way Maya explains it is that when a vampire female wants to conceive, Maya injects her with human stem cells to prepare her body," Katie started. "You see, conception was never a problem for a vampire female. But as soon as a fertilized egg tries to implant itself into the womb, the vampire's body perceives it as an injury and heals it, killing the egg. So by injecting human stem cells, Maya in effect creates a human womb. During the entire pregnancy Maya monitors the vampire female and continues injecting human stem cells to keep up the right environment for the fetus to thrive until it's time for the birth."

"That's amazing," Luther said.

"Guess they don't keep you up to date in prison," Cooper said.

"Cooper!" Katie chastised, but Luther immediately squeezed her shoulder.

"It's okay," Luther said.

Lydia looked up at Luther. "Dad filled us in. So we volunteered to bring Aunt Katie's car back."

"Thanks, honey, that's nice of you," Katie said and smiled at her niece.

She bit into a slice of pizza, ravenous now. She couldn't remember when she'd last eaten something. Oddly enough, she hadn't even noticed until now. Maybe the fact that Luther had given her his blood to heal had kept the hunger at bay.

"Though Dad did say that you can't go anywhere," Cooper added now and glanced at Luther, looking him up and down.

Luther sat down on the chair opposite Katie's, not saying anything about Cooper's obvious curiosity. For a moment there was silence.

"Have there been any developments?" Luther asked, directing his question at Cooper, treating him like an equal.

Cooper immediately sat up straighter and pulled his shoulders back. "Nothing new. They're looking into all the leads they have. Thomas and Eddie are going through all the databases to see if they can find any other hideouts this Forrester might have." Cooper sighed.

"Did they match the voice on the recording to Forrester's to get a positive ID?" Katie asked.

"Not yet. They're trying to get a sample of Forrester's voice from prison records." Cooper tossed a look at Luther. "But apparently there's been a bit of an incident at Grass Valley." His eyes shone with admiration now. "So you're some kind of badass, huh?"

"Cooper, please!" Lydia hissed. "You're embarrassing me."

"How am I embarrassing you?" her brother griped. "I'm just stating a fact. Everybody's saying the same."

"Yeah, but not to his face!" Lydia snapped, and immediately slapped her hand over her mouth. Ashamed, she lowered her lids. "Sorry."

"Don't be sorry for me," Luther said evenly. "I deserve everything people are saying about me. Nobody should have to whitewash what I am or what I did."

Katie locked eyes with him across the table, trying to tell him with her eyes that she appreciated everything he'd done to help them find Isabelle. But Luther averted his eyes and instead looked at Cooper.

"I'm an ex-con, Cooper. There's nothing romantic or admirable about that. Nothing anybody should aspire to."

To Cooper's credit, the kid didn't back down. "Do you regret it?" He held Luther's gaze.

Katie felt her heart pound out of control. Luther's eyes shifted to her. They turned darker, became unreadable.

"Eat another slice, Coop," Lydia said and broke the spell. "And don't ask questions that are none of your business." She turned to Luther. "I'm sorry. He's only sixteen. He really doesn't know when he's getting on people's nerves."

"You're one to talk," her brother protested.

Katie reached for another slice. "And people wonder why I don't want kids."

"See what you did now!" Lydia ground out, glaring at her brother. Then she put her hand on Katie's forearm. "Sorry, Aunt Katie. It's just... well, we're all under stress. And we're all taking it out on each other. The waiting... it's just killing me." Tears formed in Lydia's eyes. "Are we gonna find her?"

"Oh, Lydia." Katie rose from her chair and pulled her niece into her arms, hugging her tightly. "We're doing everything to find her. We'll get her back. We will, I promise you."

Pressing Lydia's head to her shoulder and stroking her long red hair, Katie looked past her to Luther. His eyes shimmered golden now, and she recognized the promise that lay in them. Luther would do everything in his power to help them get Isabelle back.

"I'm sorry, I'm normally not such a watering pot," Lydia wailed.

"That's okay, honey."

Unexpectedly, Cooper rose from the table and approached them. "Come on, sis, I'll take you home."

"Did you bring a second car?" Katie asked.

"No, we're taking the bus home. No worries," Cooper said and put his arm around his sister. "Thanks for the pizza. Maybe you could give Mom your recipe?"

Katie smiled and hugged him. "And lose the reason you like visiting me? Not a chance."

He pressed a loud kiss to her cheek, then whispered in her ear, "I'll tell you a secret: I've been to Pasquale's, and their pizzas taste oddly similar to yours." When he released her from his embrace, Cooper grinned from one ear to the other. Then he winked and looked over his shoulder. "Nice meeting you, Luther."

Luther, who'd gotten up, nodded. "Bye, Cooper."

"Take care, both of you," Katie said and kissed Lydia on the cheek.

"Thanks, you too," Lydia replied and glanced back at Luther. "Thanks for protecting my aunt. I know you'll keep her safe."

"Let's go, sis." Cooper walked to the door. "Or Mom's gonna get worried."

Lydia followed her brother, but pivoted at the door. "Oh, almost forgot." She dug into her purse and pulled out a manila envelope, handing it to Katie. "Dad asked me to give this to you. He said you wanted copies of the letters."

"Thank you, honey."

With shaking hands, Katie accepted the envelope and watched her niece and nephew leave. For a long moment, she just stood there, staring at the envelope, before she turned around and found Luther standing right behind her.

36

"They seem like good kids," Luther said and cupped Katie's shoulders.

"They are, and they drive their parents crazy."

Luther chuckled. "I can see that." He brushed his hand through Katie's hair, loving the feel of it. "Is that why you don't want children, or were you just pulling their leg?"

"Oh, no, I meant it. And they know it, too." She sighed. "I love them to death, but I don't think I was meant to be a mother. I don't have the patience that Yvette exhibits. I don't think I'm selfless enough to be a mother and put my own wishes behind that of a child. I didn't have the best childhood, you know. I feel that I want to live my own life, now that I can make choices for myself. Not everybody should be a parent."

She turned away and laid the envelope on the table, then started to clear the dishes.

"Let me help you," he offered.

"Thanks." She opened the dishwasher and placed the three plates in it. "Yvette wanted children all her life. Haven didn't at first." She looked up and gave him a sad smile. "He was too afraid of losing a child…"

Her words struck him as odd, making curiosity well up in him. "Why's that?" He handed her the empty baking tray, and Katie put it in the sink.

"I was kidnapped when I was a baby. Long story." She closed the dishwasher.

"Oh God." Hadn't Katie been through enough? Instinctively he reached for her hand and pulled it to his cheek. He pressed a kiss to her palm.

"Haven searched for me for over twenty years. He was eleven when a vampire took me. He became a vampire slayer because of it." A sad smile crossed Katie's face. "When he finally found me, he did the unthinkable. He sacrificed his human life so that Wes and I could live."

"What happened?"

"A bad witch. She tried to harness our witch power by performing a ritual with the three of us. You see, my brothers and I were meant to be the Power of Three, the most powerful trio of witches the world has ever seen. But that witch wanted the power for herself. And the ritual would have left one of us dead. There was only one way to vanquish the power permanently so the witch could never claim it for herself."

He understood immediately. "The power of a witch can never inhabit a vampire's body."

"Yes. I didn't know the plan Haven and Wes had hatched. Had I known, God, I don't think I could have stood by and let it happen. Haven stabbed himself." She shook her head. "He didn't tell Yvette either what he'd planned."

Luther squeezed Katie's hand. "He must have had a lot of trust in her."

Katie smiled. "Yeah, he did. They'd only known each other for a few days, but everybody could see that despite his lifelong hatred for vampires, he loved her, and she loved him. Although Yvette knew she should hate him for the things he'd done to her kind, she couldn't help follow her heart. Sometimes a heart makes its own choice and doesn't care what the head thinks. She turned Haven as he lay dying. They blood-bonded the next night." Katie sighed. "Anyway... I shouldn't bore you with family stories."

She turned abruptly, took the envelope from the kitchen table and walked through to the living room.

Luther followed. "Katie."

She looked over her shoulder. "What?"

"You didn't bore me." He caught up with her.

She motioned to the couch and sat down in one corner. Luther joined her, pulling her onto his lap, before he leaned back into the cushions, one arm wrapped around Katie, the other resting on her thigh.

"I don't have a family," he said hesitantly. "And it's nice to be reminded what it's like to have people who care about you. Scanguards was my family once."

"Is that why you came back? To remind yourself of what it was like to be part of Scanguards?"

He sighed and dropped his head back against the sofa, looking up at the ceiling. He didn't want to answer the question, but something inside him pushed him to do it nevertheless. "I came back to atone for what I'd done to them. For how I wronged them."

"So you do feel remorse."

Luther closed his eyes. "From the moment I found out that it wasn't their fault, I've done nothing but regret my actions. If I could only turn back time, but I can't." He opened his eyes and found Katie looking at him. "I erroneously believed that Amaury and Samson let my wife die. I was wrong. They offered to turn her when it was clear that she was dying in childbirth. But she refused." He'd gone half insane when he'd found out the truth. "And I failed her as a husband."

"How? How could you have failed her? Things like that happen. Medical complications…"

Luther put his finger over her lips. He didn't want her to make excuses for him. "I never wanted to be a father. I wanted a wife who loved only me. When Vivian got pregnant, I was suddenly not the most important person in her life anymore. I started resenting the child. And I started resenting her for shutting me out." He shook his head. "It's my fault that I wasn't there when she needed me. I left because we were arguing all the time. It was selfish of me not to accept that she was going to divide her love between me and the child. I'm responsible for her death."

Katie cupped his face with both her hands. But she didn't say anything. Did she understand now what a selfish bastard he was? That he wasn't the man who could keep her safe? That she should stay away as far as possible?

"I'm so sorry for what you had to go through, Luther," she murmured and brushed her lips over his. "So sorry."

"Don't feel sorry for me, Katie. I don't deserve it."

She wrapped her arms around him, pressing herself to him.

"Please, don't," he begged. "I'm not what you want me to be. I'm not your hero. In a few days I'll be gone. We both know that. You should listen to your brother. He's got good instincts. I'm only gonna cause you grief."

"I make my own decisions." She drew back to look at him, her hands laced behind his neck. "You should know that by now, Luther."

"I was afraid you'd say that." He grimaced.

"Don't look like I'm making you do something you don't want. If I remember well, you couldn't get enough of me this morning."

He groaned, shoving a hand through his hair. "It's not about that, and you know it. This physical thing that's happening between us is explosive. The sex is out of this world amazing. And your blood…" He got hard just thinking of it. Of sinking his fangs into her beautiful flesh, while he thrust his cock into her. "I'm not strong enough to resist it. That's why you should be the voice of reason. That's why I'm telling you all this. So you know what you're dealing with."

"I know who you are: a man who wants to do right. If you really came to atone, then help me save Samson's daughter. What becomes of you and me doesn't matter." She combed her hand through his hair, and the sensation sent a shudder down his spine. "Is it so wrong that I want to enjoy your company for as long as I can? Haven't we both earned a little reprieve from our past and the misgivings we have? Don't we deserve a few hours of happiness? That's all I'm asking."

He gazed into the green depth of her irises. "You deserve so much more, Katie." He cupped her nape with his hand and rubbed his thumb along her jaw. "But I'm too tired to fight with you."

"Good." A satisfied smile on her face, she reached for the envelope her niece had brought her. "Then help me figure out what Forrester plans." She pulled a handful of sheets of paper from the envelope and unfolded them. "Stalkers feel superior to their victims and have a need to boast about the things they're going to do. Somewhere in these letters we'll find where he's hiding."

Katie handed him a sheet.

He gave her a brief kiss and took the copy of the stalker's letter. "Yes, my bossy witch."

~ ~ ~

Luther put the letters beside him on the couch. Their author was a lunatic, so much was clear. He talked about *eternity under the stars, sailing into the sunset,* and *diving into a new life.* A whole plethora of bullshit metaphors spewed from the scribbled lines. Cliché after cliché sprung from the paper, making Luther's eyes hurt. As for finding any indication as to what the stalker's ultimate plan was, Luther couldn't find any clue hidden in his ramblings.

Katie had dozed off in his lap a half hour earlier, and Luther now looked at her peaceful face. How anybody could hurt a woman like her was beyond him. She signified everything that was good in this world. Katie hadn't judged him, not even when he'd tried to push her away and revealed the depth of his selfishness. Or when he'd confessed how he'd wronged the men he'd once called brothers. She made him feel that there was still hope for somebody like him. That maybe one day he could put his past behind him and start anew.

Luther pressed a kiss to Katie's forehead and felt her stir.

"Mmm." She reached up her hands and interlaced them behind his nape, pulling him down to her.

"Didn't mean to wake you," he whispered.

"Perhaps you should make it up to me," she said without opening her eyes.

He smirked. "Any preference how?"

"I don't think you need any directions from me."

"Guess not," he agreed and slid his hand underneath her T-shirt, moving north. She wasn't wearing a bra. He cupped one breast, loving how it spilled over in his palm. "You have gorgeous boobs. I'd love to sink my fangs into them again."

Katie opened her eyes. "Have you always done that? Drunk from women there?"

He shook his head. "Vivian preferred the neck. And the women before her never made me want to take blood from there." He squeezed her breast and teased the nipple, eliciting a soft moan from Katie. "But when I look at you, I can't help but want to bury my face in your breasts and gorge myself on you."

Katie winked at him. "Just as well that I stuffed myself with pizza and feel strong enough to feed my ravenous vampire."

Luther groaned. "Katie, you're not supposed to be so accommodating."

"Why not?"

"'Cause you make it doubly hard for me to keep from mauling you like a hungry beast."

"Stop talking, Luther, and kiss me." She pulled his face to her.

Resigned to the fact that he had no willpower when it came to resisting her, he slanted his lips over hers, when suddenly the ringing of a telephone interrupted him.

He lifted his head, while Katie turned and reached for the phone on the side table next to the sofa.

"Yes?"

"Katie, it's Blake."

Luther had no problem hearing the voice of the Scanguards man through the line, just as he picked up on Katie's heartbeat accelerating.

"Anything new?" Nervousness was evident in Katie's voice.

"The kidnapper contacted us. He's made demands. You need to come to HQ. Now. Have Luther drive you and park in the garage. I'll open the gate for you when I see your car on the monitor. Hurry."

There was a click on the line before Katie acknowledged the order.

Luther took the receiver from her and replaced it on the cradle, noticing that Katie's hand was trembling. He clasped it, but didn't say anything, only conveyed with his eyes what was on his mind: whatever the kidnapper wanted, Luther wouldn't allow Katie to be harmed in the process.

Five minutes later, after changing into different clothes, Luther drove Katie's Audi out of the garage, Katie in the passenger seat. The sun was just setting over the Pacific, and by the time they got to Scanguards' headquarters in the Mission district, night had descended.

Katie directed him to the entrance of the parking garage beneath the building, and when they reached the gate, it magically opened. Luther glanced at the camera and the red light on it that indicated that somebody was watching them. He drove into the garage.

"Second level, spot B5," a male voice said over a loudspeaker.

Luther followed the instructions and parked in the indicated spot. When he killed the engine, it was silent for a few moments, and all he could hear was Katie's thundering heartbeat. He met her eyes.

"I won't let you out of my sight," he promised.

He opened the car door and exited, waiting for Katie to do the same. The elevator doors opened when they reached it. Taking Katie by the hand, Luther entered and looked at the buttons. The one to the top floor was already pressed, and the doors closed.

In silence, they ascended. The elevator barely made a sound. After a soft ping, the doors opened, and they stepped into a hallway.

Before Luther knew which way to turn, a male voice penetrated his skull like a dagger. "What the fuck are you doing here?"

37

Luther whirled around, instantly ready for the coming assault, and saw Samson rushing toward him. He looked as if he hadn't slept in days, but that didn't diminish the murderous look in his eyes.

"I warned you!" Samson growled, almost upon him.

"Samson, wait, I can explain!" Luther lifted his arms in defense.

Though Samson aimed his fist at Luther, it didn't land in his face, because Katie jumped in front of him, blocking Samson's approach, shielding Luther with her body.

"Katie, nooooo!"

In horror, Luther grabbed her shoulders and jerked her to the side just in time to prevent Samson's claws slicing into her. Instead, the blow hit its intended target after all, if only marginally. Samson's fist swiped Luther's shoulder, just as he turned his back toward Samson to protect Katie.

"Damn it, Samson!" Luther cried out, glaring over his shoulder, Katie pressed to his chest. His heart pounded out of control at the thought that he could have been too late. "I don't care what you do to me, but if you hurt Katie, I'm gonna kill you!"

To his surprise, Samson froze in his next movement. His fists were still raised, his fangs still extended, and his eyes glared red. But he was hesitating.

"Stand down!"

Luther recognized Blake's voice. From the corner of his eye, he saw the young vampire run toward them, several other men following him.

"Samson, don't! I asked him to come," Blake continued as he reached them.

Behind him, Luther recognized Haven, Eddie, and Grayson. Footsteps from the other end of the corridor made him toss a quick look down that end: Amaury, Zane, and Gabriel were approaching from there, followed by several vampires Luther didn't recognize immediately.

Samson shot Blake a look of annoyance, eyes narrowed. "You did what?" he snarled.

"What the fuck!" Amaury echoed Samson's words, venom spewing from his eyes, eyes that were pinning Luther just as surely as if he were using a stake.

"You'd better have a bloody good explanation for that, Blake!" Samson growled. "Or I'm gonna rip your head off just as soon as I'm done with him."

Surprisingly, Blake didn't even flinch at his boss's threat. Instead, he inserted himself between Luther and Samson and braced his hands on his hips. "I suggest we assemble in the conference room to discuss this further."

Samson went toe to toe with his employee. "And I suggest you tell me now what's going on. My patience is at its end."

Blake nodded. "As you wish." He took a step aside and motioned to Luther. "Luther is responsible for us knowing who has Isabelle. He risked his life to get us the lead."

All the air rushed from Samson's lungs. His eyes darted past Blake and landed on Luther. Luther now turned fully, finally releasing Katie from his protective embrace. He waited silently for Samson to digest the news, just as everybody else in the hallway refrained from talking to give their boss the time he needed to come to grips with the fact that his enemy had helped him.

"I don't want a *thank you*," Luther said into the silence.

He knew how hard it would be for Samson to force words of thanks over his lips, and he wasn't going to put his former friend in that situation. If he were in Samson's shoes, he wouldn't want to be obliged to thank his enemy either. "Katie was the one who put me on the right trail. You should thank her."

Samson gave a stiff nod to Katie. Then he looked at Blake. "Conference room. Now." He glanced back at Luther. "You, too."

Like the leader he was, Samson marched down the corridor and disappeared through a double door to the right. Several of the vampires followed. Luther exchanged a look with Blake.

"Sorry, Luther, but I thought it better not to tell him in advance, or he might have prevented me from getting you here."

Luther shrugged. "Hey, he didn't kill me. Not a bad start." He took Katie's hand and walked in the direction of the conference room, when Amaury stepped in his path.

"He's not the only one you have to convince that you're worth keeping alive," Amaury said.

"I'm aware of that, brother," Luther said.

Amaury opened his mouth for a retort, but Eddie gripped his shoulder.

"This is not the time. We've got more pressing things to discuss. If you'd like to beat the shit out of my sire once all this is over, I'll be the first to stand back and watch. But if you touch him now, I'm gonna have to hurt you—brother-in-law or not," Eddie warned.

Nodding a thanks to his protégé, Luther walked around Amaury. He caught Haven's eyes zooming in on his and Katie's joined hands, before he lifted them toward Luther's face. Luther hadn't even noticed that he'd taken Katie's hand, but he couldn't let go of it now, not when Haven silently challenged him on it. Instead he met Haven's look stoically, not giving away his feelings. With a resigned sigh, Haven turned and disappeared in the conference room.

Moments later, almost everybody was seated around the large table: the full contingent of the upper echelon of Scanguards. Gabriel, Amaury, Zane, Yvette, Quinn, Thomas, Eddie, Haven, Wesley, Grayson, as well as John, who he'd met during the raid on Forrester's house. Several other vampires sat among them, but Luther didn't know them. Samson was leaning against the wall, and Blake stood at the head of the table.

Luther pulled a chair for Katie and motioned her to sit down, before taking the empty seat next to her. The tension in the room was punctuated by the silence and the looks the other vampires and hybrids gave him. Any other man would have felt nervous at so much scrutiny, but Luther ignored it. He needed to keep a cool head.

Blake knocked on the table to draw everybody's attention to him. "I want everybody on the same page. So, here's what we know so far. We know that Isabelle was kidnapped by a vampire named Antonio Mendoza, who was hired to abduct Katie, but mistook them because they wore similar clothes and hairstyles, and had changed roles. Mendoza wasn't privy to the fact that Isabelle is a hybrid and Katie a witch, or he wouldn't have made that mistake."

"We already know all that," Zane grumbled under his breath, clearly impatient.

Blake shot him a displeased look, but continued, "When Mendoza tried to pass Isabelle to the man who hired him, he was killed." He pointed to Luther. "Because of Luther's and Katie's efforts we know now who this man is."

He clicked a small remote control in his hand and stepped to the side so everybody had a view of the large monitor behind him. The headshot of a man was displayed on it. He had short dark hair, brown eyes, an oval face, and looked to be in his late thirties.

"The perpetrator's name is Cliff Forrester. He was released from the vampire penitentiary near Grass Valley nine days ago. Letters he wrote to Katie seem to suggest that he was planning for a long time to kidnap her once he was released."

"Why wouldn't he kidnap her himself, and instead hire Mendoza? Seems odd, considering he was released from prison and could do it himself," Gabriel said.

"Good question," Blake said. "We believe that Forrester was afraid that due to his stint in prison he might be recognized by council agents who keep tabs on released prisoners for a while. We must assume that he believed it was safer to have somebody else handle the kidnapping. He must have known that there was a chance that the kidnapper would be caught on security cameras."

"Any news from the council agents about where Forrester is?" Amaury followed up with a question.

"Regretfully, we have not received any cooperation from the prison authority or the council agents." He motioned to Thomas. "Do you want to update us on that?"

Thomas stood quickly. "In light of the fact that the prison authority is dragging its feet on providing us with the information we need, Eddie and I have taken the issue into our own hands and have our team working on hacking into their system. We're close and should soon have everything on Forrester, including recordings of his voice as well as his fingerprints, so we can confirm that the letters were written by him, and the voice on the recording we found at Mendoza's house was indeed Forrester's. We should know more in a few hours." He sat down.

"Thanks, Thomas," Blake said. "But we won't have time to wait for that confirmation. Forrester made contact."

A collective mumbling went through the room. Samson pushed himself away from the wall, his hands clenching, his jaw tightening. His lips moved. "Finally," he murmured.

Luther felt Katie tense next to him and instinctively reached for her hand under the table, squeezing it in reassurance.

"We know that Isabelle is alive. He let her speak to me. He wants to exchange her for Katie. But he didn't give us any information yet as to where this exchange will take place. Only the time: two hours before sunrise."

Luther exchanged a look with Katie. She appeared calm and collected. She had expected this, maybe even prepared herself for it mentally.

"Did you get a trace?" Zane asked.

"He didn't stay on the phone long enough for us to trace the call. And most likely it would have only led us to a burner phone anyway."

"What are we doing now?" Gabriel asked.

"Now that we have a picture of the kidnapper, thanks to Luther, we have patrols everywhere in the city, canvassing, searching for every possible hiding place. They know not to engage in case they endanger Isabelle's life." Blake glanced at Samson, before continuing. "But we've had no luck so far. We'll have to do the exchange. It's our only way to get Isabelle back."

Before anybody else could say anything, Katie said, "I'll do it."

Haven shot up from his seat at the same time Luther did. "There must be another way," Haven pleaded, looking at Samson and Blake.

There was a sad look on Samson's face. "I wish there were. But you heard it yourself. We've got nothing. We don't know where he's hiding her. She's still a child, Haven! Can you imagine what she must be feeling?"

"Yes, I can," Haven ground out and glanced back at Katie.

Luther knew what was going on in Haven's mind at this moment. He was remembering Katie's ordeal. And he didn't want Katie to go through the same horror a second time.

"There has to be another way," Luther interjected, drawing everybody's attention on him.

Samson tossed him a defiant look. "And what would that be, huh, Luther? I'm afraid there are no more prisons you can break into."

"It worked, didn't it?" Luther ground out. "Listen, Samson, I know you're upset, but don't allow this guy—" He pointed to the picture on the monitor. "—to cloud your judgment. You know as well as I do that there are always several solutions to a problem. I learned that from you! Don't let him defeat you into thinking you have to follow his plan."

"You wouldn't be saying that because you shacked up with Katie, would you now?"

Luther sucked in a breath of air and glanced at Blake. But the young vampire seemed as surprised as Luther himself that Samson knew about him and Katie.

"Goddamn it, Luther, I can smell her on you from across the room!"

"Samson," Haven interrupted, "this has—"

"Stay out of this, Haven!" Luther snapped, before addressing Samson again. "It doesn't matter what's between me and Katie. It's none of your fucking business. And it has no bearing on how I feel about this situation. But I'm not going to let you trade one innocent for another. That's not what you stand for Samson. You know it. Would you be able to live with yourself if Forrester harmed Katie? And every time you looked at your daughter, would you be able to forget what you had to do to get her back? To sacrifice another innocent for her?" Luther shook his head. "That's not the Samson I remember."

"You've been gone for a long time, Luther. I've changed. I'm a father now. I have other priorities."

"Other priorities, maybe. But other values, other morals? No." Luther sighed. "I've made a lot of mistakes in my life. My biggest one was not to trust you and Amaury. Because deep down I always knew you were steadfast, the rocks I could rely on for anything." He glanced at Amaury, then back at Samson. "I regret what I did to both of you and your mates. I regret every single second of it. That's why I came back. To atone. To make good the wrongs I committed. That's why I was there the night Isabelle got taken. To talk to you and Amaury and ask for your forgiveness. But I'll be damned if I'm gonna ask forgiveness of a man who's prepared to deliver an innocent into unspeakable horror. I will not stand idly by and let it happen."

There was no sound in the room. Nobody spoke. Nobody as much as breathed.

Samson's nostrils flared as he visibly tried to control the emotions warring inside him.

"You have the greatest minds at your disposal here," Luther said, making a sweeping motion with his arm. "Think for a moment. There must be another way to get your daughter back without putting Katie in harm's way."

Samson pointed at him. "You and me. Outside." Samson marched to the door and opened it.

Luther followed him outside and closed the door behind him. There was nobody but the two of them in the corridor.

"If you're playing me, Luther, you're a dead man."

"I gain nothing by playing you."

Samson scoffed and motioned to the conference room. "Don't lie to me. I'm not blind. Katie shielded you as if you meant something to her. You're doing this for her, not because you can't stand the fact that an innocent might be harmed."

"Let's not fight about who's got a nobler motive. It doesn't matter. If you're worried that you'll have to tolerate me once all this is over, don't be. I'll be leaving once your daughter and Katie are safe. I never intended to stay in San Francisco. All I wanted was absolution for my sins so I could start a new life somewhere else. I can see now that you're not able to grant me that." Luther looked down at his shoes. "Doesn't matter now. I still want to offer you my help saving your daughter."

"While protecting Katie," Samson added.

Luther lifted his eyes and met Samson's gaze. "Yes. I owe her that. She showed me that there is hope even for somebody like me. And while you may never believe me, those twenty years in prison changed me. I'm not the same angry man anymore."

Samson nodded slowly. "And Vivian? Have you forgiven her?"

"I can't blame her. She had nothing to live for. I wasn't the husband she needed. I was the husband she got." Luther sighed. "You're a father, Samson. A good one from what I can see. I'm not like you. I could have never been the kind of father my child deserved. Vivian was right to leave me. I'm only sorry that I didn't see it earlier and that I put you and Amaury through so much pain. I understand why you can never forgive me."

"You want your slate wiped clean?" Samson asked.

"Yes."

"Then help me get my daughter back safe and sound. You were always one of the best. I hope you haven't lost any of your skills."

38

Everybody was talking over each other, voicing their opinions on what the next plan of action should be. Katie eyed the door through which Samson and Luther had left a few minutes earlier. Were they arguing? Or even fighting? She couldn't hear anything. The conference room was soundproof since confidential things were often discussed inside its walls.

"Hey."

Wesley's voice made her turn her head. She watched him as he sat down in the chair Luther had occupied only moments earlier. He grasped her hand with both of his.

"I'm prepared to do the exchange," she said.

"I know that, sweetheart. But as much as I hate to agree with Luther, he's right. We can't just exchange one innocent for another. We won't gain anything by doing that. On the contrary: as soon as he has you, he'll disappear. At the moment he has to stick around, because he wants you. Once we give him what he wants, we've missed our chance to capture him."

"But Isabelle. She must be out of her mind by now. I know how scared she must be. Wes, I can't let her suffer in my stead."

From her other side, Oliver turned to them. "You know what I find odd? That Forrester would tell us so far in advance when the exchange will take place. Why even tell us? Doesn't he tip his hand by doing that and giving us time to prepare?"

Wes shrugged. "He wants us to be ready so there won't be any delays. And without knowing the location, how could we even prepare?"

Oliver rubbed his nape. "Still odd. I've got a bad feeling about this.

Blake walked up behind him, putting his hand on Oliver's shoulder. "You and me both, bro." He looked at Wes and Katie. "Ever since we got the call, I've been wondering the same thing. Why tell us the time when it's still a good nine hours until then? Why give us the time to figure out alternative rescue plans? It makes no sense."

"Maybe he's not all that bright," Wes suggested.

Katie instantly shook her head. "No. He's smart. All stalkers are. They are more intelligent than average. And that makes them feel superior. They relish that feeling. They love to dangle things in front of you, making you think you can defeat them, when in reality you can't." She'd been at the receiving end of it once before.

Blake raised an eyebrow. "You think he believes his plan is so solid that there's no way we can come up with anything better?"

"Most likely. That's why he feels safe enough to tell us when it'll happen. Almost as if the ticking clock adds to his excitement. He gets off on that, on knowing that we're counting down the minutes and are no closer to finding him. It's a game for him."

"Well, we're not gonna play his game."

Katie swiveled in her chair when she heard Luther's voice. He and Samson had reentered the room together and now approached.

Samson addressed the assembled, "Luther has an idea." He stepped aside and gave the floor to Luther.

Somewhat surprised at Samson's gracious gesture, Katie leaned forward in her chair, eager to hear what Luther had to say.

"Mendoza mistook Isabelle, not only because she changed roles with Katie, but because the two wore the same type of outfit and hairdo. They looked like sisters, if not twins. I think we can use this fact to our advantage. We'll give him what he wants. But he won't get Katie. He'll get somebody who looks like her."

"And that's not delivering an innocent to him?" Zane scoffed. "Hypocrite!"

"Not when the person we're dressing up as Katie is a vampire and knows how to defend herself."

Instinctively Katie's gaze shot to Yvette. "Not Yvette," she blurted. She couldn't let her sister-in-law put herself in danger for her. If anything happened, Haven would never forgive her for it. Nor would Cooper or Lydia.

Luther glanced at her, giving her a quick smile. "No, Yvette is too tall. And she doesn't have your curves." He gave an apologetic nod in Yvette's direction. "No offense, Yvette."

Luther was right, Yvette had a great figure, but she wasn't curvy or big-breasted, though her long dark hair matched Katie's.

"None taken. Though—" She smiled warmly at Katie. "—you know, honey, I'd do it in a heartbeat if I knew it would succeed."

Katie mouthed a silent *Thank you* to her sister-in-law.

"But we have another vampire female in mind," Samson interjected.

"Doesn't matter who it is," Amaury interrupted, standing up. "Haven't you forgotten one tiny detail?" He pointed at Katie. "Katie is human. We must assume that Forrester knows that. He won't make the same mistake as Mendoza. Anybody who knows that Katie used to be Hollywood star Kimberly Fairfax would also know that she can't possibly be a vampire. As her stalker, he'd know that. So even if we manage to make another woman look like Katie's twin, as soon as she gets close enough, he'll recognize by her aura that the person we're trying to exchange is a vampire. And the whole thing blows up in our faces."

"Amaury's right," Gabriel agreed. "When that happens, who knows how he'll react. What if he hurts Isabelle to lash out?"

Everybody started speaking at once, throwing out the pros and cons of such a move. Katie could barely concentrate on any one person's opinion. She had to agree with the skeptics of the plan. They couldn't trick a vampire, not by sending a vampire instead of her.

"It's not gonna work," she murmured to herself, wringing her shaking hands. "I'll have to do it." She looked up and pressed her hands onto the table, ready to rise and put an end to the fruitless discussion.

A wolf whistle next to her stopped her dead in her tracks. It ended all conversations in the room instantly. All eyes were now on Wesley.

"Now that I've got your attention, would you all like me to give you the solution to this problem?"

"Go ahead, Wes," Samson encouraged him.

"There's a little known spell that can temporarily shroud a vampire's aura so that no other preternatural creature can see it, making the vampire appear human. It doesn't last long. And it doesn't change anything in terms of the vampire's abilities."

The vampires in the room exchanged doubtful looks.

"You sure it works, Wes?" Blake asked.

"You've got my word."

"Good enough for me," Blake agreed.

"How long will the spell last?" Samson asked.

Wes pulled up one shoulder. "Half an hour to an hour. Hard to tell. But if I get a few volunteers, I can test it out before the exchange." He looked around the table. "So?"

Suddenly everybody avoided Wesley's gaze.

"Oh come on, people!" he growled. "It doesn't hurt! What are you: vampires or a bunch of sissies?"

"Try it out on me," Samson offered.

"Me too," Haven said.

Wes nodded. "Then we're all set." He turned to Samson. "And who's going to play Katie's role?"

There was a knock at the door. Samson went to open it.

A beautiful curvy woman stood there, long dark hair falling over her shoulders, long dark lashes framing her grey eyes. "I came as quickly as I could," she said in a soft British accent.

"Come in, Roxanne." Samson ushered her inside and closed the door behind her. Then he turned to the people in the room. "Most of you already know Roxanne. She started with us shortly after we opened Mission HQ. First in our V-Lounge, but she joined our bodyguard training program ten years ago, and has been working on various assignments since. I think she's perfect for this."

Katie noticed how Luther ran his eyes over Roxanne's body, not in a lecherous, lusting way, but in the kind of way a discerning buyer did when examining a product he wanted to purchase. Then his eyes darted back to Katie to compare.

"And the eyes?" Luther asked.

"Colored contact lenses, nothing easier than that," Samson said quickly.

Katie walked up to her. "Have they told you what they want you to do?"

Roxanne nodded. "Samson explained briefly when he called me."

Katie turned to the Scanguards boss. "Have you given her a choice about this?" She didn't want anybody to be forced into this. It was a dangerous undertaking.

She felt Roxanne's hand on her shoulder. "I volunteered."

Katie nodded slowly, relieved on one hand, scared on the other.

"Don't worry. I'm trained for this." She bent closer to Katie, and lowered her voice. "I'm better than most of the guys in this room. Just don't tell them. It'll only ruffle their feathers, then they'll start taking their dicks out to prove who's got a bigger one." She chuckled softly. "Boys."

Involuntarily, Katie had to smile. "Thank you, Roxanne."

"Well, let's get this show on the road then," Roxanne said out loud. "Who's going to help me slip into Katie's role?"

Wes grinned from one ear to the other. "Oh, that would be me." And by the looks of it, he would see to it personally that every detail about Roxanne's appearance was perfect.

"Well, well, the witch. Guess it's my lucky day," Roxanne answered dryly.

39

Luther looked over his shoulder and peered into the dark, while Katie unlocked the front door to her house. As suggested by Blake, he'd parked the car in front of the house instead of the garage so that anybody watching them would see him and Katie enter the house.

He couldn't see anybody, but it didn't mean they were alone. While the man walking his dog was clearly human and minding his own business, there were plenty of places a vampire could hide without being seen. Buena Vista Park across the street from Katie's Victorian home was located on one of the many small hills in San Francisco. It provided many such places among its heavily wooded terrain and the many view points along the path that wound its way up to the top where visitors were rewarded with a gorgeous view of the city.

When Katie pushed the door open and flipped the light switch upon entering, Luther turned his back on the park and followed her inside. He closed and locked the door behind her.

"Switch on the lights in the living room," he instructed. "Make sure you can be seen in front of the windows, before you pull the curtains shut."

"I understand."

Luther was almost certain that Forrester was watching the house. It was therefore of vital importance that he only saw Katie and Luther enter and later exit the house together.

Katie walked into the well-lit living room with the tall bay windows, crossing in front of them slowly, before pulling the curtains closed. She did the same with the curtains on the next window, until all curtains in the room were drawn.

Luther followed her into the dining room, where he helped her close the curtains. Within minutes, all curtains on the first floor were drawn and nobody from the street could look into the house anymore.

The blinds on the upper floor had already been closed.

"Ready?" Luther asked, exchanging a look with Katie.

"Ready," she answered.

He opened the door to the garage. "Wesley, we're ready for you."

Katie's brother appeared on the stairs a moment later, Roxanne on his heels. "We're here."

"Did anybody see you?" Luther asked, stepping aside to let the two enter the foyer.

"We went through the gardens in the back. We entered through a tradesmen entrance of one of the houses on the street parallel to here. Nobody saw us, but if anybody did, they wouldn't have been able to figure out where we were heading. The gardens are so overgrown we had plenty of cover. We're safe."

Luther nodded, satisfied with Wesley's explanation. He looked at Roxanne. "Thank you for doing this. I know the risk you're taking."

"It'll be my pleasure. I love kicking guys in the nuts." She tossed a sideways glance at Wes.

"Ouch," Wes commented, mock flinching. "Wouldn't want to be on your bad side."

"Well, then we understand each other, don't we?"

Luther turned away, not wanting to know what undercurrent was flowing between the vampire female and the witch. None of his business.

"Shall we start getting you ready?" Katie asked from beside him.

"Lead the way," Roxanne said.

Katie headed for the stairs and Roxanne followed her. When Wesley made a motion to head in the same direction, Roxanne pivoted and slammed her palm onto his chest, stopping him.

"We won't need you for this part," she said sweetly, but firmly.

"Uh."

Roxanne narrowed her eyes.

"Wes, why don't you come into the living room with me?" Luther asked, intent on diffusing the situation.

"Sure." Wes smiled just as sweetly at Roxanne as she had smiled at him. "Call me if you need help with a zipper or something."

"Wes, really?" Katie asked from the stairs, a twinge of annoyance in her voice.

Her brother only shrugged, then turned and marched into the living room. Luther waited until the two women had disappeared upstairs before he followed Wesley.

"Quite a stunner, that Roxanne, huh?" Wes asked.

"You do know that I can't answer that, right?"

"Because you're with my sister?"

"Something like that." Luther let himself sink into the sofa cushions.

"So what's gonna happen?"

"What do you mean?"

"I mean between you and my sister."

"You're gonna have to ask her that," Luther deflected.

"You said at HQ you came back to atone. What happens afterward?"

"I'll be leaving. I never intended to stay."

"And Katie, does she know?"

"I never lied to her about my intentions."

"And she's okay with that?"

It was a question Luther had asked himself, but didn't have an answer to. Was Katie truly okay with their arrangement? Had she really accepted that he would be gone soon, never to return?

"And how about you, then?" Wes continued. "Are you okay with that?"

"Why wouldn't I be?"

"Because of the way you look at her."

Luther scoffed. "Listen, Wes, I like you. So why don't you quit while you're ahead?"

"Just like I thought." Wes pivoted and walked to the fireplace, looking into the ashes. "She's been alone for far too long. I worry about her sometimes. It's not like she can date a normal guy. Her life revolves around her family and Scanguards. It's not something you can easily bring an outsider into. She needs somebody who knows what this life is like. And as a witch without powers she needs protection."

"Your sister is capable of taking care of herself."

Even as he said it, Luther knew he wanted to be the one to protect her. But there were issues he couldn't simply pretend to overlook. Katie deserved somebody who could fully commit to her, and given his past, he couldn't make such a commitment. It would only end in heartache. And he didn't want to hurt Katie like he'd hurt Vivian. He liked Katie. No, that wasn't even the right word. He cared about her more than he thought was possible in such a short time. He wanted her to find happiness. But he didn't believe that she could find it with him.

"So this is it then. You swoop into her life, break her heart, and then just disappear again," Wes said, pulling him out of his thoughts.

"I didn't break her heart, Wesley." *Not yet, anyway*, he added in his mind. But if he stayed, he would. Because then Katie would grow attached to him and he to her. Already now their physical connection was so strong Luther had a hard time imagining ever wanting to be with anybody else. If he let this go on, he would fall so deeply under her spell that he would never be able to extricate himself from it.

Wesley grunted.

Luther tossed him an annoyed look. "This conversation is over."

Wesley didn't reply. Instead he paced in front of the windows, brooding. Luther decided to change the subject, because the witch had gotten too close, whirled up too many thoughts Luther had tried to push back.

"Have you heard back from Samson and Haven yet on how long their vampire aura is staying cloaked?"

Wes looked back at him. "Blake called a little earlier. It lasted about forty-five minutes with Samson, and about forty with Haven. Since Haven is heavier than Samson, I'm thinking size is a factor. Roxanne weighs much less than both of them, so the spell might last even up to an hour. Won't know for sure, and I don't want to test it out on her until it's time."

"Why's that?"

"I don't have any data to tell me whether performing multiple spells within a short time frame might result in a loss of their effectiveness. I'd rather not test it out right now."

"I'm surprised you have such powers at all," Luther said, shoving a hand through his hair. "Katie told me your mother robbed you of all of your witch powers."

Wes nodded tightly. "She did."

And judging by the tone in Wesley's voice, he was still bitter about it.

"But I worked hard at getting some of them back. I'll never be as strong or as powerful as I was meant to be as one of the Power of Three, but I've harnessed a lot of the power my mother stole from me. I spent years learning, practicing." He chuckled suddenly. "Some of the guys at Scanguards can tell you a few stories about my early tries. But I know my craft now. It gives me a purpose."

"A purpose, yeah, don't we all need that?" Luther mused. He'd had a purpose once. He'd worked for Scanguards, protected people, helped the innocent. It had made him feel good about himself. He needed something like this again, something to live for, and something to die for.

"It's good to have direction in life," Wes agreed. "When Haven was a vampire hunter, I was just drifting, always getting in trouble somewhere. He had to bail me out so many times I started wondering when he'd get sick of it and would let me rot. But he never gave up on me."

"It's good to see that you all stick together." And it was good to know that Katie had two brothers she could rely on. Two men who cared about her and whose shoulders she could cry on if she needed to. Even as that thought went through his mind, Luther wanted to be that shoulder. Or better yet, he wanted that Katie would never have to cry again.

"You do care about her, don't you?" Wesley suddenly asked.

Luther met Wesley's intense gaze. "I wish I didn't." And if Wesley could see that, could Katie see it, too? Did she, too, suspect that his feelings for her ran deeper than just a casual physical relationship?

40

Pleased with her work, Katie led Roxanne down to the living room, where Luther and Wesley were waiting.

"Here she is," she said and stretched her arms out like a presenter on a TV show introducing a special guest.

Roxanne stepped into the living room and turned on her own axis. "What do you think?"

Both men looked at her with open mouths and wide eyes.

The transformation was perfect. Roxanne's hair was now styled in the same fashion as Katie's, hanging in soft curls over her shoulders. She wore identical clothes, which thanks to Katie's extensive wardrobe had not been a problem at all. Her closet carried many duplicate outfits, a habit she'd acquired during her time in Hollywood. With two inch heels, Roxanne was now the exact same height as Katie, and a little bit of padding in Roxanne's bra had boosted her cup size from a C to a D.

But the biggest change was visible in Roxanne's face. Colored contacts Blake had quickly sourced from the large vault below Scanguards HQ, which carried everything from fake mustaches to silver bullets, had turned Roxanne's grey eyes into stunning emeralds.

Professional stage make-up had changed the height of her cheekbones and plumped up her lips to make them as full as Katie's. A slightly darker foundation made Roxanne's skin color match Katie's. With a kohl pencil, Katie had redrawn Roxanne's eyebrows and shaped them so they were identical to her own. Roxanne's nose was longer than Katie's, but with the creative use of different powders and blushes, it now appeared shorter.

"Wow." Luther let out a stunned breath. "The resemblance is uncanny."

"Yeah," Wesley added. "That's totally creepy." He looked Roxanne up and down. "You look like Katie. And that's totally weirding me out."

Katie suppressed a smirk. She'd noticed how Wes had looked at Roxanne earlier. Apparently her brother had a crush on the sexy vampire vixen.

"As long as Roxanne doesn't have to talk, I think we'll be fine," Katie said. "I'm afraid we didn't have time to work on her accent."

"I've lived in this country for over three decades. I doubt even a whole semester of elocution lessons would get rid of my accent, dear," Roxanne said.

"I find your accent charming," Wes replied. "Don't ever lose that."

Roxanne didn't verbally reply to Wesley's comment, though her lips lifted into a soft smile. "I guess now the waiting begins."

Luther nodded. "I just checked in with Blake. They haven't heard back from Forrester yet. We still have a few hours until the exchange."

Katie sought Luther's eyes. "Do you, uh, could you, maybe…" She felt awkward trying to ask Luther in front of the others. "There's something…" She motioned to the ceiling, indicating the upper floor.

Finally Luther seemed to understand. "Oh, yes, of course, there's something we'll need to take care of. Uh, excuse us."

As Katie turned she caught Wesley's eye roll. But to his credit, her brother didn't make a snarky comment, though he knew what this was about: she wanted to be alone with Luther.

Because this would be their last time.

Luther didn't speak, didn't even take her hand as they climbed the stairs and walked down the corridor to her bedroom. She entered ahead of him and sensed him following her. When the door snapped shut a moment later, she just stood there in the middle of the room, not moving, not turning around.

She felt his hands on her shoulders, cupping them. His breath at her nape. She shivered.

"Katie," he murmured.

"I don't want to talk. We both know this is goodbye. Don't make it any harder than it is."

"Then tell me what you want."

"Make love to me and pretend I'm the only woman in the world who means anything to you."

Luther sighed. "Oh God, Katie." He molded his chest to her back. "I wish I'd met you twenty-five years ago."

"Let's not look back. I only want to live in this moment." She turned in his arms, facing him.

"Will it be enough?"

She forced a smile. "It'll have to be."

Luther's hand came up to stroke her cheek. "You're everything a man could wish for. Brave, beautiful, and loving."

"But it's not enough, is it?" she asked.

"On the contrary. It's too much. I don't deserve all that."

"Why don't you let me be the judge of that?"

"Because I know how this will end. With me hurting you, hurting both of us."

"History doesn't have to repeat itself."

"What if it does?"

She put a finger over his lips. "I don't want to think about what might happen. I just want to feel."

He acknowledged her demand by blinking his eyes.

Katie let her hands slide to his chest, finding the buttons of his shirt. "I want to remember everything about you." She popped the first button open, then the next. "I want to kiss every inch of your body."

Beneath her palms she felt Luther's heart beat frantically. His Adam's apple bobbed, and a strangled moan came over his lips. Katie opened his shirt and stripped him of it. She ran her fingertips over his scars.

"You're beautiful," she murmured and meant it. His pectorals flexed under her touch, responding to her caresses.

"I'm scarred, baby. There's nothing beautiful about it."

"Beauty is in the eye of the beholder." She brought her lips to his chest and pressed open-mouthed kisses onto his marred skin. "I wish I could take the pain away that you had to endure when you got these scars."

"When you touch me, I don't remember any pain." He sighed and dropped his head back. "I only feel pleasure."

Katie licked over the angry ridges on his skin. Luther smelled of power and pure maleness. He excreted a scent that drew her to him like a moth to the flame. And she didn't care if this flame would burn her, because the pleasure she obtained by being with him made it all worth it.

She ran her hands down his torso, until she reached his pants. Luther's next inhale was audible, and she felt him tense under her hands. Eager to explore him, she opened the button of his pants and slid the zipper down. Slowly, she pushed his pants down to his ankles.

Her eyes fell on his groin. Underneath the boxer briefs a large bulge was visible. It stretched the black fabric to capacity. Licking her lips, she placed her palm over it. Heat suffused her hand, and his cock jerked against it as if it wanted to leap into her hand.

Luther groaned.

She squeezed his hard flesh briefly, then hooked her thumbs into the waistband and pulled his boxer briefs down, letting them drop to his feet. His cock sprang free, curving up against his belly. His balls pulled up tightly. For the first time she could truly admire him. The times before he'd never given her a chance to look at him for long, taking her so quickly that she didn't have time to look her fill. She made up for it now.

Thick purple veins wound around his shaft, adding to its thickness. The root sat in a thick nest of dark hair. Moisture leaked from the soft tip of his cock, making the mushroomed head glisten.

Katie reached for him, wrapping her hand around his steely length.

Luther hissed out a breath. "Fuck, baby."

"I'm gonna lick you now and take you into my mouth," she told him.

With one hand he cupped her cheek, pulling her face closer and dropping his forehead to hers. "You do know that if you do that, I'm going to lose control, don't you?"

"I figured as much."

"Are you prepared for what I'll do when that happens?"

"Are you?" she challenged. Because she was ready for his bite, ready for the ecstasy he promised.

"What if I can't stop?"

"You stopped before."

He shook his head. "Because I knew I would have you again. But tonight—"

"Just pretend this is not the last time."

Katie made a motion to drop to her knees, but Luther stopped her. "Wait."

She gave him a questioning look.

"Take off your clothes."

While Luther rid himself of his shoes and stepped out of his pants and boxer briefs, Katie pulled her top over her head. When she reached for the front clasp of her bra, he gripped her hand.

"Leave your bra and your panties on." He ran a lusting look over her. "Goddamn, woman, what you do to me…"

She unzipped her pants and shimmied out of them, kicking off her shoes in the process. Finally, wearing only her black lace bra and matching bikini panties, she dropped to her knees in front of him. She felt sexy and desirable, kneeling in front of him like this, hearing him breathe heavily as if he were running a marathon.

She reached for his cock, brushing her fingers over the underside of it and back again.

"Fuck!" Luther hissed.

She scooted closer, bringing her mouth to the tip of his swollen shaft. She darted out her tongue and licked over the velvet-soft head, gathering up the moisture with her tongue. When she swallowed his taste, her nipples hardened, chafing against her bra, and her clit throbbed uncontrollably.

She felt Luther's hand on her head then, combing through her hair, caressing her scalp tenderly. "Oh, baby."

Again she licked over the head of his cock, leisurely, so she could catalogue its texture and shape, burning it into her memory. She swirled her tongue underneath the rim of his cockhead, eliciting a loud moan from Luther and causing him to tighten his fingers around the back of her head. But he didn't force her, didn't pull her head toward him.

Instead, Katie was the one to wrap her lips around him, slowly swallowing the tip of his cock and sliding down on his hard rod until she could go no farther. He was only halfway inside her mouth, but it was all she could take. He was too big.

Katie took a breath through her nose and relaxed her jaw muscles, then wrapped one hand around his root and withdrew gently, her lips puckered around his hard flesh, her tongue sliding along its underside. Her other hand lay braced on his thigh. A thigh she felt trembling now.

"Oh, Katie!" he cried out. "You're killing me."

She let him slip from her mouth, only to pull him back into it, sucking harder this time, while her hand moved up and down his erection in sync with her sucking motion. There was something about his taste that made her want more. She felt him starting to thrust, slowly at first, but beneath her hands she sensed the vampire wanting to burst to the surface. Every time she slid down on him, she felt him shudder, and every time she pulled back and withdrew, his hips flexed and he demanded more.

He was putty in her hands, surrendering to her mouth, her lips, her tongue. And for the first time in her life she knew what it was like to be powerful. To be strong. Luther gave her that power. He made her whole again. As if his cock in her mouth was the instrument that infused her with strength.

Katie licked him more feverishly now, eager for his surrender. She brought her second hand to his balls, cupped him, and felt another shudder travel through his body. His cock jerked in her mouth, and anticipation made her own body tremble.

"Stop!" Luther cried out and wrenched himself from her mouth.

He pulled her up by her elbows, and an instant later she found herself bent over the chaise longue, her torso pressed into the cushions, her ass pointing in the air. Luther ripped her panties off, tearing the thin material into shreds.

"Now you've done it, Katie!" he ground out. "Shouldn't have sucked me like that."

He sounded different now, his voice raspier, his breathing choppy.

"You didn't like it?" she teased, though she knew the answer to her question.

Luther plunged into her from behind, seating himself in her channel, before he answered, "You know as well as I do how much I liked your mouth around my cock."

But she barely heard his words, because his hard cock stretching her robbed her nearly of all her senses. "You feel good, Luther, so good."

He gripped her hips firmly and pulled her toward him, slamming his cock forward at the same time, doubling the impact. All air rushed from her lungs, making her gasp.

"See, Katie? Do you see now what you're doing to me?"

But she couldn't answer, because he began to fuck her fast and furious, plunging deep then withdrawing, his hands on her hips imprisoning her so she couldn't move. Couldn't escape his unrelenting cock. He stretched her to capacity, his erection touching places inside her that sent hot bolts of pleasure through her body. Her breasts were still imprisoned in her bra and rubbed against the cushions with every thrust Luther delivered. Her nipples were hard peaks begging for relief.

She collected all her strength and pushed herself up so she could bring one hand to the front clasp of her bra. With difficulty she managed to open it just as Luther plunged deeper into her, making her land back in the cushions. On his next withdrawal she succeeded in freeing her breasts from the cups and shucking the bra.

"Fuck, Katie!" he called out and pulled out of her.

"No!" she protested. "Don't stop!"

He gripped her legs and turned her onto her back, his eyes wild, his fangs extended. His gaze landed on her naked breasts, and she could see him salivate.

"Fuck me, Luther, please!" she begged.

He rolled over her and plunged his cock back into her. Katie let out a contented sigh, relieved that he filled her again. Without him, she'd felt empty.

Luther was riding her hard and fast. She'd never known that such wildness could give her such pleasure, but with every hard thrust and every withdrawal Luther was driving her closer to the edge. Her entire body began to tingle. All her nerve endings seemed to awaken with awareness. And inside her a fire began to burn, slowly making its way to the surface.

"Yes, Luther," she chanted, pressing her head into the chaise longue and arching her back, offering him what she knew he desired.

A growl came from him, then his breath caressed her breast and teased her nipple. When she felt the tips of his fangs scrape against her skin, she shivered with pleasure. He drove them into her, causing her a split-second of pain, but it vanished as quickly as it had come, making way for pleasure.

She felt him pull hard, feeding from her. Some of the blood spilled from his mouth, so greedily did he drink from her. She felt it trickle down her breast. But Luther didn't seem to notice. He continued to drink, while farther below, his hips thrust back and forth.

Katie let herself go. Luther feeding from her lulled her into a trance, while his pistoning cock sent waves of pleasure through her body. Her clit throbbed. Then her body erupted in a symphony of ecstasy. She heard nothing but her own heartbeat and Luther's moans. Her sex spasmed and she felt Luther respond in kind. His cock jerked inside her. Then she felt it: his hot semen filling her as he continued to move inside her. Slower now, but no less tantalizing.

She felt cool air waft against her breast, then a hot tongue lick over it. Katie lazily opened her eyes and watched Luther lift his head from her breast and retract his fangs. His eyes were still glowing red, but the moment he met her gaze they turned back to their rich brown color.

Katie opened her mouth to speak, but no words came over her lips, because the only words she wanted to say were ones he didn't want to hear. Instead she lifted her hand and ran it through his hair. It was damp from his sweat.

He held her gaze, but he, too, was silent. After an eternity, he rolled off her and stood.

She looked up at him, drinking in his perfect male form for the last time, before he turned his back to her and began to get dressed.

I love you, she mouthed silently behind his back and pushed back the tears that threatened to expose her true feelings.

41

Luther looked over his shoulder at Katie, who stood in the hallway, watching him and Roxanne getting ready to leave.

"Give me a moment," he said to Roxanne and crossed the distance between him and Katie with four long strides.

Wesley retreated into the living room, giving them privacy.

Luther put a finger under Katie's chin and tilted her face up. There was so much he wanted to say to her, but words failed him, just like they'd failed him when they'd made love. He'd sensed it then, in fact had felt it growing inside him over the last few days and nights. The feeling that he couldn't live without her. That she was meant for him. That he was meant for her. He didn't want to acknowledge it, because it was impossible for something like that to happen to him. And to happen so fast.

And why should it? Most vampires only got one chance at finding their mate. Why would he of all people get a second one, when he knew he didn't deserve it? Or was it all an illusion that would be ripped from his hands the minute he grabbed for it? He'd been down that road once before with Vivian. And he was frightened to take that same path again. What if it led him to the same horrible end? So he could be punished once more.

"Katie," he murmured, unable to turn his feelings into words.

Tears rimmed her emerald eyes. Her breath blew against his face, so sweet, so tempting that it nearly tore his heart in two.

He pulled her into his arms and brought his mouth to her ear. "I can't promise you anything, but I want you to know that what's between us means something to me." He took her hand and pressed it against the place where his heart beat out of control. "You are in here."

She sniffled. "Luther," she choked out.

He pressed a kiss to her forehead, then turned quickly, worried that he wouldn't be able to leave if he saw her cry. With long steps he walked to where Roxanne stood. He waited for a moment until he heard Katie join her brother in the living room. Then he opened the door and took Roxanne's hand to lead her outside into the dark.

Pretending to be as affectionate with Roxanne as he'd been with Katie was hard and felt unnatural, but in case they were being watched, he did it nevertheless. He was glad when they were finally sitting in Katie's Audi and driving toward the waterfront to meet up with Blake's team.

~ ~ ~

Luther pulled up at the abandoned pier and killed the engine. "Showtime."

Roxanne nodded. "Let's do this."

They exited the car. Blake was already waiting for them. Luther looked around. He saw nobody else.

"Where is everybody?" Luther asked as Roxanne stopped next to him.

"The team is in place." Blake motioned toward the water. "The exchange will take place on Alcatraz. It's not exactly the kind of place we were counting on. We had to scramble to set everything up."

"But isn't Alcatraz open for tours?"

"The last night tour would have finished at nine thirty and normally the daytime staff doesn't arrive till six am, but we're in luck: Alcatraz is closed over the Christmas break. We won't have any issues with civilians." He paused for a moment. "Forrester wants you to deliver Katie. He asked for you by name."

Luther's forehead furrowed. "He doesn't know me. How can he ask for me by name?"

"I can only assume that he's been watching us all this time and figured out that you have a connection to Katie. Or maybe he sees you as less of a threat than somebody from Scanguards. I'm not sure. In any case, we'll have your back." Blake pointed to a small motorboat that was docked a few yards away from them. "Take the boat to the main dock on Alcatraz. Once you get there, he'll turn on lights along the ground that will lead you to the location where the exchange will take place."

"And then?"

"That's all we have. Don't worry, we'll be there to swoop in as soon as he reveals himself. Your job is to secure Isabelle." Blake addressed Roxanne, "You know what to do. Keep your cover for as long as you can so you can get close to him. You need to distract him from Isabelle. Understood?"

Roxanne nodded.

"I can't give you any weapons. We must assume that he will be able to detect if you're armed. We can't risk it. It has to look like we're ready to do the exchange."

"Not a problem."

"But I have one thing for you." Blake dug into his pocket and pulled out a tiny item that looked like a button. "A camera." He reached for Luther's jacket and affixed the camera to the lapel. "That way we can see what you see. It'll help us get into the right position. It doubles as a GPS so we'll have an exact location on you."

Luther glanced at the small item. It blended in with the color of his jacket, and if he didn't know it was there, he wouldn't have been able to detect it. "Guess we're ready. Keys?"

Blake handed him the keys for the boat. "Good luck!"

Luther hopped into the boat and helped Roxanne into it. It had been a while since he'd been on a motorboat, but he still remembered how to steer one. He put the key in the ignition and started the engine. Blake untied them from the dock and tossed the rope into the boat.

In the distance, Alcatraz Island stood like a beacon in the middle of San Francisco Bay. Its main building, the cell block, which tourists visited during opening hours, was lit from the outside by large spot lights. The rest of the island, however, lay in total darkness. Abandoned buildings stood like eerie reminders of what this island had once housed: dangerous criminals.

A wooden water tower peeked out on one side of the island, a lighthouse overlooking it all. There was some vegetation on Alcatraz, a few trees and bushes near the dock where the tourists started their tour, but not much on the far side of the island.

Luther remembered a paved walkway spanning the whole island, as well as heaps of old concrete blocks that were dumped on the back end.

Luther gunned the engine and pushed the boat to its limit until he saw the dock appear in front of him. He throttled the engine down and pulled up alongside it. Roxanne threw the line out, catching one of the many hooks and tied the boat up. Luther turned the engine off and stepped onto the dock. He turned back to Roxanne and offered her his hand to help her out of the boat.

"Ready?" he asked.

She nodded, remaining silent so she wouldn't give herself away by her accent.

When they reached the end of the dock, a string of lights sitting low on the ground turned on. He pointed to it. "This way."

Luther jumped over a low railing and lifted Roxanne over it after him. She could have easily jumped herself, but they had to maintain Roxanne's cover and pretend she was human, and he her gallant lover. It was evident that Forrester was watching them. He'd switched the guiding lights on the moment they'd reached the end of the dock.

Luther glanced around as he followed the lights with Roxanne by his side. They were on a path leading not toward the cell block but away from it. They were on the part of the island that was facing away from San Francisco.

As they walked, passing a large building on their left, more lights appeared on the path ahead of them. He glanced behind him and noticed that some of the lights he was following had already extinguished. Motion-activated lamps, he assumed. He had to hand it to Forrester. He was sophisticated and had obviously meticulously planned this exchange, whereas Scanguards had only had an hour or two to come up with any countermeasures. Luther could only hope that his old friends could improvise well and outwit their opponent.

He gave Roxanne a sideways glance. He still couldn't see her vampire aura, and to him she looked entirely human. Wesley's spell was working. And he hoped that Wes was right about the length of time the spell would cloud Roxanne's aura and disguise the fact that she was a vampire. Her life depended on it. His and Isabelle's, too.

They passed the ruins of the old officer's club on their right. The water tower came into full view ahead, hovering over them to the left of the path. The old power plant appeared on the right.

Luther kept his eyes and ears open. Apart from the waves breaking on the rocks that surrounded the island and gave it its nickname—the Rock—there were no sounds. A steady cool breeze blew from the northeast, muffling even their footsteps.

The entire setting gave him the creeps. Obviously Forrester was a psycho, choosing a place like Alcatraz. A cold shiver ran down his spine. He didn't like this place, and didn't understand why Forrester had chosen it. One could reach the island only by water, which made an escape from it difficult. How was Forrester planning to get off the island with Katie (or rather Roxanne), once he had her? It made no sense. Even if he had a boat waiting for him, he had to assume that Scanguards would be easily able to track his movements on the water and follow him. Forrester was a sitting duck.

Roxanne's hand on his forearm pulled him from his musings. "There," she whispered and pointed to a spot in the distance.

He saw her immediately. A young woman dressed in a red period dress stood on a grassy, elevated area about fifty yards past the water tower, diagonally across from the old power plant and dilapidated storehouse. She was gagged and blindfolded. Behind her was a pile of rubble and from what Luther could see, she appeared to be chained to one of the rocks. She stood still, but even from the distance, he could see her chest moving up and down. She was breathing.

He exchanged a quick look with Roxanne, his heart pounding. "That Isabelle?"

Roxanne nodded.

"Good."

"Welcome!" The male voice was distorted, coming from a loudspeaker somewhere from the right.

Luther's gaze shot in the direction of the storehouse. He focused on the openings that had once held windows, but the glass had long been removed. Now the wind blew through the empty building, creating eerie sounds and shadows.

"Send Katie closer," the voice demanded. "To the storehouse."

Luther nodded to Roxanne, and she slowly walked in the direction of the voice.

"Stop!"

Roxanne stopped in her tracks. Luther held his breath, his eyes darting back and forth from Roxanne to Isabelle. He noticed Isabelle pull up her shoulders in fear. From one of the window openings, Luther perceived a movement, something reflecting for a brief moment. A mirror? Glass? He couldn't be sure.

The sound of the ocean waves and the wind was louder now. It seemed to hum a rhythmic melody.

"Did you really think I'd fall for your deception?" the voice suddenly said.

Luther instantly shot Roxanne a look, but to his surprise her vampire aura was still cloaked. She still looked human. How did Forrester realize that she wasn't Katie? From his hiding place in the storeroom he shouldn't be able to tell. Only when standing within a few feet of Roxanne would he be able to realize that she wasn't Katie.

"You're gonna pay for this!" the voice warned.

Shit!

Time for Plan B.

42

The loud sound echoed against the old buildings. Luther shot a look to Forrester's hiding place, but he couldn't see anything, only a movement behind one of the windows. A shadow shifting. Nothing more. Had he shot at them? Shit!

Luther sprinted toward Isabelle, jumping over a low chain link fence that separated him from the young hybrid, when he heard a loud whooshing sound from above. He glanced up and saw a black helicopter swoop down onto the path, cutting him off from Roxanne and in effect creating a barrier between Isabelle and Forrester's hiding place. The wind generated by the rotor blades made Luther sway for a moment, but he continued barreling toward Isabelle.

"Isabelle!" he called out to her, hoping she could hear him over the noise of the helicopter. "Don't be afraid! I'm working for your father."

He saw how she jerked her head in his direction, her body trembling. The sight reminded him of what he'd done to her mother twenty years earlier. With silver handcuffs he'd tied Delilah to a pole and gagged her, though he hadn't blindfolded her. He'd rigged the podium where she and Nina were standing to blow up once a motion sensor was triggered.

Heart pounding, Luther stopped dead in his tracks. What if Forrester had had the same idea? What if he'd set motion sensors that would trigger the countdown to a bomb as soon as somebody got close enough to Isabelle? Forrester had used motion sensors to switch on the lights to guide him to this location, why not use them to blow up Isabelle the moment somebody approached her? Why else would he leave her out here, seemingly easy to reach, rather than keep her with him in the storehouse and only release her once he had what he wanted?

Shit!

"Stay calm, Isabelle!" he instructed her, shouting over the noise. "I'll have to check your surroundings first."

She appeared to nod though he couldn't tell for sure. Maybe she was trembling and shivering too much, fear making her body shake. A twenty-year old girl, even a hybrid, had to be scared, standing in the middle of a commotion, which she couldn't even see. The noise was deafening now. Luther glanced over his shoulder. Several dark figures had descended from the helicopter and were charging toward the storehouse. Others were coming from the rocks to the left of the building, from a path leading up from the water. He focused his eyes on them. Frogmen? As they came closer, Luther realized that they were wearing wetsuits and had swum to the island, most likely from a boat not too far from the shore. They were surrounding the building now.

Luther turned back to Isabelle. About twenty yards separated them. He scanned the ground with his eyes, carefully zooming in on every shadow and every rock or patch of unevenness he saw, making sure it wasn't an electronic device. Slowly he crept closer.

"I'm almost there, honey," he said, trying to reassure her. "Nod if you're uninjured."

She nodded instantly.

He sighed in relief and took another step closer, continuously scanning the ground. "Isabelle, did you hear him setting any charges around you?"

She hesitated, but then slowly shook her head.

Gunfire erupted behind him, making him swivel. Bullets seemed to be flying, and men shouted orders and instructions. But the helicopter blocked most of Luther's view. Nevertheless he saw the Scanguards men storming the storehouse.

"Bomb!" somebody suddenly screamed above the noise.

"Fuck!" Luther cursed and charged toward Isabelle.

It was now or never. If there was a bomb, he didn't have the luxury of scanning Isabelle's surroundings for any motion detectors. He had to act.

From the corner of his eye, he saw flashes ignite the darkness, but he didn't stop to look what it was.

"I'm here, Isabelle! I've got you!"

He reached her and pulled the gag from her mouth, then jumped behind her.

"Help me, please get me out of here!" she choked out.

Luther examined her ties. She was chained to the remnants of a fence, a metal post. The blisters on her wrists confirmed that the chain Forrester had used to tie her up was silver, the only metal that was toxic to a vampire, so toxic that no vampire could break a silver chain with his hands, no matter how thin.

"Stay still, I'm gonna break the chain, okay?" He searched the hovel of rubble behind her and found what he was looking for: a piece of metal rod slim enough to insert into one of the links of the heavy silver chain. As long as he didn't have to touch the silver himself, the metal rod would do the work for him.

"Hold still, Isabelle," he instructed her and slid the rod into position. He twisted it, and the link broke, separating the chain. Snatching the bow of her dress and wrapping his hand with it, he grabbed one end of the chain and unwound it from Isabelle's wrists. Even through the fabric he felt the silver burn him, but he was able to untie her completely.

Isabelle pulled her arms forward. "Thank you!" She reached for her face, pulling her blindfold off. Her eyes fell on the helicopter and the firefight beyond it. "Oh my God!"

An explosion rocked the island. Instinctively, Luther threw himself over Isabelle, tumbling to the ground with her. He felt her breathe hard underneath him, but he knew she wasn't hurt.

Listening for the sounds coming from the storehouse where Forrester had been hiding, Luther heard voices he recognized. He realized now why. The helicopter's blades weren't turning anymore. The pilot had switched off the engine. Suddenly it was quiet.

Blake's voice drifted to him. "He's dead. We got him."

Relieved, Luther lifted himself off Isabelle and helped her up. "Blake, we're here. I've got Isabelle. She's fine."

Several people came running toward them. Samson was the first to reach them. He only had eyes for his daughter.

"Daddy!" Isabelle cried out and threw herself into his arms. "You came!"

Samson pressed her to his chest and stroked her hair. "Of course, sweetheart." Then he turned his head and looked at Luther. "Thank you, Luther. I owe you so much."

Luther shook his head. "We're even now." With a nod at Isabelle, he walked toward the storehouse.

Blake met him halfway. "Good job."

Luther motioned to the structure the explosion had originated from. "What happened there?"

"He blew himself up when we charged the building. Guess he didn't want to be taken alive," Blake replied and walked alongside him.

Luther shook his head. "I don't get it. He put himself in a position he couldn't escape from."

"Maybe he wasn't as smart as we assumed after all."

Several men from Scanguards were already extinguishing the flames. Luther pointed at the storehouse. "Can't have been a very large explosion."

"Didn't even blow out any of the walls," Blake confirmed. "No collateral damage. None of us got hit."

"In there?" Luther motioned to the door and entered upon Blake's nod. He glanced around and noticed a spot close to a window where some debris pointed to an explosion. "Suicide vest?"

Blake came closer. "Kind of looks like it, doesn't it?"

Though there were no remains of the vampire, there was other evidence: pieces of shiny metal, fabric, and wood. Even what looked like part of a radio or a speaker.

"You sure he was here and didn't just blow up a doll?"

"Positive. We got a visual on him before we went in. It matched the photo we had of him. It was definitely Forrester. You can see for yourself when we get back to HQ. We got it all recorded on our personal cams and were feeding it back to Thomas. He confirmed via the comm system that he's our guy. No doubt about it."

"Hmm." Luther rubbed his chin. Something was bothering him. "He didn't make any attempt to harm Isabelle. Why didn't he keep her with him in here until he knew he had Katie? Why tie her up out there, where we could get between him and Isabelle. He was practically giving up his bargaining chip before he even had a chance at getting Katie."

"Blake," a man said from the door. Luther recognized him as John. He was dressed in a wet suit, his hair wet.

Blake pivoted. "Yeah?"

"My team is ready to leave. Clean up outside is done. I radioed for the boat. It's pulling up alongside the power plant. Are we good to take care of the inside now?"

Blake nodded. "Go ahead. I've seen everything I needed to see."

John waved to somebody outside, while Blake stepped out. Luther followed him, tossing a last glance at the remains on the ground. A few links of a chain sparkled silver for an instant when the light from the helicopter fell onto it.

Blake was waiting outside for him. "You can ride back in the helicopter with us. I think Samson will want that." He waved Roxanne closer. "Nice work, Roxanne. Are you okay with taking the small motorboat back? One of John's team can ride with you."

Roxanne nodded. "Sure. No problem."

Luther stretched his hand out to her. "Thanks for everything, Roxanne."

She smiled and shook his hand. "My pleasure."

Blake patted him on the shoulder. "Let's go back to HQ. My guys will finish the cleanup and make sure we don't leave any evidence behind."

By the time Luther got into the helicopter ahead of Blake, Samson and his daughter were already sitting in it. The pilot had switched on the engine and the rotor blades were turning, picking up speed.

Luther took the seat opposite Samson.

Blake slid in next to him, then gave the pilot a sign. "Back to HQ."

It was too loud to talk in the chopper, and Luther was glad for it. He looked out through the window, looking back at the location Forrester had picked for the exchange. His forehead furrowed. It was an odd stage he'd set for himself. He'd basically set himself up for failure by choosing a spot he could neither defend nor escape from. It seemed like a suicide mission.

"Something bothering you?" Samson suddenly said from across the aisle.

Slowly Luther turned his face to him. "Lots of things. It was too easy." He glanced at Isabelle, who pressed herself to her father, seeking comfort in his arms. "No offense, Isabelle, I know it must have been horrendous for you, but that—" He pointed down to the island. "—was a clusterfuck by Forrester. He had no way out. And no way to fight us. If I'd try to pull something like that off, I sure wouldn't have chosen a place where I was totally exposed."

"And as we all know, you're speaking from experience." Samson's voice remained even, though his jaw seemed to tighten.

"Listen, Samson, I just want to make sure that what happened down there was real." He turned to Blake. "You said you piped back the video feed to HQ?"

"We did."

"With your permission, Samson, I'd like to have a look at that. I want to see Forrester with my own eyes. Peace of mind, you know."

After a few seconds, Samson nodded. "Fine. Blake will debrief the team anyway. You can join them and see for yourself that it was Forrester." He smiled at his daughter and pressed a kiss on the top of her head. "He won't hurt you anymore, Isa."

"I can't wait to see Mom."

"She already knows you're safe. She can't wait to hold you in her arms. She's meeting us at headquarters."

43

Luther followed Blake into the situation room, where they were greeted with cheers by Scanguards' inner circle. Blake was instantly surrounded by several young hybrids, Gabriel, Amaury, and Zane as well as a few other vampires.

Several monitors graced one wall, replaying different parts of tonight's rescue mission.

"Well done!" Thomas said, nodding at Luther.

Eddie walked up to Luther, slapping him on the shoulder. "It all went smoothly. Thanks for helping us."

"Does Katie know yet?"

Eddie nodded. "We called her the moment we knew Forrester was dead and Isabelle safe. She's very relieved."

"Good." He looked past Eddie. "Are those all the recordings you have from the mission?"

Thomas joined them. "Yes, why?"

"Can you show me the beginning? I want to see Forrester."

Thomas raised an eyebrow, but motioned him to the console that controlled the monitors. Eddie followed them.

"Is there a problem?" Thomas asked quietly.

"I'm not sure. I just want to make sure it's him. From where I was I couldn't see him."

Eddie nodded. "I know. We watched your movements via your camera." He pointed to Luther's jacket, reminding him that he was still wearing the hidden camera.

Thomas pressed a few buttons and pointed to one of the monitors. "I'll feed everything we have that shows Forrester's position into here."

Luther lifted his head and examined the images on the screen. The action started when the helicopter touched down and somebody jumped from it, either Blake or Samson. Moments later the frogmen appeared from the other side and were caught in Blake's camera angle. Then the shooting started. One camera zoomed in on the window. The light from the helicopter hit just right, suddenly illuminating a face. Forrester. Luther recognized him from the picture Thomas had distributed before the mission. There was no doubt.

Luther watched as Forrester opened his mouth as if to scream.

"When he started shooting, we had to act quickly," he heard Blake say to his colleagues.

Luther spun around. "Are you sure Forrester shot at you?"

Blake nodded. "Yeah, we heard the shots. Wasn't one of our guys. They had strict orders not to shoot until I gave the okay."

"That's impossible." Luther pointed back to the monitor. "Where's his gun?"

For a moment Blake said nothing.

"Did your guys remove Forrester's gun before I walked into the building?" Luther asked.

"No. Nobody touched anything until after you and I left."

"Then how could he have shot at you when there was no gun? The explosion wasn't strong enough to pulverize his weapon. Hell, I saw parts of a radio and some metal bits. But nothing that looked like a gun."

Blake ran a hand through his hair. "Fuck!"

Luther turned back to the monitor, staring at it again. He felt the other vampires in the room come closer, also looking at the monitor.

"Play it again from where we see Forrester's face."

Thomas followed his request and replayed the image.

"It looks like he's screaming," Eddie said next to him.

Luther looked over his shoulder at Blake. "Did you hear him scream?"

"No. Not a sound. And we were close enough. We would have heard him."

"Thomas, can you zoom in on his mouth?"

Luther focused his eyes on Forrester's mouth as Thomas increased the image by two hundred percent. That's when he saw it.

"Oh shit!" Luther slammed a fist on the desk. "You know what this is?" He pointed to the charred looking inside of Forrester's mouth. "Forrester's mouth and throat were burned with a UV ray gun to prevent him from speaking." He pivoted, facing the other men in the room. "Forrester was a patsy."

"But how?" Blake stared at him in disbelief.

"Get Isabelle in here. She can identify her kidnapper," Luther ordered.

Gabriel rushed outside, leaving the door open.

"Thomas, put the photo of Forrester up on another monitor."

Without a word, Thomas executed the command and displayed the picture. Footsteps came closer a moment later and Luther looked to the door. Samson rushed in, followed by Delilah who had her arm around Isabelle. Samson's two hybrid sons were behind them.

"What's going on?" Samson asked, his voice tense.

"I believe Forrester was a scapegoat." Luther looked at Isabelle. "Isabelle, was this the man who kidnapped you?" He pointed to the screen.

Isabelle took a few hesitant steps closer, clutching her mother's hand. Her eyes moved, looking at the picture on the screen. Then she met Luther's gaze. "No. That's not him."

Luther felt as if a vise was tightening around his heart and squeezing all life from it. "Shit!" The wheels in his head began to turn. There had to be a way to figure out who had been using Forrester to lead them on the wrong trail. "Thomas, you said you had a recording of when the kidnapper killed Mendoza and took Isabelle. Let me hear it."

"Give me a sec." Thomas clicked on an icon on the computer, then opened various folders, until finally, he clicked an audio file and turned up the volume for all in the room to hear.

"Here she is."

"That's Mendoza," Thomas said.

Somebody grunted. *"Who the fuck is that? That's not Kimberly Fairfax! What am I paying you good money for?"*

"That's him," Isabelle said, her voice shaking. "That's the man who took me after killing Mendoza."

Luther's heart turned to ice. "Turn it off, Thomas." He stared at the people in the room. "I know him. It's one of the guards from the prison. It's Norris."

No wonder he'd been able to use Forrester. Norris knew everything about him. It all made sense now.

"He would have known about Forrester's obsession with Katie, but I don't think Forrester was the one who wrote the letters. Norris was. He set it all up. Forrester had movie posters with Katie in his cell. Maybe Norris saw her there for the first time and developed his own obsession." Luther ran a shaky hand through his hair. "Norris went on leave the night I was released. He must have hired Mendoza to snatch Katie for him, and then when he realized that Mendoza got Isabelle instead, he changed his plan and grabbed Forrester."

"But why?" Samson asked.

"He knew he needed to do an exchange. And he needed a fall guy for that. So he got Forrester, tied him up and let us believe he was the kidnapper." Luther pointed at the monitor. "I saw something blink silver in the light when I was in the storehouse where Forrester supposedly blew himself up. There were remnants of a speaker or a radio. My guess is that Norris piped all the sounds in remotely via a radio, the gunshots you heard. He must have been watching via a camera. He made us believe that Forrester spoke to us and shot at us. That's why there was no gun. Forrester was a sitting duck. Norris waited for us to get close enough and then blew him up. And so Forrester couldn't warn us, he singed his mouth and throat with UV rays."

Luther had done the same to Bauer in the prison, so he knew it worked.

"Shit!" Samson cursed. "But how did he know that Katie wouldn't be there and we'd be sending a vampire disguised as her?"

"He was counting on it. That's why he gave us so much time to tell us when the exchange would take place: so we would come up with the idea to send in a double." He shot a look at Blake. "Who's with Katie?"

"Wesley," Blake replied. Then he motioned to Eddie. "Send reinforcements to her house immediately. And warn them. Now!"

"I'm going there myself," Luther said and charged toward the door, when he almost ran into Wesley. "What are you doing here?" He looked past him, but he was alone. "Where's Katie?"

Wesley's eyebrows snapped together. "At home, why? I left when we got word that the mission was a success and Forrester was dead."

"Oh fuck!"

"She's not answering her phone," Eddie said from the other end of the room.

Thomas dialed on another phone. "I'm trying her cell."

Luther's blood froze in his veins. For a few seconds there was no sound in the room. Only a faint ringing sound coming through Thomas's cell phone. Then it went to voicemail. A look of regret colored Thomas's eyes as he shook his head.

Luther felt a cold shudder race down his spine. "Oh God no, he's got her. Norris took Katie."

44

For a few seconds, Luther was in shock. He'd failed to protect Katie. And now she was in the hands of a madman.

"Fuck, fuck, fuck!" Wesley cursed.

Gasps and curses flew through the room. Isabelle started to cry.

"Ok, everybody listen up," Blake said loudly. "We've gotta find her." He looked at the clock on the wall. "We have less than one and a half hours until sunrise. We need to find out where he's taking her before the sun comes up or we risk losing them." Blake started to issue orders. "Wes, scry for her. Now!"

"I've still got some hair from her in my office," he mumbled to himself and ran down the hallway.

"Thomas, get us everything you have on this Norris."

Thomas nodded. "Already on it. My team just hacked into the prison authority's computer system. We should have all they have about him in a few moments." He motioned to Eddie and the two started typing away on their computers.

"I've already sent two guys to Katie's house," Amaury confirmed. "They'll call us in case she's still there."

Luther knew it was a long shot, but Scanguards was thorough and couldn't just dismiss the possibility that Katie was asleep and had switched off the ringer on her phone. In his heart though, he knew that Norris had snatched her while all of Scanguards had been occupied on Alcatraz. He would make good on his threats now: to take Katie away.

All of a sudden remembering something, Luther said out loud, "He's sailing into the sunset with her. That's it! The marinas!"

Blake and several others looked at him. "What about the marinas?" Blake asked.

"Norris told the other guards that he was going to leave everybody in his wake. That's a nautical term. And in the letters he talks about sailing into the sunset with Katie. He's gonna be on a boat." He walked to where Thomas and Eddie were sitting. "Can you find out if he has a boat registered to him?"

Eddie looked over his shoulder. "Already on it. Give me a minute."

Luther looked back at Samson and Amaury. "How many marinas are along the Bay?"

"Too many," Samson said instantly. "Sausalito, Larkspur, Oakland, Alameda and a few others on the East and South Bay. There must be around a dozen."

Luther shook his head. "Forget everything but San Francisco. He doesn't have time to cross any of the bridges. He planned this ahead of time. He knew he only had a short window of time to grab Katie. He wouldn't risk having to drive through half the city. What's the closest marina to Katie's house?"

"Thomas?" Samson asked.

"Monitor four," Thomas said.

Luther looked at the screen, where suddenly a map appeared. A red dot was blinking in the Haight Ashbury area: Katie's house. Blue lines flashed from her house, all leading toward the water. Then one line turned bold.

"South Beach, the yacht club behind AT&T Park," Samson said.

"I got a photo of Norris," Thomas announced and projected it on a monitor.

Luther looked at Isabelle. "Do you recognize him?"

Shivering visibly, Isabelle nodded. "That's him."

Eddie swiveled in his chair. "No boats registered in Norris's name. Sorry."

Luther cursed. Nonetheless, he knew his hunch was correct. Norris was going to take Katie on a boat.

Somebody stormed into the room. Luther spun around. It was Wesley.

"I've got an approximate location, but she's still moving."

"Where?" Luther asked frantically.

"On Bryant Street, driving toward the water."

"He's heading for the marina. Let's go. We've gotta reach him before he can leave with the boat." He looked at Samson. "Can we take the helicopter?"

With a regretful sigh Samson shook his head. "The pilot already parked it in the hanger in South San Francisco. We don't have time to bring it back."

"I'm parked out front," Wesley said, already running toward the elevator. "Let's go."

Luther followed him, his heart racing. He had to get to Katie before it was too late. He owed her that. She'd trusted him to keep her safe. And not only that: he *needed* her to be safe. He needed Katie to be alive and happy. He regretted now not having told her how he felt. Regretted having been a coward and not having confessed that without her he was nothing, just an empty shell, because she had crept into his heart and made herself at home there, without him even noticing at first. But once he'd realized it, he'd done nothing to push her away. Instead he'd started craving that feeling she gave him, the feeling of being worthy of love. Katie's love.

"I'm coming with you," Blake called after him, then barked more orders to his team. "Check who's on patrol in that area and send them to the marina at South Beach Park. Then alert our contact at the Coast Guard. And have weapons ready for us in the lobby."

The elevator doors parted and Wes stepped in. Luther was on his heels. Blake came running and jumped in just before the doors closed.

All three exchanged concerned looks.

"Can't you put a protection spell on Katie?" Blake asked Wesley.

Katie's brother shook his head. "Takes too long. I don't have all the things here that I need for that. We don't have that kind of time." Wes hit his hand against the wall. "I shouldn't have left her alone."

Blake grunted. "You couldn't know."

"He fooled us all," Luther said. "But I swear, Norris isn't gonna get away with this. He's not gonna take Katie away from me."

When Blake and Wes stared at him in surprise, Luther realized what he'd said. But he didn't back down from it now. He wasn't going to deny any longer that his heart belonged to Katie.

"I'll kill him."

The elevator stopped and they exited on the lobby level. A vampire was waiting for them, handing them a bag. "Your weapons."

Blake took the bag. "Thanks, Rob."

Luther charged out the door ahead of the other two. He looked over his shoulder at Wes. "Which car?"

Wes pointed to a BMW, clicking his key simultaneously. The lights of a black BMW seven series blinked. "Hop in."

Luther marched toward the car, when two vampires stepped in his path.

"Luther West," one of them addressed him. "You're under arrest."

The other stranger jumped behind him, slammed him over the hood of the BMW, and cuffed his hands behind his back so fast Luther could barely comprehend what was happening to him.

"Shit!" he cursed. "Let go of me!"

"What's going on here?" Blake interrupted.

Luther twisted his head to the side. "Tell these idiots to let me go. I need to get to Katie." He pushed back, trying to get the vampire who'd cuffed him off his back, but the guy was of massive proportions. He knew exactly who these two were: trackers sent by the council to apprehend him.

"Stop struggling, West! Let's go!"

The other tracker addressed Blake, flashing him a badge. "We're from the council. Enforcement Division." He jerked his thumb in Luther's direction. "West broke into the prison and assaulted several guards. We're taking him back to charge him."

"You can't do that!" Blake protested. "We're in the middle of a rescue operation. A woman will die if you don't let him go."

"Nice try," the vampire said.

"He's telling the truth!" Wes shouted and charged at them. "Let him the fuck go, or I'm gonna turn you into a toad!"

"Fucking witch!" was the tracker's reply.

From the corner of his eye, Luther saw the guy aim his weapon at Wesley.

"Don't, Wes!" Luther warned and kicked back, using the vampire's momentary surprise at seeing a witch to push him off his back. He managed to stand up and barreled against the tracker brandishing the gun at Wesley.

"Stop! Drop your weapons!" Samson's authoritative voice sounded from behind them.

The eyes of the other two trackers widened instantly. Luther looked over his shoulder and saw Samson, Amaury, and Gabriel standing in a line, all of them armed with semi-automatics pointed at the two vampire enforcers.

Luther breathed a sigh of relief. "Thank God you're here."

"We saw the incident via your camera feed." Amaury pointed to Luther's jacket.

Samson motioned to the two strangers. "I want you to call the head of the council and tell him Samson Woodford wants to speak to him."

Neither of the two vampires budged.

"Now!" Samson ground out.

One of them reached into his pocket and pulled out a cell phone. He punched in a code, then put the phone to his ear.

"Sir," he said stiffly, "this is Rigsby. A Samson Woodford insists on talking to you." He paused, then nodded and handed the phone to Samson. "Here."

Samson took it. "Watch them," he instructed his friends and turned away. "Sir…" He walked back to the entry door of Scanguards, making it impossible for Luther to follow the conversation.

It took only thirty seconds though it felt much longer, until Samson came back and handed the phone to Rigsby. "I've arranged for a delay in Luther's arrest. I'm personally vouching for him. He'll turn himself in when this is over. The head of the council will confirm our arrangement."

Rigsby grunted and pressed the phone to his ear. "Sir?" Displeasure spread over his face as his listened to his superior. "But, sir…" There was a short pause. "Yes, sir," he ground out. "I understand." But it was clear he wasn't pleased about the development. He turned to his colleague. "Tolliver, take off his cuffs."

When Tolliver freed him of the cuffs, Luther rubbed his wrists. "Thanks, Samson!" Then he opened the car door. "Let's move. We've lost enough time already."

"We'll follow you," Rigsby said, narrowing his eyes.

"I'll turn myself in just as soon as Katie is safe. You have my word." Luther jumped into the passenger seat, while Wes slid into the driver's seat and Blake hopped in the back, throwing the bag with the guns on the back seat.

Wes gunned the engine and raced down Sixteenth Street.

Luther stared straight ahead, urging the car to go faster even though the needle was already passing sixty.

I'm coming for you, Katie.

45

South Beach Harbor consisted of seven docks, or fingers, south of Pier 40, each of which had approximately eighty slips for small sailboats and motorboats. The marina was framed by a concrete wall on the bay side, acting as a breakwater, with one exit to the south and one to the north. Blake had given him a quick overview of the area on the drive there, and now Luther reached for the door handle, ready to leap from the car.

Blake disconnected his call. "Okay, two of our guys are already there. They saw movement on the sixth finger at the southern end of the marina. But they weren't close enough to even see if the guy was a vampire."

"I'm going there." Luther jumped out of the car the moment Wesley brought it to a stop near the sidewalk. He didn't even bother closing the door and raced over the grass surface that separated King Street from the walking path along the water. He sprinted past the children's playground, his eyes already scanning the boats in the water.

To his right the clubhouse lay in darkness. Luther charged past it, heading for the row of slips where Scanguards' men had seen somebody. He prayed he wasn't too late. He focused all his senses on the sixth dock, checking each boat for any indication of recent movement, searching for any boat that generated more waves than its neighbor.

At the same time he inhaled deeply, trying to pick up Katie's scent. Her blood still permeated his cells and led him closer to the dock.

There, he could smell her. She'd been here not long ago. Her scent was still fresh and strong. She had to be close.

"I'm here, Katie," he murmured. "I won't let you down."

A sound came from one of the boats on the far end of the dock. Luther's ears perked up and he focused his eyes on the direction of the sound. Somebody was turning a key in an ignition. An instant later, the low humming of an engine reverberated against the other boats.

Luther ran to the gate and pulled on it. It was locked. He kicked his foot against it, but the damn thing didn't give way immediately.

"Shit!"

He hooked his fingers into the chain link fence and climbed it, jumping over at the top. He ran down the plank to the individual docks. Toward the end of the sixth finger, he saw a motorboat pull out from its slip. Luther estimated the length of the dock and realized that he couldn't outrun the boat and would be stuck at the end of the dock without being able to reach it.

He had to cut Norris off at the exit of the marina, at the narrow opening between the breakwater and the pier that ran parallel to the seventh finger. Luther sprinted down the dock, feeling the planks shift slightly beneath his feet as they rocked with his movements. He swerved at the last finger and ran down the long dock. His lungs were burning, hungering for air, but his legs were eating up the distance, his focus on the end of the dock, where a large sailboat blocked his view of the breakwater.

Without stopping he catapulted himself onto the deck of the sailboat and traversed it with three long strides. Just in time as it turned out, because the motorboat was passing it at that very moment. The man at the helm turned his head, and his face froze as their eyes met for a split-second.

"Norris!" Luther leapt off the sailboat, pushing off it with all his might.

He crashed into Norris, tackling him to the floor. Luther's gaze immediately shot to the open cabin door. There was no light, but Katie's scent was stronger here. She was down there.

"West," Norris ground out, already pulling back his fist for a punch.

Luther pulled his knee up and thrust it between the guy's legs, but Norris was fast and rolled to the side in time to avoid the kick. Norris got back on his feet, and Luther braced himself against the bench to get leverage to kick his foot at Norris's midsection.

The guard staggered backward and hit the steering wheel. The boat suddenly tilted the other way. Norris jerked forward, his fists aimed at Luther when Noris's jacket got caught on something. Norris pulled frantically, as Luther charged him. Just as Luther was upon him, there was the sound of something breaking. Norris was free and slammed his fist into Luther's face.

Simultaneously the boat took a leap forward, its speed increasing with every second.

"Shit!" Luther cursed and delivered a series of blows, alternately punching Norris in the gut, then landing uppercuts to his chin and whipping his head sideways. But the guy kept coming, grunting with every punch and every blow.

"Never liked you much, West!" Norris said between intakes of air.

"Likewise, asshole!"

Norris grinned coldly, then flashed his fangs. "How about a real fight now? See who's got what it takes to win the prize." He motioned to below deck where Katie was probably tied up.

Luther glanced past Norris. They'd cleared the breakwater and were heading toward the opposite side of McCovey Cove, where a large parking lot lay deserted. Knowing he didn't have much time before the boat hit the shore, Luther feigned a move to the left, then reached into his inside pocket and pulled out the stake he'd stashed there while in the car.

"Yeah, a real fight," Luther repeated as if agreeing with Norris. Then he jerked his shoulder back and launched himself onto Norris.

With one arm he blocked Norris's claws, while he drew back the other. With a grunt, Luther drove the stake into Norris's chest, watching with satisfaction how the vampire froze for a split-second as he realized his fate.

"Don't have time for your sick games," Luther said.

Norris dissolved into dust.

Luther didn't lose a second but reached for the wheel. He turned it, but it didn't move. It was locked in its position. He reached for the lever to throttle down the engine, but the lever was gone. Broken off.

"Shit!"

One glance at the approaching shore and he knew he only had seconds left.

He raced down into the cabin. "Katie!"

A muffled sound came from a corner, but he'd already spotted her. She was bound to a rail and gagged. He willed his fingers to lengthen into claws and sliced through her ties. Luther grabbed her and pulled her with him, lifting her out of the cabin. Katie tore on the gag and pulled it down. Luther stepped onto the bench at the back of the boat and with Katie clutched to his chest he jumped into the water.

"Hold on tight, baby."

He felt her shudder as they hit the water and dove beneath the surface. Better that than a fiery death. Luther kicked his legs, propelling him and Katie away from the boat, before breaking through the surface.

Katie gasped for air. "Oh Luther!"

The explosion ignited the night sky as the boat hit the big rocks lining McCovey Cove and was blown to bits. Flames shot high in the air and Luther shielded Katie from the fire as debris hit the water.

His heart raced and with Katie in his arms he swam away from the explosion toward the other shore.

"Luther, this way," a male voice called out to him.

Luther turned his head and saw a boat come toward them. Blake was waving at them from the bow, Wesley next to him.

Finally, Luther felt relief course through him. He looked at Katie and brushed wet strands of hair from her face.

"I've got you, baby." He stroked his hand over her face while he continued to tread water. "It's over now. He's dead. He can't hurt you anymore."

"You came back for me."

"I would always come back for you."

"We'll pull you out," Blake interrupted as the boat pulled alongside them.

Moments later Luther and Katie were sitting on a bench in the Coast Guard boat, wrapped in a large blanket. Feeling Katie so close to him felt right. He pulled her against his body, not concerned about Wesley, Blake, and the man from the Coast Guard watching them.

The boat was already heading back to the dock, where two people were waiting for them. Luther recognized them immediately. Tolliver and Rigsby. They weren't giving him much time. And he wasn't going to waste it with meaningless things.

"Oh Katie, I thought I'd lost you." He captured Katie's lips and kissed her. She shivered, but he rubbed his hands over her back, warming her. He didn't feel the cold himself, not like her human body did.

It wasn't the right place for this, but he had no choice. He kissed her, wanting to memorize everything about her, her taste, the texture of her tongue, the softness of her lips. He couldn't get enough of her, but when he felt the boat stop and dock at the pier, he knew his time was up.

Luther separated his mouth from Katie's and looked into her emerald eyes.

"West!" Rigsby called out to him.

Luther looked over his shoulder. "In a minute."

Then he looked back at Katie, whose gaze had shifted to the two men on the dock. "Who are they?"

"Trackers. They're here to take me away."

Katie gasped. "No! Why?"

"I broke into a prison, I assaulted two prison guards, I destroyed their equipment. And I brought an outsider into the prison. I have to pay for that."

"No! That wasn't your fault. It's my fault. Let them punish me!" she wailed, trying to get up.

But he pulled her back. "No, Katie." He stroked his fingers over her cheek. "Please listen to me. It doesn't matter what happens to me. As long as you're safe."

"But, Luther—"

He put a finger over her lips, preventing her from speaking. "Please hear me out. I don't have much time. And there's something I need to tell you."

She stilled.

"I love you, Katie. And if I were a free man, I would ask you to be mine, but I'm not." He paused. "I can't ask you to wait for me. It wouldn't be fair. You have to live your life. But know this: you'll always own my heart."

He saw tears rim her eyes. "Luther..." she choked out, but her voice failed her as tears started streaming down her cheeks.

He kissed her and tasted the salt of her tears. It broke his heart.

"West."

Luther let go of her lips and peeled himself out of Katie's arms. "I'm coming." He locked eyes with her for one long last moment, before turning his back and stepping off the boat.

He was glad that they handcuffed him, or he might have jumped back onto the boat and made a run for it with Katie. But he wasn't fool enough to believe that they wouldn't catch him.

Though he was fool enough to hope that Katie would wait for him despite his plea for her not to.

46

One week later

The tears had dried though they always returned once she was alone. She'd heard nothing from Luther since the two enforcement agents from the prison authority had taken him away in handcuffs. It had been hard enough to see him leave, but what made the whole situation heart-wrenching was Luther's confession. He loved her.

Katie choked down a sob and pushed back the tears. No, she couldn't break down again and cry herself to sleep. Not tonight. All of Scanguards and their families had assembled in her house to ring in the New Year and to celebrate Isabelle's rescue. Tonight was a night for happiness, and she would draw on everything she'd learned as an actress to show the world that she was fine.

Pulling a deep breath into her lungs, she pasted a smile onto her face and walked back into the packed living room, carrying a tray of hors d'oeuvres. Dance music was coming from the loudspeakers, courtesy of Damian and Benjamin, Amaury's twins, who were acting as DJs. She had to give them credit; they weren't blasting the music so loud that conversation was impossible.

Katie glanced around. The men were wearing tuxedos, the women had donned elegant evening dresses. Even the teenage hybrids were looking festive and had turned into mirror images of their respective parents.

When Damian and Benjamin spotted her, they waved to her, pointing at the tray in her hands. She smiled and walked to where the two were mixing the music.

"I'm famished," Benjamin said.

Damian snatched a smoked salmon tartlet from the platter. "Ditto." He shoved it into his mouth.

"Thanks, Katie," Benjamin said, taking a tartlet and eating it with gusto.

"Your parties are the best. And there's food!" Damian grinned.

Katie laughed. "You make it sound like your parents don't feed you!" She glanced around and saw Amaury and Nina slow dancing in one corner of the living room. They looked like a young couple who couldn't wait to be alone.

The twins followed her gaze.

"Those two sometimes forget we're around," Benjamin claimed.

"Yeah," Damian added and winked, "we give them space, you know, and still they haven't thanked us by giving us a little sister."

Benjamin chuckled. "And trust me, they *are* trying."

"Yeah, like all the time!" Damian said, rolling his eyes.

"Is that a way to talk about your parents?" Katie recognized Maya's voice immediately and turned to her.

"You're taking the words right out of my mouth," Katie said and embraced Maya. "So glad you're here."

"Wouldn't miss it for anything," the stunningly beautiful vampiress said, tossing a strand of her long dark hair over her shoulder. Then she looked back at the twins. "I seriously hope you guys don't rub off on my boys."

Damian and Benjamin exchanged a conspiratorial look. "At least you guys gave Ryder and Ethan a little sister to tease," Damian claimed. "And what have we got? Nothing."

"You have each other," Katie interjected. "I wouldn't call that nothing."

Maya shook her head, laughing. "Let's leave them to themselves, shall we, Katie?"

"I agree."

"Leave the tray," Benjamin said and reached for it. "We're still growing."

Katie pressed the tray into his hands. "Please share it with the others."

"Sure," Benjamin promised, but his facial expression said otherwise.

Maya put a hand on Katie's arm and they walked away.

"You doing okay?" Maya asked.

"You asked me that already last week when you examined me," Katie said tersely. "I'm fine."

"Well, I just wanted to follow up. It's hard for me to forget that I'm a doctor. And looking after everybody at Scanguards is in my blood. You're part of my big extended family."

"I know. I'm sorry, I didn't mean to snap at you." She sighed. "I'm really fine. I didn't even get a cold after that nighttime swim in the Bay. Guess I'm more resilient than I thought."

"Yes, you are." Her gaze suddenly drifted away, and a lovely smile curved her lips upward.

Katie turned her head to the side and saw Maya's mate Gabriel approach. Despite the large scar that marred the left side of his face, there was something attractive about the big vampire with the ponytail as he locked eyes with his wife.

"I hope I'm not interrupting anything important," Gabriel said. "But I just put a song request in with Damian and was hoping to dance with my wife."

"Don't let me stop you," Katie said.

He nodded. "Everything all right, Katie?"

Why did everybody keep asking her that? Didn't they already know that she was hurting? That with Luther gone all her hopes had been destroyed. That she barely knew how to get through this day, let alone the coming year. And there was nothing she could do about it. Samson had told her that as a non-Vampire she wasn't even allowed to visit Luther in prison. Besides, at this point it wasn't even clear where they'd taken him or how long they were going to hold him. They didn't even know if there would be a trial and a sentencing.

"I'm sorry for asking," Gabriel suddenly said. "I know this is hard on you." He put a hand on her forearm and squeezed it. "Don't give up."

Tears shot to her eyes and she pushed them back, trying to be brave. "Have you heard anything at all from him?"

Gabriel shook his head. "There's no news."

A new song started.

"Go and dance; enjoy yourselves. I have to check on something in the kitchen anyway."

Katie caught Maya's pitying smile before turning and walking toward the kitchen. She didn't get far.

"Hey Aunt Katie," Cooper greeted her. "Do you have any more food? Damian and Benjamin are hogging that tray."

Katie hugged him and kissed him on the cheek, then ruffled his hair. "I thought you stopped at Pasquale's on your way and had pizza."

"That was hours ago!"

Lydia appeared behind her brother and patted him on the shoulder. "Don't bother Aunt Katie. She's got enough on her plate. You know where the kitchen is. Fix yourself something if you're hungry."

"Fine!" Cooper spun around and marched toward the kitchen.

"Honestly, that boy is like an eating machine!" Lydia gave one of her long suffering sighs. "I don't know what to do with him."

Katie laughed. "You sound like his mother."

"Sometimes I feel like it. I swear I'm never gonna have kids. I'll be like you. Footloose and fancy free. No commitments. No strings."

"No, Lydia," Katie said softly, brushing the girl's red hair out of her face. "Commitments are good. I just wasn't lucky enough to find somebody I wanted to commit to. Hollywood wasn't exactly conducive to forming lasting relationships."

"Was it really that shallow there?" Lydia asked with interest.

"People used each other to get ahead. There was always an ulterior motive to any relationship. Trust was hard to come by."

"Is that why you left?"

"Partially. I guess I was tired of that life." She sighed and looked past her niece. "Oh look, there's Grayson and Isabelle."

Lydia turned her head as the entire Woodford family entered the room. "Grayson looks kind of grown up now, doesn't he?"

Katie nodded. Grayson had changed since his sister's abduction. Suddenly he seemed more like a man than the hybrid teenager he'd been before. "He's going to be as dashing as his father."

Lydia turned back and chuckled. "I like Patrick better. He's a much nicer guy." Then she quickly added, "Not that I'd ever date any of them. Hell, I've practically grown up with them. I feel like their older sister."

Katie laughed. "Lydia, you're sounding much older than your age."

"Mom often says that. I don't mind." She paused. "Let me go say hi to Isabelle."

"Go," Katie encouraged her and watched her greet her best friend.

Katie caught Samson and Delilah looking at her and approached them.

Delilah hugged her. "Thanks for throwing this party. I just couldn't face arranging anything in our house. Too much going on."

"I really don't mind. I love having people over." Katie smiled at Samson. "I'm glad you came."

Samson took her hand and squeezed it. "We haven't had a chance to thank you yet. The last week has gone by so fast." He exchanged a look with Delilah. "We're very grateful for all you have done for our family. I want to apologize for how I reacted when Isabelle disappeared."

"Don't—"

"No, please," Samson interrupted. "I was distraught and needed to let out my anger on somebody. You were just a convenient scapegoat. I'm sorry for that. None of this was your fault." He paused. "Norris never laid a hand on Isabelle. I think he knew once Isabelle told him who I was that if he hurt her, I would chase him to hell and back. That's why he tied her up at a safe distance from where he blew up Forrester. He just wanted you. He was sick. But we got Isabelle back, because you, Katie, were brave. You took so many risks for us. For that I'll always be thankful to you."

"I wish people would stop saying that I'm brave. I don't feel brave." Luther had called her that, too.

"But you are," Delilah said softly. "You helped get my baby back. Thank you."

A tear escaped Katie's eye and ran down her cheek. "I'm glad it's all over," she choked out. "Will you excuse me? I need to check on something."

It was an excuse and they knew it, but they were gracious enough to let her escape. When she opened the door to the kitchen, she instantly saw that she wouldn't be able to find any solitude there either. Not only was her nephew raiding the fridge, three more boys were helping him: Adam and Nicholas, Zane and Portia's twelve- and thirteen-year-old sons, and Sebastian, Ursula and Oliver's ten-year-old half-Asian son.

All four boys whirled their heads in her direction, looking like deer caught in headlights.

"Oops," Sebastian said, looking absolutely adorable with his sheepish facial expression.

"Don't worry," Cooper said. "Aunt Katie said it was okay to make ourselves something, right?"

"Yeah, yeah, that's fine. No worries, kids," she said quickly and walked through the kitchen, exiting through the other door.

She almost bumped into Haven in the corridor. "Hey, sis, don't you wanna dance?"

Katie sighed. "I can't, please, Haven. I just can't." Another tear escaped her eye and ran down her cheek.

Haven wiped the tear away with his thumb. "I think you should, sweetheart."

She shook her head and tried to squeeze past him. But he took her by the shoulders, stopping her.

"There's somebody who wants to dance with you," Haven insisted.

"Haven, don't you understand? I can't pretend any longer that nothing is wrong."

"Then let me make it right," he said and turned her to face the hallway leading to the entrance door.

There, in the foyer, stood a vampire.

"Luther," she whispered.

Haven let go of her shoulders. "Happy New Year, sis." She heard him walk away.

Her feet carried her to Luther, who met her halfway.

"Katie," he murmured, pulling her into his arms. "Oh God, I missed you."

His lips were on hers before she could say anything. His kiss was brief, but hungry. When he released her lips, he pressed his forehead to hers.

"They let you go?"

"Kind of."

She pulled back, staring at him, gripping his arms to hold on to him. "I can't let you leave again. Luther, please."

He brushed his hand over her cheek. "I'm not leaving, baby. I made a deal."

Her heart beat into her throat. "A deal? What kind of deal?"

"The council dropped all charges against me in exchange for me working for them."

"Doing what?" Striker Reed and the dangerous work he'd done for the council suddenly flashed in her mind. "They want you to be a tracker for them?"

Luther threw his head back and laughed. "A tracker? No. That's not my specialty. They want me to consult on prison security for them. Considering I was able to break in and out again, they figured they need to upgrade their systems."

Relief flooded her.

"I can work from San Francisco," he added. "If that's what you want."

Katie threw her arms around him and pressed herself against him. Suddenly she lost the ground under her feet. Luther was lifting her up.

"I take that as a yes."

"Yes," she said into his ear.

"Good. I hope you don't mind if I skip the party. But I don't feel civilized enough right now to be among people."

She shifted her eyes to the staircase.

"I'm glad we're on the same page." Luther pivoted with her in his arms, when he suddenly froze, his eyes directed toward the door to the living room.

Katie followed his gaze and saw Samson standing in the open door.

"I'm glad you're back, old friend," Samson said.

Luther's voice cracked slightly, when he answered, "It's good to see you, brother."

Katie saw it in their eyes. Their old friendship was restored. They were like brothers again.

Samson turned with a nod and a smile and went back into the living room, closing the door behind him.

47

Luther set Katie on her feet and locked the bedroom door behind them. Only the lamps on either side of her bed were lit, otherwise the room was dark. The music from downstairs was subdued and just loud enough to give a little background ambience.

He couldn't believe he'd actually made it back. After he'd presented his plan to the council to negotiate his release, he'd taken a vicious beating from Bauer and Patterson, the guard who'd stabbed Katie. Once they were satisfied that they'd caused him as much pain as he'd caused them, the council had debated for several days. Days he'd spent in a dark cell, thinking of Katie and praying he'd see her again.

And now that he was back, he could barely believe that he wasn't dreaming.

Luther brushed his fingers through her hair, holding her face in his hands. "Oh, Katie, I know there's so much you don't know about me, and I promise you I'll tell you everything you want to know, but I need to hear one thing from you. Please tell me that I'm not just imagining what I think you feel for me. Please tell me it's real."

"I've waited half a lifetime for you. I would have waited another lifetime." She lifted herself on her tiptoes. "I love you, Luther."

Her lips were soft, warm, and welcoming. She tasted of ripe woman and innocent girl. Of seduction and comfort. Of love. His desire for her instantly spiraled out of control. But he stilled, forcing his breath to gentle.

"I need to ask you something."

He let go of her face and took one step back. As he dropped to one knee, he pulled out a small box from his jacket pocket. When he looked up at her, she stared at him with wide eyes and an open mouth.

Katie gasped. "Oh, Luther."

"I haven't asked you yet. I want to do this right." He took a deep breath and locked eyes with her. He took her hand in his. "Katie, you've shown me that there is redemption, that even I deserve love. You've taught me that the demons of our past only have power over us if we let them. And I'm not going to let them have that power any longer. I'm free of my past. I'm ready for a new life. And I want to share this life with you. As my mate, my wife, my everything." He opened the box to present the diamond engagement ring he'd picked out for her. "Will you blood-bond with me?"

Katie pressed her lips together, visibly choking back tears. "Yes."

Luther slid the ring on her finger and rose, tossing the box to the side. He rid himself of his jacket and pulled Katie into his arms. "I'll do everything in my power to make you happy."

Her body molded to his. Through the thin fabric of her evening dress, he could feel every curve and every muscle of her luscious body. He slid one hand to her nape, the other to her ass, holding her to him, letting her feel what she did to him. A soft gasp told him that she could feel the outline of his cock press against her center.

"Take me," she begged.

Her words fueled the fire in him, the fire that was raging, threatening to incinerate him if he didn't make her his.

He brought his mouth to hover over hers, inhaling her sweet breath. Without haste, he slanted his lips over hers and took her mouth captive, kissing her with a passion he thought he wasn't capable of anymore. But Katie had awakened his heart just as surely as she was causing his cock to harden and thrust against her with unquenchable need.

When her tongue touched his and they began a passionate dance as old as time itself, waves of pleasure coursed through his body. He delved deep into her delicious caverns, soaking up her taste, getting drunk on it. Every sigh and moan she released, he captured and swallowed, wanting to take everything she was willing to give him.

He was crazy about Katie. Needed her like his next breath. She nourished his heart and made it awaken again just like she would nourish his body from now on. Because once they were bonded, he would only drink from her. She would be his only source to sustain him, to keep him alive. In turn, she'd partake in his immortality and remain as young and beautiful as she was now. It was a perfect symbiosis. A flawless connection. He didn't have to explain it to her. She'd been living with vampires. She knew what a blood-bond entailed.

Slowly, Luther began to undress her. He found the zipper of her dress and slid the straps off her shoulders, letting the silk fabric pool at her feet with a soft whoosh. He looked at what he'd unveiled, drinking her in with his eyes. She wore a red bra and matching panties. His cock leapt at the tantalizing sight.

"So goddamn perfect," he murmured.

Katie reached for him and started to unbutton his shirt. He helped her until he could finally take his shirt off. When she reached for his pants, he put his hand over hers.

"Easy there, baby. It's been a week since you touched me. I'm liable to go off like a rocket."

Katie smiled at him from under her long lashes and pushed his hand away. "Oh, you'd better be going off like a rocket, or I'm not doing it right."

He groaned, but let her proceed stripping him of his pants and boxer briefs. He kicked off his shoes. Seconds later he stood naked in front of her.

He reached for her, brushing his hands over her tempting boobs, feeling her nipples pebble under his light touch. He grinned and opened the front clasp of her bra.

"Looks like you'll be exploding like a rocket, too, baby," he said, dipping his head to her breasts.

He licked over one nipple, then the other and felt how Katie dropped her head back and moaned. While he captured one hard peak between his lips and sucked, he let his hands glide down her back, slipping underneath the silky fabric of her panties. He filled his hands with her ass, squeezing gently, and pressing her against his cock.

The contact of skin on skin nearly robbed him of the last thread of his control. For a second he stilled, taking a deep breath to steady himself. But he couldn't deny his body for long. He needed this woman. He needed Katie.

Luther pushed her panties down, then rid her of her bra, letting it fall to the floor. He lifted his head from her breasts and looked at her.

"I'm going to take you in your bed."

"Our bed," she corrected.

"Our bed." He lifted her into his arms and carried her to the bed, gently placing her on the cover.

For a moment he looked down at her. Like a halo, her dark hair framed her face. She was spread out for him like a feast. A feast he would partake of every day of his life from now on. Because every day he would feed from her while making love to her. But tonight would be special. Tonight she would be drinking from him at the same time.

"There won't be any foreplay, Katie, I just don't have that much patience tonight," he warned her.

Katie spread her legs wider, letting him see her glistening sex. "Foreplay is overrated."

"I'm glad you think that." He lowered himself over her and sank his cock into her warm and inviting channel. Involuntarily, he groaned out loud. "Fuck!"

"Yes," she said, her voice raspy, her torso arching off the mattress as if she was offering her breasts to him.

Luther buried his head between them, luxuriating in their softness and warmth. Then he began to thrust, his cock dictating the rhythm, sending pleasure through his body.

He lifted his head from her breasts and watched in fascination how they bounced up and down and from side to side while he continued to drive his cock into her. Katie's lids were half closed, her mouth open, sounds of pleasure rolling over her lips.

"You're mine, Katie. I won't allow anybody to take you away from me," he promised.

She met his gaze. "And you're mine."

Bracing himself on one elbow, he lifted his hand and willed his fingers to turn into sharp claws. From the corner of his eye he noticed

Katie stare at them, not in fear, but admiration, while her interior muscles squeezed him more tightly, indicating the approach of her orgasm.

"Wait for me, baby." With his claw, he made a small incision on his shoulder and felt blood drip from it. "Drink from me now."

He lowered his shoulder to her mouth and felt her latch onto it immediately. He groaned from the instant pleasure he felt. His fangs descended automatically and he nuzzled his face in the crook of her neck.

"I'll love you forever," Luther vowed and drove his fangs into her flesh.

The moment Katie's blood ran down the back of his throat, he could feel her soul. He reached out to her, offering himself to her. He felt her essence wrap around him and draw him closer.

Katie, my love.

Her thoughts drifted to him, filling his mind. She was opening herself to him, inviting him in to a place no other person had ever been. He let himself fall. He was home.

I'm yours, Luther. Forever yours.

~ ~ ~

SCANGUARDS
FAMILY TREE

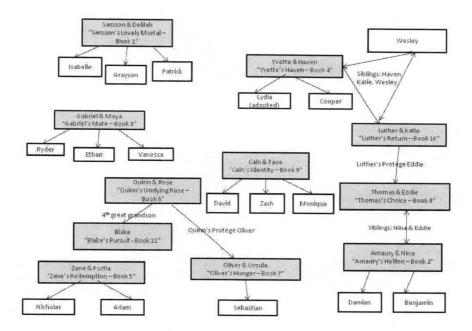

Samson & Delilah
"Samson's Lovely Mortal – Book 1"

Isabelle

Grayson

Patrick

Yvette & Haven
"Yvette's Haven – Book 4"

Lydia
(adopted)

Cooper

Wesley

Siblings: Haven, Katie, Wesley

Gabriel & Maya
"Gabriel's Mate – Book 3"

Ryder

Ethan

Vanessa

Luther & Katie
"Luther's Return – Book 10"

Luther's Protégé Eddie

Cain & Faye
"Cain's Identity – Book 9"

David

Zach

Monique

Quinn & Rose
"Quinn's Undying Rose – Book 6"

4th great grandson

Quinn's Protégé Oliver

Thomas & Eddie
"Thomas's Choice – Book 8"

Siblings: Nina & Eddie

Blake
"Blake's Pursuit – Book 11"

Zane & Portia
"Zane's Redemption – Book 5"

Nicholas

Adam

Oliver & Ursula
"Oliver's Hunger – Book 7"

Sebastian

Amaury & Nina
"Amaury's Hellion – Book 2"

Damian

Benjamin